The Flavor of Cultures

Weam Namou

HERMiZ
PUBLiSHING

Hermiz Publishing, Inc.

Copyright © 2015 by Weam Namou

Library of Congress Cataloging-in-Publication Data
2 0 1 5 9 0 3 5 5 2

Namou, Weam
The Flavor of Cultures (Literary Fiction)

ISBN 978–0-9752956–6-3 (paperback)

First Edition

Published in the United States of America by:
Hermiz Publishing, Inc.
Sterling Heights, MI

For my ever so sweet son

Chapter 1

Fi youm min al-ayam—In a day from amongst other days . . .

I was nineteen years old. I had a closet full of brand name clothes and high-heeled shoes and a dresser stacked with uniquely shaped perfume bottles, fruit-scented lotions, musical jewelry boxes with dancing ballerinas, and six-inch dolls wearing lace, ribbons and hats. Although my family was barely middle-class, the fabric of my dresses and the softness of my hands could have fooled the most brilliant fortune teller.

By that age, I had acquired eloquence, manners and poise, but that was not enough. I wanted from life my own distinctive story of love, passion and freedom. I did not know exactly what those words meant aside from the definitions given in the dictionary but they were said so often and with such romantic attachment that I was certain they had tremendous value beyond human lips and great literature.

I had no story of my own. Fortunately, because of the women in my life who'd poured as much information into my ears as they did tea into china cups, I grew up knowing everyone else's story. My favorite was about my blue-eyed Uncle Sabir. He lived in Telkaif, a Christian village in Northern Iraq inhabited mostly by Chaldeans (Christian Iraqis), and was famous for having married a green-eyed, blond-haired girl twenty-five years his junior.

"There are people in Iraq with blonde hair?" was the first question I'd interrupted my second oldest sister, Layla, with when I was a child.

"Well, not blonde-blonde, Mervat," she'd said in her gentle yet ardent way. I learned that in Iraq, people with honey-colored hair were considered blondes and that they were rarer than the eggs and milk available in the *souk* once a week.

Layla knew everything about Iraq because she'd spent twelve years there. I'd spent only two. This was a great disadvantage, since I wasn't qualified to be an Iraqi by experience or an American by law. I'd never visited my homeland and although I had applied for American citizenship, the immigration officials hadn't yet called me for a naturalization exam. I was stuck between these two worlds like a secret between a gossiper and her neighbor.

I'd never met my Uncle Sabir, but I knew his history, which, in my eyes, began when he was nineteen months old. He'd fallen ill one afternoon and was taken to the hospital. The village doctor promised to cure him by giving him half an injection of medicine each visit. The visit before the last, however, the doctor decided to inject the entire shot at once. He wanted to be kind and spare my grandmother the extra trip she'd have to make the following week.

This decision dramatically altered my uncle's fate by crippling him for life. He started losing sensation in his leg, and then his body became numb. There was, of course, much agony in the house and a priest was sent to help. He prayed for the infant and gave his blessings to the family who knelt day and night beside Uncle Sabir's bed and massaged his body with ointment. After months of such remedies, my uncle regained feeling from the waist up. While his upper-body developed normally, his legs grew more slowly and remained paralyzed.

I don't know whether the doctor was ever confronted about his malpractice because my grandmother didn't blame him. She believed a woman named Hassina had jinxed her son the day she'd first set eyes on him.

"Why didn't the blue-eyed trinket Nanna pinned on his pajamas protect him like it was supposed to?" I asked, remembering the ones my mother had sewn on my nieces and nephews' pillows, clothes and cribs before they were born.

"Not a gold trinket or a crucifix could've broken that woman's evil eyes," Layla answered. "A tomb, though, might have."

I was curious about what evil eyes looked like and wished there were illustrated books about them, but the school library had books only on birds, reptiles, wars, countries and presidents. I wondered if perhaps, one day, some scholar would come along and fit a small section about them into the encyclopedia in order to warn those from cultures that weren't familiar with them. And while the scholar was at it, he might also add a paragraph or two describing how my grandmother, on special occasions, pealed an apple and divided it between her nine children, or how she'd once bathed a neighbor's toddler who was smeared with his own excrement because his father, who'd stay at the *souk* all day to sell olives, asked her to.

My grandmother drew her allegations from the way in which Hassina, startled by my uncle's blue eyes and white flesh, had praised him endlessly without once uttering the word *mashallah* (may Allah's name be upon him). "Oh, the baby is beautiful!" she'd cried. "Oh, his eyes! Oh, his nose! Oh, he's darling!"

Two months later, he was paralyzed.

"Was Nanna being too hard on her?"

"No, Mervet, everyone knew Hassina was Telkaif's finest jinxer," Layla said, and in defense of my grandmother she presented me with proof. Through dozens of events, Hassina had earned her title. For instance, she'd once seen a lantern in my grandmother's house and with an awkward grin complimented it a thousand and one times. The second Hassina left the house, my aunt picked up the quilt they'd eaten breakfast over to shake off the bread and cheese crumbs. The quilt struck the lantern and shattered it.

"Could it have been a coincidence?" I struggled with the concept of invisible eyes being able to cause such mischief.

"Once," my sister went on, using all her passion to convince me that this woman was not falsely accused by the village of Telkaif, "she complimented her guest's outfit so much she frightened her. 'Don't jinx me, Hassina,' the woman warned. 'This took me three months to design and today is my first time wearing it.'" My sister paused, but her eyes twinkled. "Do you know what happened next?"

"No, tell me."

Layla's face came nearer to mine and she whispered. "When her guest reached for the bowl of roasted cantaloupe seeds, her skirt ruptured three inches."

"Huh!" I gasped.

"The woman accused Hassina of having jinxed her outfit before she walked out of the house with loose threads hanging between her thighs."

I was chewing my fingernails, tasting the garlic from the *turshi*—pickled vegetables—I'd eaten at supper.

"Do you want me to tell you more?" Layla asked with a taunting smile.

"I do!"

"Once, our youngest uncle found a dog and decided to keep it. He didn't have enough money to take it to a veterinarian, so he asked a friend of our father, who worked at one of Baghdad's universities, to have a chemist or scientist or physicist look at it."

"Why?"

"To make sure it was clean."

"Of what?"

"Rabies, flees—chicken pox," she added with a grin.

"Oh."

"So the man did our uncle the favor and after neutering the dog and giving him a few shots, he delivered him back in perfect condition. The pet lived in Nanna's backyard for forty days. Hassina admired it so much it vanished."

"Where?"

"Died."

"Completely?"

She frowned. "Mervat?"

"Oh," I'd said. I was affected by the loss of the dog, but more by the sorcery of Hassina. "Tell me more."

She clasped her hands together, as though ready to pray, and rested her chin on them. "Are you sure?"

"I'm sure!"

"Once our cousins bought two pairs of sandals for a hundred dirham each. On their way home, Hassina met them and her eyes fetched their new sandals as quickly as chickens do wheat."

"Oh."

"She congratulated them on their new purchase until her lips turned blue," Layla said. "And do you know what happened the instant they got home?"

The suspense had muffled my vocal cords, and I kept silent in anxiety. Layla didn't respond. She traced the rim of the bed ruffles with her finger, tilted her head towards the star-filled window, and took in a deep breath before handing me the conclusion.

"They were stooping over a green and orange turtle that our grandfather had brought home from his hunting trip, and suddenly, both the sandals' thongs snapped."

"Ahhh!" I was convinced. Once again my sister, using

mostly English, had woven Chaldean (Neo-Aramaic) and Arabic myths into my heart. Layla never told me stories in the daytime because legend had it that in Iraq whoever did so risked growing horns and having his gold turn to iron.

It might have seemed detrimental, but my blue-eyed uncle's paralysis was certainly not. Although in a wheelchair, he was the house's sole provider after my grandfather passed away. It was said that without him my grandmother's family wouldn't have survived. He worked at a post office in the daytime, sorting mail. In the evening he rode a motorcycle, specially built for the handicapped, to Mosul and sold the cheap cigarettes he'd bought earlier in Telkaif.

Uncle Sabir was considered a great blessing to the family until he turned forty-five years old and found he had a desire to marry. His loved ones' happiness spoiled as quickly as milk soured. He chose a beautiful girl and, despite her age and without inquiring about her reputation, he married her within a week.

Those who heard the news were automatically suspicious of the bride's intentions. They questioned why a young green-eyed blonde girl would want a man who was incapable of consummating the marriage. The answer became evident a few weeks later when she ran away from home in the morning and didn't return until night.

After that she fled home repeatedly. Uncle Sabir's family would search for her each time she disappeared and either they'd find her (no one ever discussed where) or she'd return on her own a few days later.

These occasions confirmed that the green-eyed blonde woman had married in order to establish a respectable name while, having a handicapped husband, gaining freedom. When I heard this part of the story, I envied the woman more than I pitied my uncle. She'd attained both freedom and respect in one face.

"He deserves it!" my great-uncle on my mother's side growled in Chaldean one evening, lifting himself a few inches from his chair as he drooled from his denture-less mouth onto the tray of stuffed grape leaves. "He was so desperate to get married, he would've wed a cow!"

It was Nameera, my third oldest sister, who'd caused his rage. When Uncle Sabir was mentioned, she'd said how sad his situation made her, a sentiment which my great-uncle vastly disapproved of.

"He's right, Nameera," my mother said, appeasing my great-uncle's temper. "Your Uncle Sabir should have used caution. Marriage is not a game. It requires enormous thought and consideration. And it needs family approval."

When my mother finished her speech, my great-uncle took his eyes off her and returned to his seat, his face quivering. "When I tried to find him a wife, he said 'That one has a mole. That one is bald.'" He raised his arms high and lifted his body a few inches again. "What did he expect? He doesn't even have testicles!"

My sisters and I had been restraining ourselves from laughter since my great-uncle's fury had begun and could stop ourselves no longer. We burst into laughter, despite my mother's stare and my great-uncle's seriousness. Seeing we couldn't be controlled, my mother tried to distract my great-uncle by polishing his comments with nice words.

She really shouldn't have bothered. My great-uncle wasn't acknowledging our laughter or her encouragements. He was still too preoccupied with condemning Uncle Sabir the way countries would spies. My sisters and I, with our hands covering our mouths, continued giggling.

Even when I went to bed that night, I had to keep my hands pressed against my mouth, my great-uncle's words still tickling me. But that wasn't the only time I went to sleep with stories tucked against my head like hair rollers. Every night, bakers and barbers, cheaters and liars, hunters and navigators performed for me. They satisfied my senses so completely that I didn't need theater tickets for sparkling wit or brilliant acting. All I needed was to offer my sisters Egyptian seeds and milk them until every drop of fable was emptied into my inexperienced heart.

Then, *fi youm min al-ayam,* I encountered the story I'm about to write, which caused me to live life through my own senses.

Chapter 2

Al-bedia—The beginning

The event that changed my life began on a warm spring afternoon in the early 90's, two weeks before my older brother's wedding. I was working part-time in my father's party store for spending money and family duty, taking two summer classes at Macomb Community College for an associate's degree for the attainment of independence, and flipping through travel brochures for inspiration and future destinations. I was also one of the eight bridesmaids standing up in the wedding.

I had been looking forward to the party even though I had loathed having to wear the off-the-shoulder mauve dress and white-flowered hairpiece. I envied my three sisters for buying their own gowns from Middle Eastern boutiques. They would stand out like princesses amongst the party crowd.

Together, they had spent $2600 on dresses they'd wear only once. My sisters weren't extravagant in general, but since an only boy was getting married, it would have been a disgrace not to be as done up in gold and paint as the churches of Sicily.

I was displeased that afternoon about having to drive my mother to a party store owned by her friend's son. Chaldeans don't mail their invitations, thinking it impersonal, so my mother had to hand deliver a card to a woman named Aunt Evelyn. Because the family is the core of respect, everyone in the Middle Eastern culture is addressed as "aunt" or "uncle," "brother" or "sister," "son" or "daughter," depending on their age.

Aunt Evelyn lived in Arroyo Hills, a wealthy suburb on the west side, which was twenty-seven miles away from our home in Detroit. My mother tried to spare us by contacting a few east side people and asking them whether they were going to encounter Aunt Evelyn at a wedding or funeral, and if so, could they kindly pass her the invitation.

"Oh, no, Saleema," they all said, showing their regrets. "I doubt if I will see Evelyn anytime soon—but tell me, dearest, how is your health and your husband's? And how is your son and daughters?"

"We're all well, *al-hamid ila Allah* (praise be to God)," she'd replied, and then politely asked about their immediate families' welfare before ending the conversation by calling upon the next Chaldean who lived on the east side and was acquainted with Aunt Evelyn. It appeared no one was going to see her before my brother's wedding. Just when we were about to personally deliver the card to her home, Aunt Evelyn supplied a solution.

She suggested she and my mother meet at her son's store, only five miles north of where we lived. We were to visit her before four o'clock, when her daughter's shift ended and the two of them left for the day.

I'd planned on studying until my mother and I left the house, but by one o'clock I'd barely read a few pages of my philosophy book when Maysoon, my closest acquaintance (I was not intimate with people outside my family, so I couldn't honestly call anyone a friend), unexpectedly showed up. We sat on the front porch, though it was as unwise to be seen with her as it was to date a married man.

The problem was that Maysoon had a reputation the size of my ego and since we lived amongst half the Chaldean community in the little Detroit area of Seven Mile and John R, where everyone knew everyone else's business, I didn't want people to think I was *wakiha,* naughty, like her. I'd tried convincing her that my bedroom was cozier and more private, but the way she'd pinned her buttocks against the porch's cement said that even if she was offered the bribe of a magic lamp, she wouldn't budge.

"Listen to this lesson real carefully now," Maysoon said. She and I spoke what most people our age felt at ease with, English. "I won't repeat anything 'cause it won't sound as good the second time around."

Maysoon chewed her spearmint gum, then rotated it to the other side of her mouth with her tongue. Her eyes fell on my eight-year-old niece, who'd been drawing a lavender fish just a minute ago but was now gaping at Maysoon's brightly painted lips.

"Ashley, leave for a minute," I demanded.

Ashley puffed a breath of air, gave me a look, and with her notebook tucked in her arms, walked grudgingly off the porch. My attention returned to Maysoon. Before she could continue, however, a clunky green Oldsmobile with four hooting boys came by. Maysoon arched an eyebrow and lifted her leg over the porch railing, her short skirt moving higher.

After the boys drove off, Maysoon shrugged and resumed her speech. "You start off with their ear, kissing it wildly with your tongue. Then you go down to their nipple . . ."

"Ooooh," I interrupted, squinting my eyes and clenching my teeth. "You're being too detailed."

"Hey, there's more to a blow job than just sucking on a guy's thing."

I gasped, nearly fainting and causing a scene worse than

she'd had with the boys a minute ago.

We'd started talking about hair wax, but that must have been too ordinary for Maysoon because she quickly diverted it to sex, claiming that such talk would benefit me when I one day had a boyfriend. So I listened, not imagining that what she would describe as foreplay revolved around the genitals.

I tried to change the subject. "Would you like some tea, Maysoon?"

She looked at me as though I'd insulted her mother. "Jesus, I'm crowing like a rooster and you're not even listening."

"I am listening." I suppose it was my rudeness that made her take a while to go on, rolling her eyes and twitching her lips in the meantime. I wanted to ask if I should slice an onion and flatten it against her nose, but before I could, she returned to her normal smutty self.

"You slide your tongue to their stomach–" she began and, to make the visit to the sexual arena more tolerable I buttoned my legs and tightened my jaws.

The rest of what came out of Maysoon's mouth was nastier than the dried lemon broth my mother forced me to drink whenever I had a stomach ache. It was also shocking; I thought every Chaldean girl had been raised to keep away from a man's masculinity until her wedding night.

"Raed, throw back the ball," Ashley shouted at her brother, attracting the attention of half the neighborhood who, like us, had left their old homes to take advantage of the warm weather.

Raed, my seven-year-old nephew, smiled impishly while he stood in the front yard with the ball in his grip. Placing her hand on her hip, Ashley waited for him to respond.

"Raed!" She was louder this time, but he still refused to yield. They started to wrestle and she ended up crying for help.

"Leave her alone," I demanded as I stepped down from the porch. I was so happy to be rescued from Maysoon that I wouldn't have minded their fight lasting longer.

Raed released his sister's hair and they both managed to stand complaisantly in front of me. Ashley was now holding the ball.

"Give it back to him," I ordered her, knowing she'd caused the entire ruckus out of mere boredom.

Defeat written on Ashley's face, she looked as though she was about to surrender, but then Raed's smile widened. Again angry, Ashley dropped the ball so hard it bounced over everyone before falling in the neighbor's front yard.

Raed hurtled after it while I gave my niece the fiercest look I could. That house, recently painted white, was owned by a Polish man who'd mistaken it for a deceased Egyptian queen. He tried so hard to preserve its frame that he would've built a pyramid around it in order to protect it from the children, drugs and guns in the neighborhood. I couldn't understand the man's great fondness for it when I was eager for my father to finish paying off the store loans so our family could move someplace prettier and farther away, like Barbados or Acapulco, where my sisters Ikhbal and Layla spent their honeymoons. My sister Nameera went to Hawaii for her honeymoon but she advised everyone against it. The beaches were nice, she'd said, but everything else was boring. Although I wouldn't mind boring if it were different from Detroit.

After Raed retrieved the ball, I returned to the porch. My nylons irritated me in the hot sun so I pinched them a few inches away to let my skin breathe. I wished my legs and stomach were toned enough to be exposed without this sweltering material. I was a size four but feared people wouldn't realize it unless I showed them the clothes tags.

"Oye, are you going to sit still and let me finish or are you going to fidget like a guy's thing before it gets it?" Maysoon snapped.

I took a big breath. Like my great aunt who, I'd been told,

had so much strength that for her son's wedding she'd slaughtered twenty-two chickens in less than an hour, this girl had no mercy.

"I'm going to sit still."

Maysoon tucked in her shirt, causing her breasts to bulge, and gazed around. "Do you have potato chips?"

"What?" I asked, caught by surprise.

"I'm starving"

"Oh."

I went inside the house and grabbed a bag of Better Made from the kitchen closet.

"Why are you taking that outside?" my mother asked in Arabic. She never spoke English with us—what little she knew of it—and generally used Chaldean with my father and elders.

"The porch is dirty and we need something to sit on," I said, annoyed that I had to explain to my mother every step I took.

My mother tightened her lips as I walked outside. I opened the bag, sniffed it with all my might and restrained myself from touching what was inside before I handed it to Maysoon. She grabbed three large chips and chewed them fervently. I longed to be as carefree about food, made of potatoes and deep-fried in oil, as she was. Obsessed with my weight, I couldn't afford such luxury.

"Where was I?" she asked, her cheeks puffed out.

The sound of chips so mesmerized me I couldn't answer.

"Did I tell you about this part?" She placed her hand, which glistened from the grease, between her bare naval and panty line.

I still couldn't answer.

"Did I?" she demanded.

I shook my head, floating in a cloud of the junk food I'd enjoyed before I turned fifteen and began to define the meaning of beauty as thin.

"See—" crunch, crunch. "You first—" crunch, crunch, crunch. "Do you have Pepsi?"

Her request brought me back to earth. As good a hostess as the Bedouin who killed his finest and last camel in order to serve his guest a grand meal, I sauntered inside to bring her a drink.

"What's that for?" my mother asked when I walked out of the closet with a bottle of Pepsi.

"What?" I was still hypnotized by the potato chips.

She looked at the bottle. "That."

"Oh," I sighed, too preoccupied with food to be exasperated. "Maysoon said she'd rather sit on this instead."

My mother wasn't pleased at my answer but before she had the chance to respond I walked outside and served Maysoon the Pepsi. Watching her gulp, I thought I would go mad from the heavy smell and the sound of her heart beating joyfully to its cold taste. I didn't dare take so much as a sip of such drinks for fear of round bellies and pimples.

Maysoon rolled her eyes and moaned. I suffered miserably. Then, in the middle of her ecstasy, she jerked her head forward.

"Oh my God, is that Tony?"

I turned and saw a white Trans Am coming towards us through a narrow street. "It's his car."

She set the Pepsi down, shuffled her palms together, curved towards me and adjusted her maroon v-neck shirt. "Do I look okay?"

I observed her quietly. Her hair was too gelled, her nails too long and her thighs too wide. I wondered where she got her confidence and how she kept her boyfriends. "You look good," I said, then glanced casually at the approaching car.

Maysoon had told me she and Tony hadn't talked for five days now. They'd fought about her going to a girlfriend's birthday party without his permission. "It was a last minute thing," she'd lied. "It was too late to get hold of you."

The real reason she hadn't told him, however, was that her friend's brother was her ex-boyfriend. And knowing what a flirt his girlfriend was, Tony would've forbidden her to go. Tony had stopped calling her at work—although, in any case, it's not proper, and in most instances, it's troublesome for a Middle Eastern girl to receive calls from men who haven't yet made their courting formal.

The Trans Am pulled to the side of the curb. We noticed Imad, Tony's best friend, sitting in the passenger seat. Maysoon spit out her gum, glazed with potato chip crumbs, stood up and again pulled her shirt down, showing more cleavage. "Come with me."

Her command startled, even scared, me. "Why?"

"So I don't look like a slut talking to two guys, dummy."

I hesitated. I didn't want to risk my reputation for guys who meant less to me than a comb to a bald man. Besides, it was unrealistic of her to believe she wasn't already considered a slut, and I didn't want to contribute to her denial.

"Come on," she insisted.

Knowing her perseverance would ultimately win, I checked both sides of the street to make sure no one was watching and forced myself to follow her. I wished I were wearing a watch to time our encounter and insure its brevity, though being observed by the neighbors for a split second would not be less lethal to my reputation than a whole ten minutes.

Tony smiled.

"Hi." His voice was so deep and his face so handsome that I couldn't understand what he liked about Maysoon.

"Hi." We greeted Imad, not nearly as attractive as Tony.

"So what's up with you girls?" Tony asked.

Her hands clutched behind her waist, Maysoon lightly swerved from side-to-side. "Oh, just nothing."

"Yeah, same here." Tony's right hand slowly stroked the steering wheel and I imagined it against Maysoon's breasts, over her purple lace brassiere, the one with a black bow and white pearl between the size D cups.

Maysoon managed both to frown and smile devilishly. "You don't love me no more over some stupid party?"

He stared at her and then looked ahead. Fidgeting with the radio dials, he changed stations, passing up good songs and repeating the process again.

"I just got off of work," he said. "I thought I'd stop by and see you."

"Looks to me like you just came back from a ho," she said. He was a mechanic and yet looked as tidy as a custom-made cake.

He grinned while glancing over his ivory shirt and blue jeans. "I took a shower at Imad's house."

"What'd you take a shower for?"

"'Cause I knew I was coming to see you, baby."

Her face brightened and my heart was blinded with jealousy. I couldn't understand how the two of them could talk this lovingly when I'd never even flirted. He wasn't even planning to marry her. It was obvious he was only putting up with her until he became a grown man and was ready for a respectable lady.

Maysoon's lashes fanned Tony as she murmured provocatively. Then her eyes fell on me until I got the hint and walked to Imad's side of the car. Maysoon had tried to hook me up with Imad several times so we could double date, but I'd refused. He lacked education, financial stability and an honorable family name; although he was Chaldean, he was from the village of Alkoush, which I'd learned from elders and relatives was much less civilized than Telkaif.

"Oh come on," she protested. "It's just for fun."

"No, that's okay," I'd said. "But thanks, anyway."

She continued to try to get us together, but there was no convincing me. I'd put my life into a crystal bowl to be perfect for future suitors and please God and my culture. I wasn't about to spill an ounce of it for the sake of fun.

Maysoon said my fussiness was why I hadn't yet experienced a strong and meaningful relationship with a man. Her comment hadn't bothered me then: relatives praised my will power, describing it as virtuous, honorable and sweet. They'd even gone so far as to promise that my discipline would one day be rewarded with a prestigious husband, adorable babies, exotic vacations, ultimate freedom and possibly servants.

But recently I doubted such guarantees. Seeing my parents' and sisters' day-to-day workings of marriage, I was beginning to accumulate a poor opinion of it. There was hardly passion and romance there, let alone freedom, vacations and servants. If I wasn't limited by my gender and culture, I thought, I would not depend on that institution for anything. But, as it was, I had no other choice. The trick, then, was to have a husband who could provide me with a remarkable married life.

For some reason, watching Maysoon and Tony talk that day was more painful than having a usually loose skirt snug at my waist. Under normal circumstances I would have teased Imad for a while, pampering my ego before I walked away, but seeing Maysoon's playfulness as Tony worked to win her back sickened me.

"My father is coming from work soon and he'll kill me if he sees me talking to you guys," I said. This wasn't true. My father never came home before closing the store at eleven o'clock, and being much more lenient than my mother, he would, regardless of my misdeeds, never kill me.

"Just say we're Maysoon's cousins or something," Imad suggested, pushing his charm desperately.

"No, I really should go. I don't want to be caught." I waved goodbye.

I sat on the porch and observed Maysoon's behind tilt like

a pendulum as she twirled her curls, smacking my confidence so badly I needed something quick and accessible to restore it, something like a Ralph Lauren suit.

She came back five minutes later, squinting in the sun. "Guess where we're going tomorrow?"

I cleared my throat and was careful to speak without jealousy. "Where?"

"A hotel."

I was so enraged I couldn't help showing it. "You're going to lose your virginity, just like that?"

"I've been losing it little by little."

I glared at her.

"Oh, don't be so stunned," she laughed. "I've been to a hotel before."

I was baffled. She made this sound no more dangerous than washing a tomato. "Maysoon, how on earth do you expect to get married?"

"Is that what you're worried about?" she asked, simply. "That's easy. I'm going to have a doctor stitch me."

At first I didn't believe her, and then, after my initial shock was over, I was terribly frustrated. Knowing that a girl's honor—with a little time and a few instruments—could be repaired as easily as a torn dress meant that I had to work harder to keep away from the opposite sex.

Perhaps it would be smarter to run away from my family, I thought, the way Gulnare of the Sea had done, and be sold to a great king who'd be so captivated by my beauty that he'd bathe me with treasures and affection. But surely a Middle Eastern girl who followed in Gulnare's footsteps couldn't live happily ever after in twentieth century Detroit.

Chapter 3

After she'd finished half the bag of potato chips, Maysoon left me with bitter, even wicked, feelings. I didn't care what being virtuous had in store for me. It was unbearable to be thought attractive as a gazelle yet be as neglected as fruit pits.

I was tired of getting stares but never kisses, and I wished Maysoon would start menstruating tonight and spoil her hotel plans. I hated her for occupying a position I had more right to. The old saying "God gives walnuts to toothless people" must be true.

Inside the house, I prepared a bowl of fat-free vanilla yogurt with a sliced banana and one apple. The food erased a few ounces of pain while I watched my mother put on her glasses and dial the party store so I could ask Aunt Evelyn's daughter for directions.

I couldn't dial the numbers myself because they were written in Arabic. Thanks to my parents, I could speak the language fluently, but I couldn't read the alphabet. I wanted to so I could partake of my family's heritage more. I was born in Baghdad, but I knew as little about the country as I did about love. Perhaps the fact that my name wasn't Arabic, although that of a famous Egyptian actress, had something to do with it.

"Mervat" had a European origin, whereas my family's names were rich with Middle Eastern culture. My mother Saleema, a feminine version of peace; my father Jalaal, majesty; my sister Ikhbal, greeting; Layla, a feminine version of night; Nameera, tigress; and my brother Isaam, a type of sword.

I often wondered why God had chosen Iraq as my birthplace. I only followed its traditions because I liked the characters of those who came before me. Their stories inhabited my heart, and I wanted desperately to one day have their passions, although none of their misfortunes. And what if I had been born in America? Would my thinking have been more individualistic than tribal? Would my decision to kiss someone have been based on my own desires rather than that of a society? To these questions, my sisters once responded, "Never imitate."

"Take Seven Mile to Nine Mile Road," the girl on the other end of the line said in a cold voice with a light Arabic accent. "Make a right at the light. Once you pass MacNaughton—" and she spelled as I wrote—"you'll see it on the left corner. Azziz's Party Shoppe."

I grabbed my purse from over the kitchen counter and was about to follow my mother when the telephone rang. I hesitated but worried the call might be important. I picked up on the fourth ring.

"Mervat, my dad—" my niece Ingham, Ikhbal's daughter, interrupted her sobbing and took a deep breath that nearly strangled my throat. "He is—" She took another deep breath and I felt the rope around my neck tighten. "He is yelling hard, and he is–"

Her words were overlapped by intensified crying and her father's shouting, and I could no longer understand her. The telephone clicked and there was a dial tone. My body stiffened as if I'd just seen a demon.

Within seconds, my nerves turned soft and I didn't know what to do. My mother yelled that we were running late. I squeezed my eyes shut, trying to think. The sound of my mother's heels interrupted me. She appeared at the door looking impatient.

"Aunt Evelyn is leaving by four o'clock."

I toyed with the phone. "Just give me a minute."

"What's the matter?" she asked, her face changing from angry to curious.

"Nothing, I just need a minute."

She paused and looked suspiciously at me before walking out. The instant she was gone I called Layla—whom I counted on to resolve every dilemma—and told her what had happened. She barely gave what I considered a catastrophe a thought. "Call Ikhbal's home right now and talk to Ingham. Have her tell you exactly what's wrong."

"What if Ikhbal's husband picks up the phone?"

"He won't."

"But what if—"

"He won't," she stressed.

Despite my throbbing heart and sweaty palms, I complied. There was a busy signal, which both relieved and tortured me. I telephoned Layla again and she suggested I drive over since she couldn't do it herself with her husband at work and her daughter too young to be trusted with the baby.

I kept quiet. I was too embarrassed to admit that my lack of experience didn't permit me to be the mediator of a dispute. "I could watch your kids, if you like."

"Mervat, don't worry. Mom will be there. The second he sees her, he'll hide his anger and you'll see nothing but meekness." She obviously sensed my fear and I felt foolish for having believed she could count on me to settle a problem. I was just the chauffeur for my mother.

I agreed and we hung up. My mother returned, growing

angrier.

"What's the matter with you?" she asked.

"Ikhbal and Salem are fighting."

She asked no questions and showed no grief, which surprised me. She usually made a fuss if I ate two bananas in one day, or drank tea in my bedroom, or kept my hair down while eating a bowl of cereal, or left my travel magazines scattered on the floor, claiming one was a form of gluttony, the other neglect towards the safety of my carpet and furniture, the third barbaric, and the fourth unnecessary messiness.

"Who told you about the fight?" she asked.

"Ingham called crying."

She mumbled something I couldn't hear and was about to walk outside when she paused and glanced at me. "Come on, let's go see what's stirring that man's blood."

Her calmness confused and scared me. Major arguments were too ordinary a thing amongst couples. This ruffled my impression of marriage. The institution could give me a house of my own, respect and attention from elders, but maybe it wouldn't lift my curfews and need for permission. Perhaps it would give me a headache rather than my ideal of freedom.

Before we left, the telephone rang once again and I rushed to it. It was Layla, telling me that she'd just spoken to Ikhbal and we needn't bother going to her house.

"She wants to work the problem out herself," she said.

"But she shouldn't want that."

"If she needed us to get involved, she would've asked us to." Layla was calmer than my mother, which, at that moment, inspired me against marriage altogether. Shouldn't everyone rush to Ikhbal's rescue no matter what she said? Wasn't it boorish to abstain from helping her?

Because I was the youngest and my voice the least heard, I obeyed. What she said vexed me, for my sister's sake and for myself. If this was the definition of marriage, I wanted to stay single, a ludicrous idea since I'd have to live with my parents for the rest of my life and be called *ibnaya*—girl—until I start to turn gray, or at a more mature age, *anisa,* lady. Females in the Arabic culture are not considered women until they either grow old or surrender themselves to a man. Since it's shameful for the latter to occur outside marriage, whoever is unwed is, out of respect, called a girl regardless of whether or not the label actually applies.

At the store, an elderly woman greeted us with hugs and kisses.

"Your daughter has grown so beautifully, so magnificently," she praised me to my mother in Chaldean. "She has become a bride."

This meant I was physically developed enough for suitors to knock on my door and ultimately slip a ring on my finger and gold around my neck, wrists and ankles. My mother thanked Aunt Evelyn and the two of them went off together to the canned food aisle, leaving me to wander the store alone.

I paced in front of the counter, studying loaves of bread, boxes of cereal and bags of chips on the shelves. There was a man and girl behind the cash register, evidently brother and sister. They resembled each other with their blue eyes, light skin, and tall, large-boned frames. I was certain they were Aunt Evelyn's children since the man, aside from being handsome, looked too self-assured to be anything other than an owner. And the girl, with her thick gold necklaces and countless little charms, was too pretty and too proud to work for anyone outside the family.

"You look familiar," she said to me as coldly as she had over the phone. Her fingers, with gold crawling around them, dropped empty bottles into a shopping cart with the rest of the customers' returns.

I studied her face carefully, but I couldn't remember having met her. And I couldn't imagine where she would've run into me since we lived so far apart.

"I know I've seen you before," she said.

"I don't know where that might have been."

She stared at me suspiciously, as if I was lying. Then she took a bottle of Windex, sprayed the pop and beer stains on the counter, and wiped them with a paper towel. "Were you at the communion party of Salwan's son-in-law's cousin last month?"

"I don't know who Salwan is."

"His son-in-law is Kehldoon," she clarified, but that didn't make the puzzle easier.

Embarrassed at being cornered in front of her brother, I was tongue-tied. Confusion bounced off me so palpably I thought he'd want to put a box of cereal between us to prevent contamination.

"I don't know who Kheldoon is," I brought myself to say as confidently as I could.

"I think his cousin's name is—ah, I think–" Her brows creased, and I was frightened that she'd eventually remember the name, mention it, and I'd still be lost.

"In'am," she pronounced with great joy.

I felt hot, pretending to consider the name, even though I hadn't a clue who it belonged to. "It sounds familiar, but–"

"The party was at Miro's banquet hall."

I strained to recall the names and party, but I couldn't in the face of her snobbery and perseverance. "My family and I went to at least four parties at Miro's this summer," I said.

"But this was a communion. On a Wednesday."

She was irritated, and I wanted her to crumble this subject and toss it into a well where the *djinns*—invisible beings created by God out of smokeless fire—would catch it, season it with salt and pepper, and gobble it for supper.

"Oh, yes," I said with relief. "I was there, but only because my sister wanted me to go with her. I didn't really know the people and that's why I couldn't recall their names," I finished victoriously.

Just when I thought I'd painted a better impression for her brother, she quizzed me again. "So then you do remember seeing me there?"

"Uhmmm . . . What were you wearing?"

"A short black dress with a diamond chain around the waist."

I worked harder than a murderer in front of a sultan to find a clever evasion. "Oh, yes! I think I do remember you."

I wasn't lying, either. I wouldn't dare to a girl like her. Her persistence had actually forced a single clear image before my eyes of her dancing. "But you look different now," I added like an idiot.

Her eyes opened wide and locked onto mine. "How? How do I look different now? Tell me."

If she became so savage towards this harmless comment I wondered what she would do if someone insulted her by calling her "*mara*," woman.

"I don't know," I said. "Just different."

"But how?" the girl insisted, and I tried to keep my feet on the ground in case I received a blow. I'd never received one yet, so I might not handle it well. Or it might ruin my brother's wedding pictures.

"Sou'ad," her brother intervened, his voice sedate and his accent lighter than hers, "maybe she's thinking about Cousin Nora." He gave me a charming smile that assured me I needn't worry; his sister's tactlessness was equipped with words but not bullets. "People mix them up all the time."

I pondered his remark. "Well, now that you mention it, there were two girls who looked similar."

"What was the one you're thinking of wearing?" his sister continued as though it was her honor we were discussing.

"I—I don't remember," I stuttered. "Black, I think."

"I think she's mixing you up with Cousin Nora," her brother repeated, his first rescue attempt having failed.

From the authority of his voice and the tyranny of his eyes, it was clear that this time his assistance was going to be more effective than her inquiry. The girl abandoned the subject and he took over the conversation, asking me all sorts of questions about where I lived and worked. It was difficult to tell him my home was on Seven Mile when he lived in a wealthy suburb somewhere near my Cousin Nadia. She'd once said of our neighborhood that she wouldn't mind living here between three and six o'clock. The vicinity of Seven Mile and John R was most exciting during those hours as Chaldeans sat on their front porches and observed each other while drinking tea and eating seeds, or driving the narrow bumpy one-way streets to show off their fancy cars or new hair-dos.

"I just wouldn't want to stay overnight," she'd added, knowing that thieves, muggers and gunshots occasionally grazed the area during that time.

Aunt Evelyn's daughter rang up customers while her brother and I chatted. Sensing his interest, I became reserved, taking care not to smile too often or answer questions with lots of words. His sister was so perturbed by his attention that she took measures to stop it.

"Johnny, guess who called me the other day?" she asked as he told me a story about a customer who'd argued with him over the deposit price for a keg of beer. "Remember Azhar? She really likes you, you know. She keeps wanting me to set the two of you up."

Johnny avoided her comment by asking me what sort of customers came to our store, a question common among Chaldeans who enjoyed comparing locations, prices and shoppers.

"Seriously, Johnny, she wants me to hook you guys up,"

she interrupted. "She really likes you."

"Fine, then go and tell her I like her too," he said with sarcasm.

"No, Johnny, that's mean," she cried. "You know she's a nice girl and you don't want marriage."

He ignored her by fixing his eyes on the register. I was astounded. Until now I'd thought girls weren't jealous of their brothers, but perhaps that wasn't what'd led her to be cruel. Maybe she didn't think I deserved him. I felt like telling her she needn't panic; I was more virtuous than my slim figure and stylish outfit suggested.

"Honestly, Johnny, you shouldn't say such things," she urged him. "You know you don't want marriage."

"No, with Azhar, I don't want marriage."

And to his sister's displeasure, his eyes braced mine so directly that I blushed and lowered my head. Their blue was so powerful they plucked a large nerve from my heart, leaving it swollen hours after we said goodbye.

My mother and I went to Ikhbal's house but before parking in her driveway, I checked to see if her husband's car was there. Only when we were certain that he wasn't home did we ring the doorbell. Ingham opened the door and we followed her into the kitchen, where my sister was at the stove, frying eggs with palm dates.

"Are you hungry?" she asked as we sat down.

"A little," my mother said. "But I need a hot glass of water and a spoon first. I've got a terrible headache."

My grandfather had taught my mother to cure headaches by dipping a spoon into hot water and then pressing the back-end of it against her head. I'd once asked her why she didn't just take aspirin instead, and she'd accused me of being disrespectful.

My sister brought the hot pan of eggs and dates to the table and placed it on a wet rag. "You must taste these dates. My sister-in-law sent them from California."

My mother, sister and niece made themselves pita bread sandwiches and ate earnestly while they drank cardamom tea. I only had the tea, wary of the egg yolk and palm dates fried in oil.

Ikhbal put her sandwich down and brought the tea cup close to her chin. The steam washed a healthy color over her pale cheeks as she began telling us how an hour ago she'd melted a pound of Spanish cheese and stuffed it with the green garlic stem she'd sowed in her garden last year, the plant being unavailable in the market. Not yet prepared to discuss the dispute she'd had earlier with her husband, she described in detail other ordinary tasks she'd done that day.

I found myself drifting away from the dull talk and looking at the backyard instead. There was a ditch filled with baby apples that Ikhbal's children had gathered from a tree perched two feet away. The apples, which had been green last autumn, had shriveled into the size and color of chestnuts. I'd once asked my sister why the birds hadn't eaten them, the way they did bread crumbs and rice, and she'd answered, "Because their insides are packed with worms."

At the time, I'd winced at the image, but now I wondered whether the apples, when the weather turned cold and windy, preferred having worms crawl into their wrinkled skin, eat pudding, drink soup and share the apples' quarters, rather than rot alone on the ground or be poked at and devoured by sharp beaks. I considered this until I shivered as I suddenly pictured my insides being forever empty and my heart always uninhabited.

I wished that all I had to do to sample love and be in the spotlight was hand a man like Johnny an invitation with fancy engraving. He'd appear at the church, wearing a tuxedo and grasping a set of wedding bands and plane tickets. I'd then be the wife of an eminent so-and-so and be allowed a voice.

"So how did you catch him doing it?" I heard my mother ask after the kitchen had fallen silent and I'd awoken from my daze.

Ikhbal tucked one arm beneath her breasts, the other under her chin. "I went to the grocery store for fifteen minutes and when I came home, I found him sitting on the kitchen table, holding a newspaper."

We all looked at her and waited.

She arched a brow. "He can barely read a utility bill much less an article."

My mother leaned back in her seat and shook her head disapprovingly, yet her face carried a grin.

"I know he's looking at the sport's section to find the basketball scores," Ikhbal said. "So I accuse him of gambling, and he says, 'Why can't you believe I'm just reading the paper?' I tell him because he's a liar and he starts spinning in front of me like a ceiling fan. So I tell him again he's a liar, and he growls like a bear and scares the kids to death."

My mother pressed her palm on her forehead and bent her head. She must have wanted to cover her laughter since she usually reprimanded us for this type of merriment in serious situations. Ingham ducked her nose into the tea cup and laughed aloud. I alone was grave. The scene Ikhbal had just described did not charm me.

"So the poor man was outraged that you caught him gambling?" my mother asked.

"I think he was more insulted that I assumed he couldn't read English," Ikhbal said.

This caused all three of them, even my mother, to burst into laughter. They continued musing over it, but I couldn't see the humor in my educated sister, who in Iraq had been chosen by the Bishop to teach to catechism children in his church, having to tolerate a man who didn't know his ABC's. He had been raised in a Baghdad family who owned a booth that sold spiced pickled vegetables and imported olives.

All three of my sisters, despite their beauty and intelligence, had walked happily down the aisle knowing they'd spend the rest of their lives with very common men. From the start, everyone was aware of the fact that Ikhbal's suitor exaggerated his wealth, Nameera's pampered his ego, and Layla's worshiped his poverty. And if that wasn't enough, after marriage, their husbands' faults multiplied.

Had I had any voice in the matter I would've stopped my sisters from marrying, and then I would've dedicated the rest of my life to finding them men more worthy. But I hadn't had a voice, not at nine years of age, nor at nineteen. And since I'd failed at protecting my sisters' lives, I figured the least I could do was not hurdle into their trap.

I'd vowed, especially since divorce was forbidden to us, never to marry a man who lacked wealth and prestige. I hoped that through such a masterpiece plan, I'd simultaneously acquire constant freedom and an adult type of popularity, as my Uncle Sabir's green-eyed wife had.

Chapter 4

On the morning of my brother's wedding, Jacqueline, the beautician, extended my long hair towards the ceiling while studying me disapprovingly at the mirror.

"Honey, you know what's going to happen with these split ends?" she asked. "They'll keep breaking until your hair is this short." And she pressed her long-nailed fingers slightly above my bra strap.

She'd dampened me from shoulders to waistline while washing my hair so I didn't trust her. I insisted she cut only an inch. Jacqueline shrugged. "Whatever you like, honey, but really, these here could ruin your hair worse than perms and bleaching."

"Uh-huh."

"Really, honey, that's what they'll do."

Jacqueline's surprise wouldn't fade and neither did my stubbornness. Then she tried convincing me to at least style my hair with her authentic recipe: spiked bangs, a French braid in the back and spiral curls hanging from the ears.

"We'll put the flower right here." She placed the hairpiece on the top-left of my head.

"I want it simple," I said, knowing that every girl at the party would have it the exact opposite.

"But it's your brother's wedding!"

This made me refuse even more. If I agreed to look as crowded as a map at my brother's wedding, I'd surely be wheedled into resembling the entire galaxy at mine.

"I don't want to look like a fountain," I said.

Jacqueline was exasperated. With her thumb against her large white teeth, she wearily exhaled. "Honey, don't you want everyone to notice you?"

I wondered from which *souk* this woman had obtained her license. The fountain hairdo would garner stares from women, not men. And since I was old enough for a suitor, only the opposite sex mattered here—although another girl would argue that attracting women, who often arranged marriages, held more significance. In my case, however, this custom was not effective because pampering intimidated most mothers and sisters. They preferred finding their sons and brothers ordinary brides, confident that such girls would be better at cooking okra stews and sweeping kitchen floors.

When Jacqueline realized I wasn't going to submit, she softened and began brushing my wet hair. "That's okay, honey. I'll make you look beautiful anyway."

She sprayed water on my hair and measured its length with a comb. As her arms crossed over my face, the scents of her mint-colored blouse—nicer than the Hudson's entrance at the mall, where women with heavy make-up and black clothing passed out business cards sprinkled with perfume—lulled me to sleep.

But the sound of scissors rapidly clipping at my hair startled me. I wanted my sisters, who were asking Jacqueline questions about her fiancé while they drank coffee and ate raisin bagels with cream cheese and grape jam, to set aside their personal interests and examine her work instead. I didn't want to look like a donkey and disappoint Johnny.

I tried to voice my complaints myself, but before I could gather the courage, the job was done. I watched the blow dryer cough hot air against my scalp and neck, and my eyes watered. My longest strand had easily stretched to my naval, but now it barely touched the tip of my breasts.

"Because these curls are so tight, honey," Jacqueline said when she saw my face reddening. "They'll all unfold the minute you shower."

Then, acting as though her scissors and arrogance hadn't just chopped away a part of myself, she gave me a lollipop and without further delay removed me from the barber's chair. I took a seat elsewhere and to stop myself from crying flipped through a dozen magazines, feeling as resentful towards Jacqueline as the merchant's son had towards the barber of Baghdad. Layla first told me this story when I was in third grade, and she'd begun it, as she always did when reciting fables, with this sentence:

"Kan ma kan, fi qadim azzaman—there was, there was not, in the oldness of time—a merchant's son who saw a girl watering a flower pot from her balcony and he instantly fell in love. He sent a messenger to ask her if they could meet but the girl said no. The man was heartbroken and bedridden until she agreed he could visit her chamber while her father was out.

"Wanting to make an excellent impression," the story continued—in my adult and less-detailed version—"the merchant's son called for a barber to trim his hair and beard. But rather than using his razor, the barber, who had a tongue as long as the road to Mecca, talked endlessly, despite the young man's desperate pleas for him to stop. The hour became very late, and the meeting with the girl was impossible."

Thanks to Jacqueline's absent-mindedness, my fate with Johnny might be just as disastrous.

"You guys let her cut my hair too short," I cried as we walked towards my car.

"What?" I heard at once from all three sisters. And before I could say another word, they defended themselves as vociferously as if they'd been accused of infidelity; Layla explained she'd been busy finding a style to suit Nameera; Nameera said she'd had her eyes on the ceiling while Jacqueline's assistant washed her hair; and Ikhbal claimed she had no problem whatsoever with my hair's length.

"Actually, it looks better that way," she said, caressing my hair as though it was a fur coat.

"No, it doesn't!"

"Mervat, darling, it's gorgeous," one lied, while the other asserted, "It looks just like that Egyptian actress's hair—oh, what's her name?" and as she tried to remember, another sister commented, "Now that it's fuller and thicker around the face, it makes you look healthier."

"I don't care. It's ugly. I know it is."

"No! No! No!" they protested. "It's lovely. It is."

Although I wouldn't admit it, their praise revived the confidence Jacqueline had shaken and by the time we left the shopping center, I felt better. I'd driven my sisters to the salon because although they were the deepest and wisest souls I'd ever encountered, they were as unfamiliar with highways as they were with the Declaration of Independence.

I rushed up the stairs the minute I got home, my mother's complaints trailing behind me. "Had one of you girls come to the salon I'd gone to, you wouldn't be running late right now."

"Okay, Mom." And I closed the bedroom door.

My mother had accompanied my brother's fiancée, Zena—who'd insisted on a different hair stylist than the one we'd chosen—because it is the duty of the groom's family to personally pay for the bride's salon expenses.

My mother tried to hasten my preparations by telling me to hurry but as my brother and father hadn't yet returned from the barber, I ignored her and dressed in leisure. On the bed I organized the mauve gown, the strapless black brassier, the nude colored nylons and the jewelry—a burgundy, lime and sky-blue rhinestone necklace with matching earrings and bracelet. I coated my face with lots of cover-up, lipstick, kohl, mascara and a rose blush. My sisters had warned me that, without so much makeup, the camera's bright flash would make me look like a ghost in the wedding video.

"Hurry up, Mervat," I heard my mother call again.

I closed my eyes as I doused my hair with extra spray, in case Jacqueline had been economical, then, stretching the bridesmaid's dress through the sleeves so the deodorant wouldn't touch the fabric, I tip-toed into it and drew it cautiously over my shoulders.

"And bring down the *kefiyat*," she hollered.

I paused in the middle of zipping the dress as I tried to remember where I'd put the *kefiyat* that Nameera, the creative sister of us four girls, had made. Last week I'd sat on the floor beside her as she cut colored sheer fabrics into squares and decorated their edges with sequins, beads, tiny cow-bells and shiny paper. She'd made seventeen of them—one for each sister, a few for cousins, and some extras to be given to the closest, dearest people outside the immediate family. And since it is the groom's responsibility to make these ornaments available at the ceremony, she'd made fifteen of them for the bride's side as well.

Because *kefiyat* are meant to be seen, whoever has one raises it high while dancing, keeps it to her side when walking, or leaves it on the dinner table if she's tired of it. It was important to me which *kefiya* I carried.

"I want that one," I'd announced excitedly, pointing at a white *kefiya* with red sequins and gold cow-bells.

"*Iddalalie,*" my sisters had responded, which meant 'Ask, I'll do anything for you'—a caring phrase Iraqis often use when addressing one's requests.

After Nameera had finished the *kefiyat* that day, she'd proudly exhibited them over her floor, like a tradesman would his Persian rugs. We'd all ah'ed at her work and each sister chose the color she liked best.

After I polished my nails, my toilette was complete. With my hands in the air, I cautiously walked down the stairs and into the kitchen where my brother and father were standing over the counter eating cold *biryani*—rice mixed with chicken strips, potato cubes, peas and onions.

"Hi, Babba."

Looking up from the pot of food, my father was taken aback. "*Subhanallah!*" he said, meaning 'Glory be to Allah.' "What have they done to you?"

"Babba, I'm supposed to look like this."

He shook his head and mumbled negative phrases about Muhammad and his Quran. My father always aimed his anger at the prophet even though he himself wasn't a true supporter of Christ. He defined all religions in his own terms and often disregarded the stories in the Bible and Quran, inventing new ones.

A good example was his reasoning about why Muslims outlawed pork from their diets. "*Fed youm min al-ayam,*" he said, "when Muhammad was being chased by men with swords, he saw a herd of pigs and hid between them. Instead of protecting him, the pigs fled east and west, north and south. Muhammad was so upset that they'd deserted him, he swore to make the rest of their lives lonely, degrading and wretched."

"Don't forget to lock the front door," my mother told them. She and I left much earlier than they did because men need only appear at the church minutes before the ceremony, but the ladies who have significant relationships to the groom festively escort the bride and her family to the church.

The bride had chosen her brother's house to walk out of since its opulence—with its chandeliers and mirrors, thick drapery and new furniture—were worth flaunting in front of in-laws and the camera. When we arrived, however, Zena's brother did not permit us to enter.

"In the name of the Messiah," he said in Arabic from behind the door, "you must first pay five hundred dollars."

The women on the other side of the door assumed he was joking and laughed. They realized differently ten minutes later when he again demanded the money as boldly as one would an overdue payment. My mother asked him to be a good man and allow us into the house in peace.

"No, I won't hear of it!" he declared, upsetting some of the women but still amusing others. "I won't be taken advantage of!"

"I'm not paying, Adel," my mother said. "So you better open the door."

"If you think I will be manipulated by your threats, I won't."

My mother, outraged, was going to attack but luckily the women beside her stilled her tongue by addressing Zena's brother themselves. "Please Adel, let us speak with your wife," they said, "or any of the other women inside the house."

"They can't budge my final word," he snarled. "I said five hundred dollars and I mean five hundred dollars."

The women moaned and sighed in distress but decided to wait in hopes that Adel would return to sanity. I was worried that the sun would soon boil my makeup and hair spray over to stain my dress.

The women fanned themselves with paper, tree leaves and *kefiyat* as they chatted. But when their patience didn't produce results, they became bewildered and they started knocking on the door and shouting at Adel's foolishness. Still he would not surrender.

"*Ya goura,*" an elder woman tried to reason with him by calling him a man in Chaldean instead of by his first name, "these things went on in my days, and they were done for humor. Back then, people didn't request money. They asked for a bottle of *arak* or a box of chickens, or–"

"Times have changed. In America there are no appetites for *arak* and no farms for chickens."

"What about chocolate or flowers?" someone teased, and the crowd of women laughed.

"No!" we heard him growl. "I will not accept scraps!"

This outraged my mother more. Before she spoke she called upon Jesus Christ and the Virgin Mary to help her. I didn't hear either of them answer, but she must have because her face became serene. She held the large thick cross that dangled near her stomach along with the rest of her gold.

"I swear on this cross—" and she paused, kissed it and dabbed it with a little lipstick. "If you don't open the door this very minute, we'll go our separate ways and there will be no wedding, not today or ever!"

The entire street fell silent. The door squeaked open. Some chuckling and others swearing, the women stormed inside the house and nearly hammered Adel to the ground. They began climbing the stairs until they were stopped by Zena's little niece, who informed them that the bride wasn't there.

My mother looked astounded. "Where is she then?"

"She's still at the salon," the girl replied.

"But when I left her, she was almost done, and–" Some thought distracted my mother as she paused and turned towards Adel. "Have you no shame? You ask for a gift in order to hand us the bride when she's as far away from here as your brain is."

He cleared his throat and slightly bent his head.

"Never mind," she said, to spare him further humiliation.

He was, after all, her son's future brother-in-law. "Just be a decent host and serve us water before we charge you five hundred dollars for our dehydration."

The bride's arrival caused a great deal of ruckus as four of the strongest women shoved everyone else away and shooed her to the bedroom.

"Ladies, you must hurry," the cameraman pleaded while he paced in front of the bedroom door. His equipment and assistant were beside him, eager to begin shooting.

I snuck out of the crowd and stood at the entrance where I could catch a breath of fresh air. Not a minute passed before I heard my name being called. I raised my eyes and saw my sisters gesturing for me to come upstairs. "Hurry, they need all the bridesmaids."

Everyone stared at me when I entered the bedroom, like I was a guest no one knew. I noticed the bride sitting on the bed and I was disappointed about the image that she, her stylist and her seamstress had lumped together. Each strand of hair was over-teased, four huge flowers flocked the top of her veil, and from head to toe, too many layers of ruffles surrounded her dress.

"Go there," the cameraman instructed, pointing to where the bridesmaids stood. I stopped worrying about the bride's appearance and joined the rest of the girls whose costumes resembled mine.

"Smile," the photographer said and the bright flash raised the temperature in the bedroom.

"Smile." Snap. Snap. Then he dropped the camera around his neck and approached the bed. "Okay, girls, you two sit next to the bride. You two stand to the side—lean that way—the bouquet is too close to your chest—bring it right—yes, there."

Snap. Snap. Snap. My vision was blurring and the room started to look like an abstract painting.

"Okay, girls, each one of you now walks to the bride—she gives you the bouquet—you kiss her on the cheek—you move away," he said, orchestrating wildly with his arms. "Okay, girls? Okay!"

"Don't give her a real kiss and mess her makeup," I heard a woman caution. "Give her a fake one."

"Yes, a fake one," another chimed.

Each girl acted out her part, except for Dura, who almost fell on top of the bride while trying to give her the most pretentious kiss possible.

"Okay, stand still girls," the video camera man said. "I'm getting close shots of you." He rotated the instrument, which darted a burning heat and a blinding light, from one person to the next. "Okay, third bridesmaid"—me—"your face is dripping with sweat."

Out of thick fog, a hand with Kleenex immediately stretched towards me. I took it and tapped it against my forehead and upper lip, then hid it behind my bouquet.

"Okay, I want the bride to start downstairs—followed by the flower girl, candle girl, maid-of-honor, bridesmaids." He dashed out of the room and added, "Don't come down until I have the equipment set up. Okay, girls? Okay!"

As the bride slowly and delicately made her way downstairs, the women surrounded the bridal party and did the customary ululation, a high-pitched tongue trill uttered at weddings and happy occasions. Everyone met in the family room afterward where they danced to Arabic music and opened a bottle of champagne. The eldest women chanted Chaldean folk songs. "This is it, and there'll be no other like it, and when Mervat's day comes, there'll be another day where there's no other like it."

They repeated this song until they'd mentioned all the unwed family members' names that were of marriageable age as a way to wish them the same happiness. Through it all, the bride stood in front of the fireplace with sparkling eyes, watching everyone honor her special day.

Half an hour later, the cameraman reminded us that the church ceremony was starting in forty-five minutes. "Ladies, we must hurry!" he begged. "We must hurry!"

Some complained about having to be rushed, but I didn't mind. I wanted to see Johnny and I was anxious to get to the banquet hall. I imagined him waiting, ready to be as clever about winning my heart as Ali had been with Kawthar when he'd instructed his three servants to stand beneath her window and describe out loud their master's fairness and strength. The servants had done such a superb job that Kawthar, upon hearing them speak of him, fell in love with Ali before she'd even set eyes on him. The two married shortly afterwards and they lived happily ever after.

Actually, the truth was that I hoped Johnny would put twice as much effort into gaining my love because, although I was eager to start a new lifestyle, I didn't plan on giving into him as easily as Kawthar had to Ali.

Chapter 5

After the priest chanted and read verses from the Chaldean Bible, after he asked my brother and his fiancée a few questions and they replied *"na'aam,"* and after he fed them both the body of Christ and placed a crown on each of their heads, he pronounced them husband and wife. This process, performed for an hour in front of the altar, was as splendid as the romance between Antar and Abla, the Romeo and Juliet of the Middle East. It helped reduce my skepticism of marriage.

Later in the evening, when everyone was at the banquet hall, I sat comfortably in the lounge area watching people mutter complaints as they glanced at their watches. The grand entrance, in which the bride and groom are welcomed into the banquet hall with much celebration, was delayed half an hour. One of the ushers, Rami, and the partner he was escorting to the party hadn't arrived on time.

"Maybe he dropped his bow-tie in front of the Virgin Mary and went back to get it," one of the men said, and someone laughed.

"Maybe he dropped it someplace more private and his bridesmaid went to get it," another said, and there was louder laughter.

When the missing usher finally appeared, everyone demanded an explanation. "Brother, we thought something bad happened to you," they lied mischievously. "Maybe a flat tire, or a police officer pulled you over, or your bow-tie got stuck between your zipper."

Rami stood confounded until the cameraman interrupted their sport by running towards him and crying, "Where have you been? Where have you been?"

Rami casually explained he'd gotten hungry after the long ceremony and had stopped for a pizza. This caused laughter, from the men in particular who could be blunt in public about frivolous matters, and it tormented the camera man whose pleas for the bridal party to gather around a fountain were left unheard.

"Tell us, brother, what toppings did you order on your pizza?" the men teased as they posed for the camera. "Olives or mushrooms? Anchovies or jalapeno peppers? Necks or hearts?"

Rami's story must have sounded as plausible to them as the story of Saint Rita had to my father. As a little girl, I was told that Saint Rita, wanting to be as much a part of Jesus' life as the crucifix, had decided to surrender all her belongings and become a nun. She moved into a convent, and there she'd knelt in front of the cross and prayed for Jesus to bestow her with the pain He himself had endured.

"What did this pain feel like?" I'd asked Layla.

"I don't know," she'd answered. After a brief meditation, she added gracefully, "I assume, though, that since He died for our sake, there was a delicious, delicious sweetness behind His suffering."

If that was true, I thought, then Saint Rita wasn't altogether mad for praying twenty-four hours a day so God would grant her a tiny bit of what Jesus had felt. Layla told me the nun's request was finally honored one day when a powerful ray bounced off the cross and onto her forehead, creating a wound which bled for a week. Her wound didn't heal for a long time and such an unbearable odor came from it that the other nuns refused to come near her. She was isolated until two miracles occurred and changed her life. First the bad odor evaporated and a spicy scent of incense flowed from her body. Second, oil started dripping from her palms like water from a broken faucet.

"From that point on, this nun possessed the power to heal and comfort people," Layla said, "and so she was called a saint."

After hearing this story, I wondered whether I too could heal and comfort people if my body was wounded by God. Although tempting, the notion was frightening. It would be smarter, I thought, to be the opposite of Saint Rita and, by using all sorts of precautions, prevent catastrophe from my life.

"Checking, one, two." The band signaled for the bridal party, the guests and the cameraman to take their places.

The guests made a row wide enough for the bride and groom to parade through when their names were announced. Then the loud, rhythmic beating of the music dove its passion into the women's hips and torsos, and together they moved like exotic caterpillars.

"Talaal Putris and Sana Jebbo." A male relative who stood on the stage and held a microphone introduced the best man and maid-of-honor into the banquet hall.

Their arms interlocked, the couple sauntered through the crowded lines of sequined women, tuxedoed men, bright *kefiyat* and fancy canes (hand-decorated walking sticks which Chaldeans, usually men, hold at weddings while dancing). Then they separated, the girl to the right, the boy to the left.

"Lateef Sito and Mervat Putris."

When our names were called, my partner and I mirrored the first couple's steps. I was not unfamiliar with the role of a bridesmaid. This was the fourth time I'd stood up in a wedding.

The other three, however, were for people I'd barely known because their relatives were in my sisters' bridal parties. As though it was a matter of exchanging sheep for goats, my parents owed them a member of our family to do an equal deed.

In all those weddings, I remember loathing the dresses the bride selected, but I always treasured the part where I'd openly join arms with a man, and with my head raised high, saunter into a crowded church or ballroom. Those brief moments felt so wonderful I wished they could've been permanent—except in this case, where I'd heard that my usher was a refugee counting on me for his future green card.

After all six couples' names were called, the bridesmaids, who stood facing their partners, lifted their flower bouquets as high as they could reach. The ushers then touched the tip of the bouquets' white ribbons to form a sequence of eight triangles for the bride and groom to walk under.

"And now ladies and gentlemen," the relative announced enthusiastically. "I introduce to you the beautiful, the lovely, the new Mr. and Mrs. Isaam Putris!"

The bride and groom appeared from behind closed doors, and the various *kefiyat* and canes started swaying in the air. The clapping, cheering and dancing was so fervid it could have embraced the entire world had it been invited. People packed as closely together for this moment as I was told they did to buy milk and chickens in the Baghdad market.

In this spirit, everyone led the bride and groom to the dance floor and eventually to their table. The band started playing milder music as people took turns congratulating the bride and groom and blessing the bridesmaids and ushers with the Arabic words "May this day be for you," since Chaldean weddings have unmarried bridal members.

It's disrespectful for a husband or wife to be escorted by someone whose obligations towards them resemble those of their spouse, and even if both are invited to play this role together, married couples feel too dignified to be told what to wear and how to act in a party. That's why such positions were handed to less mature persons, like me.

I was greeting the people who shook my hand and blessed my future with a good man and a superb marriage when I noticed Johnny and his family standing in line. I was both happy and terrified, wishing I could sneak away and hide in the bathroom where I could sharpen witty remarks for him.

Such hopes were destroyed the instant I noticed Aunt Evelyn extending her hand to me. "May this day be for you, my daughter," she blessed me in Chaldean.

"*Shukran,*" I thanked her.

Johnny's father, whom I hadn't met before, only nodded and moved on.

"Congratulations." His sister, who'd shown such dislike for me a few weeks ago, softly shook my hand, looked at me warmly, and left me baffled. I wondered if I'd hallucinated at the store or if, fearing her brother's reprimands, she'd rehearsed her courtesy for today.

Johnny appeared, stroked my heart with a match and threw the flame onto my whole body. I wanted my usher to take the pitcher of Pepsi beside our empty plates and pour it over me so the fire wouldn't spread to my brain, but the fool was busy swirling a carrot in the onion dip while gazing at his sleeve. He must be thinking up a scheme, I thought, that would induce me to accept his marriage proposal and forever nail him to American soil.

But I discovered I didn't need my usher's assistance to cool off. Johnny's gentle handshake and smile hushed the blaze inside of me. His eyes lifted me to a far away land, as though I was being kidnapped.

"Congratulations," he said.

"Thank you."

He followed his sister, leaving me in wonder. It was a

heavy mixture—confidence and kindness, and it made me want to explore life outside ancient tales, healthy food, pretty clothes, school books, cash registers and travel brochures. His perfection was that of the moon's, and I figured that camping in his blue sky would be my best opportunity to flourish into a star.

After I'd shaken too many peoples' hands and listened to enough blessings, I left the table and joined my sisters on the dance floor. A train of the easiest *depka*—there are six popular ones in all—was already in progress. I took my place between Ikhbal and Layla and I danced in accordance to everyone else's shoulder, waist and foot steps, a performance I savored because of the union it created amongst sisters and brothers, husbands and wives, friends and strangers.

Unless it happens by coincidence, these intimate dances do not allow men to take places beside girls whom they aren't closely related to because it means holding her chaste or served hand. Of course, there are always those who, in order to slip their telephone number to a girl they'd been exchanging glances with, overlook the rules. And then there are those who simply delight in doing what's prohibited.

"He came to the party," I whispered to Layla.

"You must show me who he is."

"Of course. But first tell me," I said timidly, "should I help him find a way to talk to me, or should I make him do it on his own?"

She winked. "Help him."

Her answer produced such a flurry inside me I thought of connecting Layla's hands to Ikhbal's so there wouldn't be a gap in the *depka* and then heading off to follow each and every one of his steps.

Curious to know what we were discussing, Ikhbal tilted her head in our direction. "What is it?"

"I'll tell you later," I said, not yet comfortable about introducing the subject of Johnny to her.

I loved my sisters equally, but my friendship with each differed. I told Nameera little of my affairs because I rarely spent time alone with her. She lived quite a distance from Detroit and having three vigorous boys and hating to drive, her husband dropped her off at our house only once a week, on Sundays. Although I told Ikhbal a lot more about myself than I did Nameera, I didn't share any secrets that dealt with boys. Ikhbal often mistook me for one of the catechism students she'd taught in Baghdad. Her philosophy about living a pure and noble life sounded nice, but sometimes seemed to clash with my real feelings. It also contradicted her own mind which was restless with overflowing future projects and her husband's numerous faults.

But I told Layla everything. She was the last to get married, so she and I had shared a room for many years. We'd even slept in the same bed, where I'd confessed all the day's events at school and on the playground and she'd spoiled me with nonconforming advice and breathtaking new stories or treasured old ones.

"Excuse my language," my usher said in broken English as he dunked a piece of bread into the salad bowl, "but do you have a boyfriend?"

I lifted my head from the plate of steak and potato that I was determined not to touch but had allowed myself the pleasure and torture of examining thoroughly. I was about to snub the question when he went on to explain that his intentions were trustworthy, that his uncle might loan him ten thousand dollars to buy a liquor store, and that his family owned two vehicles and four television sets in Baghdad.

"You'd have the privilege of meeting them once I bring them here from Iraq." He tried to entice me, now using classical Arabic to prove I wasn't just a pick-up.

"I can't marry until I finish college," I lied. I couldn't be so ruthless as to show my real feelings to an illegal immigrant. He'd surely gone through plenty of hardships with language and immigration and didn't need me to humiliate him further, but I worried that he was the type who'd be impressed by my rebukes.

"If you don't mind asking, when you think that will be?" He returned to English.

"In two or three years," I lied again. I only had one year left to get an associate's degree and I didn't plan on going to a university, but I did want him to lose all hope.

"But, excuse my language, this is wrong." And he preached in Arabic to me about how a girl could accomplish much more with an understanding husband who owned a liquor store and a beeper than she would alone. "Pretty girls should secure their future with marriage, before Satan—far be from you a thousand times—gets a hold of them."

I watched salad dressing drip from the bread he held in the air as he vented a dozen other opinions and examples concerning marriage and education. I was getting a headache. My responsibilities as a bridesmaid that day were too great to cope with. Not only was I trying to be polite to my usher while I smelled and heard people eating delicious food, but I was also scanning the banquet hall for a glimpse of Johnny.

Later in the evening, as the waiters cleared away, my usher went to paste his face against the camera lens so he could send the video to his family in Iraq. I was left feeling sad. I hadn't seen Johnny throughout dinner, nor afterward, nor did I see him during the bridal dance and the cutting of the cake, an event as lavish as the grand entrance. I wondered if he was with friends in the lounge, or if he'd gotten bored and left. Perhaps he hadn't come for me after all but just for sheer entertainment.

To honor my brother's wedding, I pushed Johnny from my mind and danced with my sisters, returning to my seat an hour later because my new shoes were choking my toes. As I caressed my injured feet beneath the table, I saw my usher running towards me with a medical kit.

"Hello," he said, carrying a ridiculous grin. "You seem hurt, so I came right away."

I rolled my eyes and turned my face. "I'm fine."

"Are you definite about that?" he asked, probably trying to impress me with a new word he'd just learned.

"Yes, I am definite," I said, tightly.

"Oh, I'm so very glad." He then made himself cozy on the chair beside me and began to talk endlessly again. As much as I tried, I couldn't figure out a way to silence him. My empty stomach, my bruised feet and his jarring voice made me dizzy. I was also frustrated by my failure to track Johnny.

I stood up, pardoned myself and hurried to the bar. There were only a few children and no men—luckily, since it is taboo to be seen at the bar when herds of the opposite sex are standing idly around. If the waiter isn't available, a lady asks her father, her brother, her cousin or her husband to get her a drink or she simply dies of thirst.

"Just water please," I said to the bartender.

I hungrily observed a plate of sliced lemons and a bowl of salt as he poured water into a glass. I wanted tomorrow to arrive so I could eat my vanilla yogurt with a blueberry bagel again. The instant the bartender handed me the water, I drank it. I even bit into the ice, hoping it would cure my dizziness before I dropped to the floor and wrecked my brother's wedding.

I'd drunk half when I noticed Johnny leaning against the wall, slowly stirring his liquor with a straw and looking at the ground. When he lifted his eyes I became so nervous that my glass might have fallen had I not been accustomed to not breaking a single object, belief or rule even if it meant my chance at happiness, or better yet, experience.

"I never did learn your name," he said after he greeted me. "It is something like Marlene or Magdalene, isn't it?"

I was so overwhelmed by him and so weak from lack of food in the past few days that I simply looked at him. Dressed in an olive-colored suit, he was exquisite enough to touch. I wanted to smell his cologned wool jacket and rest my hand against his clean-shaven face to see what such gestures could do to a girl's heart. I'd kissed a boy once before, but it was something I preferred not to remember.

"In other words," he said as he smiled and pinched the edge of his chin, "what is your name?"

"Oh, yes," I stammered. "It's Mervat."

"Like the actress, Mervat Amein?"

I nodded. "Uhm-hum."

We were quiet for a few seconds before he complimented my name, saying it suited me as it did the elegant and popular Egyptian actress. Then he complimented the party, saying it was the fanciest and liveliest he'd attended in quite a while.

"Thank you," I said. "My sisters and brother put it together, though, not me."

"Why not you? You would've done an excellent job."

"I don't know," I said modestly. "I suppose my taste isn't mature enough yet."

He frowned. "You think so?"

"Yes, I think I think so."

His frown was about to turn to laughter but he smothered it by tightening his jaw and clearing his throat. "You must show me who your sisters are, so I know whether you're an exaggerator or just sweet."

"I'm not an exaggerator," I defended myself. I would've added that I wasn't sweet either, so he wouldn't think me gullible, but I was afraid he'd think I was wicked.

I glanced towards the dance floor and pointed out Ikhbal, Nameera and Layla by describing their dresses. He tried to watch as they danced in the center of the *depka* where the immediate family of the bride and groom often belly-danced to express their joy in a more intimate manner.

"You are right," he said. "You're not an exaggerator. They're very beautiful and very, very graceful."

"They are magnificent." I watched my sisters with the warmest heart, recalling how they loved and pampered me. "That's precisely why I've allowed them to sketch my mind and figure," I murmured to myself.

Johnny turned and studied me so earnestly I felt I was being dissected. I considered borrowing someone's blue-eyed trinket to guard myself from his scalpel-eyes but I didn't want to draw attention and ruin my chances. "You give out generous, but unusual compliments," he said.

"They're not compliments. They're the truth."

His expression became so severe it was as if he knew exactly how much I liked him and how little I knew myself.

"I should walk away now," I said. "I might get strangled for standing here this long with you."

"Or I might be forced into marriage."

His expression remained solid and serious and I blushed and looked away.

"You are now being an exaggerator," I said. "If you truly suspected that might happen, you'd never have taken the risk."

"No, you are wrong. I never let risks slip away. Risks are too fun and too natural to avoid."

My eyes jumped to his. "They might be fun—I don't know—but they are not natural."

He laughed. "Of course they are. Besides, you do know. You too are taking a risk."

I scowled and fluttered as I realized my hypocrisy. His enigmatic mischief indulged and frightened me. I collected myself and prepared to take my leave. "If that's what I'm doing I should go. I'm not very fond of risks."

And smiling to disguise my embarrassment, I placed the half-empty glass on the counter, thanked him for coming to my brother's wedding and turned to walk away.

"Mervat—"

He called my name without urgency and I pretended not to hear him. I kept walking, but very slowly.

"Stop by the store sometime," he said, loudly enough for me to get the message but quietly enough not to get me in trouble.

I paused momentarily as I held my breath and smiled. Then I continued to walk towards the dance floor, knowing that something meaningful had begun and a daily routine had ended.

Chapter 6

Once the fuss of my brother's wedding was over (there were half-a-dozen other, more private, ceremonies held in the newlyweds' honor after their honeymoon), I neatly folded Johnny's memory and placed it next to my prohibited foods and distant legends. I didn't plan to visit his store for several months so that it wouldn't look as if I was anxious.

By autumn, I'd become quite comfortable with my restraint. As though I was crash dieting, I challenged myself not to see him for increasing periods of time. That wasn't the only reason I stayed away however. Dating was such a complex matter I feared I couldn't handle all that was involved. To keep my reputation, I, like any other Middle Eastern girl, had to first design solid blueprints, which needed effort and courage to keep my rendezvous a secret. Otherwise I would shame my family name, like the woman whose husband caught her feasting and entertaining other men and was stabbed to death with a dagger.

Although in these days such crimes were usually punished only with slaps and a scolding, matters worsened as time passed. My doubts and apprehensions about seeing Johnny began to exceed my affection for him. I was distraught with trying to decide which approach would get the best results and considered scraping the handsome son of Aunt Evelyn off my mind like a layer of mayonnaise on a slice of toast and trusting to coincidence to bring us together. Then, one afternoon in October, a student named Sonia tempted me into wanting a man in my life and I became impatient with my own logic.

That day, my philosophy professor analyzed Socrates for an hour before he took a break from his lecture to pace back and forth in front of the black board. Suddenly he paused and turned on us. "This man," he roared. "This man was absolutely massive! He was just massive!"

I watched the white-bearded, round-bellied teacher go into a spell, talking about Socrates and Plato the way I thought of my grandfather Thomas, the best fisherman and quail hunter of Telkaif. My siblings were once taken on a long train ride to visit our grandparents. In Telkaif they'd met the quietest culture and the most loyal church-goers, and Ikhbal told me how our grandfather attended six o'clock Mass every morning and afterwards stopped at a nearby farm to purchase cheese and melons.

"We used to cry, 'why didn't you take us with you, *Jidu*'?" Ikhbal imitated in a child's voice. "And he'd say, 'I tried to wake you up, *ibrati,* but Nanna said you are from the city and your eyes are not used to opening before sunrise."

My sister went on to describe how my grandparents took great joy in accommodating people. "We once heard *Jidu* tell Nanna to cook us *pickouta*—large yellow grains—for breakfast and she said to him, 'No Thomas, no. The children are from the city and they are used to having *pickouta* for supper'."

"*Jidu* ate *pickouta* and not eggs before he went to church?" I asked in amazement. Such a meal, digested at that hour, sounded as absurd as eating barbecued chicken during cartoons on Saturday mornings.

"Church-goers don't eat before Mass, Mervat," she pointed out.

"They don't?"

"No, they don't."

"Oh." Imagining the anguish of sitting on a bench with an empty stomach for an hour, I was glad my family wasn't churchgoing.

"The first thing that enters their heart should be Jesus' body, given to them through a piece of bread," she explained. "So they'll be purified."

"What's purified?"

"Cleaned."

"Like when Mamma scrubs my elbows and knees with soap and *leefa?*" A fish-shaped rag made of fibers that my parents brought with them from Baghdad.

"Yes," she replied with hesitation, "only with Jesus' bread, your inside is scrubbed."

The idea of having a piece of bread scrub my liver and lungs the way *leefa* did my belly button and toes amused me. "Can I eat my body through a piece of bread too?"

"Of course not!"

"Then how can I get cleaned?" I asked. "We don't go to church."

My sister glowered and not until I dropped my eyes to the ground as a form of apology did she continue. "When you take First Communion we'll start taking you to church."

"But what about Mamma and Babba?" I couldn't help asking, worried that without Jesus' bread, their kidneys and intestines would get old and dirty, buried beneath fungus and mildew. Or they'd rust.

"Don't be concerned. They can take care of their hearts through other methods."

"Like what?"

"Like beads and rosaries, candles and incense."

"And that takes the place of Jesus' bread?"

"Of course not!"

"Oh." Seeing I'd somehow flustered Ikhbal, I dropped the subject altogether even though I ached to ask more questions. I waited my turn impatiently to taste this bread, expecting it to be more fun than cereal or sour candies, but when I took the dry, hard circle into my mouth and sucked on it until it slithered down my throat in fragments, I was disappointed. Nothing had happened. Nothing.

I was unable to fathom why a hot shower felt nicer than being washed by Jesus' body, yet I didn't dare ask any more religious questions. Not only did they upset people but I didn't trust that the answers given could satisfy my curiosity. If only Socrates was still alive! He'd say, "Ask away, child, to your heart's content," and then provide me with decent answers.

"Now the Native Americans, for example, don't believe in god," the professor said. Having wandered off to my grandfather's village and Jesus' bread and the idea of asking Socrates questions galore, I didn't know how he'd introduced Native Americans into the world of the Greeks. Perhaps he'd read my mind and wanted to tell me it was alright that I was as unfamiliar of God's ways as I was of Maysoon's ways. "No, they don't. Not *the* God. They believe in the sky, and the trees, and nature."

I wondered what my grandfather would have thought of that, he who attended Mass a second time at eight o'clock in the morning for the sake of taking his late rising grandchildren, and a third time before supper with the rest of the village.

The professor's eyes tilted to the clock on the wall. It was seven minutes before noon, and, as usual, he was late dismissing us.

"Okay, you're excused," he said, but he seemed sad at time running out.

I wondered what it was that made him want us, the students who sometimes found his passions comical, to keep our seats and drink up knowledge. I pondered that even as I headed towards the cafeteria where the Middle Eastern students gathered at two tables. Although I always sat in their group, I said nothing. Being quiet is one of the nicest qualities for a Middle Eastern girl.

"Supposably, she lost her virginity falling off a bike," Sonia, a Lebanese girl, said to her boyfriend, Ahmad, a Syrian, while she puffed on a cigarette. She was one of the bad girls who, apart from smoking, was a Christian publicly dating a Muslim.

Ahmad grinned as he took a pack of Marlboros out of his leather jacket. "Yeah, that's what every Arabic girl says. And by chance, they all suffered this accident at age ten."

The guys laughed and made comments that none of the girls, aside from Sonia, understood. Ahmad interrupted their noise to ask if anyone had matches, and the other guys checked their pants and shirts until someone at the end of the table passed him a lighter.

I watched his large dark hand cover the cigarette as he focused on lighting it. His throat contracted as he drew a deep breath. I imagined he looked that way when he kissed Sonia. His cigarette flared and when he exhaled, I sighed.

"Oh Waleed," Sonia cried, turning to the table behind us. "Can I have your spoon, please—if you're not going to use it."

I glanced at the tray of roast beef, mashed potatoes and gravy, green beans, biscuits and butter staged in front of Waleed. It was during such occasions that I longed to be a boy and eat as casually as one blinked.

After handing Sonia the spoon, Waleed lifted his fork and knife and sliced the roast beef. He delivered the small pieces to his mouth and chewed them without showing an ounce of gratification. I wasn't able to take my eyes off him until I caught a glimpse of Sonia wiggling back to her original posture, like a plump worm swimming the sidewalk on a rainy day.

She took a sip of her heavy creamed and sugared coffee and I was mesmerized again. The way she dipped the spoon into the cup, raised it to her mouth and glided it between her teeth so her lipstick would remain flawless intrigued me. Her behavior wasn't that of a girl who was conceited, but of one who knew how to spoil herself.

"You want something to drink?" Hassan, a Yemeni, asked while I looked at Sonia. By then Sonia's boyfriend's arm was around her shoulders and her knees rubbed against his left thigh. Never before had I been so tortured that I wanted, if only for a day, to be her.

"Mervat?"

I looked and saw Hassan. "Huh?"

"You want something to drink?"

"Just water." And even though I knew it would be psychologically harmful, I quickly turned back to the couple's fondness for each other.

"You don't want coffee?"

"I don't drink coffee," I told him for the twelfth or fiftieth time. He always forgot because I suppose no other student in the whole cafeteria didn't drink coffee.

The instant Hassan disappeared, my eyes returned to Sonia's giggles and teasing. I wanted to dive into her private life and explore, but I was not permitted. Her reputation forbade me from getting close to her so I was left to guess how she had enough courage to date a Muslim. Or to date at all.

"*Itfatheli.*" Hassan welcomed me to the glass of water he'd brought from the drinking fountain.

As I took the glass, a heated discussion began at the other end of the table. It was started by a Chaldean who'd corrected a Palestinian for innocently labeling him Arabic.

"Chaldeans existed seven thousand years ago—long before Iraq appeared on the map," the Chaldean explained, rigidly. "We have our own language, our own traditions, our own–"

"That, my friend, does not matter," the Palestinian interrupted. "The question is, where were you born?"

"In Mesopotamia."

Everyone laughed and the Chaldean accused them all of being ignorant. "You know nothing about history!"

While some disputed his claim and others apologized for the jests, Sonia leaned closer to her boyfriend and asked whether or not he knew why Chaldeans became offended when called Arabs.

"Because they think it implies they're Muslim."

Hearing this for the first time, I wanted to enter the dispute. Not all Arabs are Muslim. If they were, the Christians from the other Middle Eastern countries would also have drawn their swords and marched into battle whenever they were identified as Arabs. I didn't argue my point, however, fearing they'd suspect I didn't mind so much being called an Arab because perhaps, like Sonia, I'd once dated a Muslim.

"Our heritage played an important role in the Bible," the Chaldean stressed. "We were one of the first who believed in Jesus. We came to him with wool to sleep on and herds to eat from. Abraham himself was Chaldean."

His information was correct but his boasting reminded me of the day my father had given a most odd biblical interpretation of black Africans. He said they'd descended from anthropoid apes and were born before Adam and Eve. When my mother tried to explain that climate and region were what changed people's skin color and features, he thought she was insane.

"After Cain—Adam and Eve's first child—killed Abel, God put a mark on Cain so that no one would kill him too," he'd said. "Now if his brother was already dead and his parents were not murderers, who was the 'no one' that God had to protect Cain against?"

My mother looked at him but couldn't answer.

"Don't you see? There were others on this earth." While

she remained speechless he continued to quiz her. "Cain was then sent into another land, and there he got married. Who do you think he married?"

"His sister."

"His sister wouldn't be living alone on an island," he snickered. "Besides, if he did have a sister, which he didn't, she'd be a child, and he wouldn't marry a child."

My mother nodded as though she understood but I didn't think she was convinced. I, on the other hand—especially after reading the first few pages of the Bible and seeing that Cain and Abel's story matched my father's version—was. But how could my father, a non-churchgoer—claiming all he did in the temple was stand up when a certain Bible verse was read and sit down when it wasn't—discover this when priests and bishops were still oblivious? And if this theory was true, shouldn't blacks, being God's first choice, be favored over whites?

I didn't dare upset my father by asking him these questions, but the idea that God created my race second caused me to feel a bit inferior and bitter. And it helped prove He was not fair.

As the discussion continued, half in Arabic and half in English, my attention drifted to the thick hand resting over Sonia's hem and her chest leaning against Ahmad's jacket. I imagined him smelling her French perfume while she breathed in his Indian leather. He must buy her pretty trinkets all the time and kiss her often, I mused. She probably draws him hearts and arrows in class and teases him on the phone.

The notion that Sonia and Maysoon enjoyed their youth more than I did stung me painfully. That day I drove home a most unhappy and envious girl. I suddenly realized that even if I did have a boyfriend, I wouldn't be able to enjoy him the way a bad girl does. Then I looked at the bright side. Sonia and Maysoon might always have boyfriends but they would never have husbands to take them to the Virgin Islands or Mexico.

Chapter 7

Although seeing couples hold hands, kiss and flirt depressed me, I remained a coward and put off my visit to the store as deliberately as one would the dentist. I turned to Layla for inspiration and a sense of direction. We had a three-hour discussion about it, but were unable to untangle the knot of doubts in my mind. I kept finding objections to her recommendations until she finally said, "Just go when you're ready, Mervat."

I didn't understand what being ready meant. But it was two o'clock in the morning, her husband was being neglected and we had to end the conversation.

The following night I went to Ikhbal for a second opinion which was useless because she ignored the question of how long playing hard-to-get was reasonable. Instead she said it would have been nicer if Johnny had asked me to Big Boy's for coffee.

"I don't drink coffee," I said.

"Alright, then ice cream."

I was about to remind her I didn't eat sweets either when a stronger argument arose. "I thought it was rude for a man to ask a girl on a date because it means she's the type who dates."

"It's not very rude. And it's more proper than going to a strange man's workplace."

We were quiet for a few seconds as anger at Johnny maneuvered itself to every bone in my body. How dare he insult me this way? I may have stood at the bar with him for all of five minutes and unconsciously loosened my self-restraint, but that didn't justify his impudence. Not only should I stay far away from his store, I concluded, but I ought to forget him altogether! Then I remembered that Layla approved of Johnny's invitation and my anger deteriorated.

"So what do you suggest?" I asked.

"If I were you, I'd do nothing. Wait until you meet again. He'll appreciate you much more this way."

Then she went on to give me places we might run into each other: the Chaldean parties held every week, the Detroit fair in August, the Arabic festival in June. It's true that Chaldeans meet many friends and relatives during these events, but winter was approaching and my patience was dissolving.

I went to bed that night thinking of an Iraqi myth Layla had told me when I was a child. A saint was eaten by a whale and survived in its stomach for three days (some scholars argue it was forty days) before escaping.

"There are no whales in Iraq!" my father had declared when he overheard Layla.

"I think there are, Babba," she said.

He shook his head. "There couldn't be. Iraq doesn't have an ocean. All it has is a gulf the size of a pool." He laughed merrily. "Why, our rivers are so small, the fishes' asses stick out when they swim."

"If you say so, Babba." Layla agreed and smiled to humor him, but she assured me in a whisper that the whale who'd eaten the saint was as real as the black beauty mark on her neck.

Recalling this story now, I wondered why my father had been astounded by the details of the ocean and not by the unbelievable hero; how could a person get himself out of a huge mammal when I could not bring myself to meet a man?

Things improved the next morning when a flock of birds and Matthew's crudeness helped me arrive at a decision. I'd opened the store at nine o'clock, but Matthew, the stock boy, came in at noon. I was relieved to see him because I couldn't bear counting another bag of sticky bottles that customers had returned. When I told him this, he asked me to show him my "asparagus fingers" so he'd see what harm the tin and glass had caused.

Not having waxed my hands for almost a month, I hid them safely behind my back and glared at him. "We shouldn't be wasting time," I said. "I have eight Italian subs to make, four corned beef, seven pastrami—"

"Let me see your hands," he insisted, making me as nervous as the day my fifth grade schoolmates convinced me to play volleyball with them. I'd spent hours that day trying to resolve how I could wear a pair of shorts, since my mother, who considered me old enough to care for my sisters' newborn babies, thought I was too young to wax my legs.

I remember having cried about the injustice of my mother's strictness while she kept assuring me, "They're all girls, Mervat. They won't notice or care."

It was terrible how my mother couldn't understand that we lived in a culture that frowned upon unwanted hair as much as it did upon thirty-year-old virgins. Infuriated, I swore I'd use my brother's razor as I stormed into the bathroom and locked the door, but she wailed as if I'd announced I was about to dishonor myself with a man, and so I hesitated.

She telephoned my sisters and had them talk some sense to me. Meanwhile I sobbed over the sink, wanting to be like the American girls who only had hair on their heads and between their thighs, or the rare Middle Eastern girls who were naturally hairless and, therefore, placed in art museums.

Matthew irritated me with his request once more.

"I have to slice lunch meat now," I said and hurried behind the counter. "You should start on the carts of empties before my father comes."

"Oh, how I love to take orders from women."

"I did not give you an order, and I am not a woman!"

"She did not give me an order and she is not a woman," he echoed, raising his eyes to the ceiling and pushing the piled cart to the back room.

The Hostess man walked in, placed a tray of pastries on the counter and began counting. I gazed at the tray until I realized he was looking at me for approval. He'd finished counting, but he'd done it so fast and my mind had been so busy with sugar, cream filling, crust and sponge, that I hadn't checked the order.

"All set?" he asked.

I nodded and signed the pink inventory list. I walked between the aisles, skipping between the Spam and jams, pancake syrups, chips and salsa dips until I reached the canned vegetables. Choosing a can of green beans for lunch, I wondered if I'd ever be able to eat normally, no longer restricting myself as much from food as from boys.

There were a few days during the month in which I came out of my diet prison for a breath of fresh air, but I couldn't really call this normal. Before menstruating my appetite grew so huge that fat-free food couldn't sustain me for five minutes. I'd hide myself in nightgowns and sweaters and without an ounce of guilt eat chocolate bars, beef jerky, pizza with steamy bread sticks, French fries and strawberry shakes. I would not stop gorging until the enormous mixture of heavy oily foods harvested a ten-pound weight gain.

Despite the pain, I always looked forward to these days. They absorbed a month's worth of cravings, granted me a bit of freedom, and prepared me for another fasting marathon.

It was a little past two and I was slicing salami when a towel smacked my behind and startled me. I turned and Matthew jumped back and grinned.

"You scared me," I said irritably.

I nudged my hair away from my face with my shoulders and returned to work, taking the stack of salami over to the Provolone and Polish ham. I was about to grab another package from the cooler when Matthew gently circled his arms around my waist and pulled me close. A tingling sensation weakened me and I half-heartedly tried to free myself.

"You know how I can really scare you?" he whispered.

I couldn't stir, much less struggle. His grip tightened and his almond-scented breath brushed against my neck. He was an American and no threat to my reputation, and I wanted his fingers to climb my ribs and touch my breasts. I'd finally know what Maysoon boasted about. But then his hands dropped around my pelvis, and as though the gesture was water spilling over my face, I came to my senses.

"You can't fool me, Matthew," I said, unlocking his arms and glancing for an instant towards his pants. "You know you don't have one."

I started towards the register but he leaped in front of me.

"Stop being a devil," he said, his claws pressing against my skin, "and let me kiss you."

"I am not a devil, and I will not let you kiss me," I said haughtily.

"If you're going to be a prima donna," he said angrily, "I suggest you stop wearing short skirts and tight jeans."

Outraged, I looked frantically for something sharp to throw but the buzzer saved him. A customer walked in and like a good clerk, I followed.

"Two Virginia Slim Menthol Lights 100's and three Benson & Hedges Gold."

I reached for the cigarettes and Matthew skulked away. My

anger faded as I thought how my pride might have hurt him, and when the store was clear of customers, I went to the door and stared out at the parking lot. There were no cars, aside from mine and Matthew's, but there were sixteen tiny brown birds hovering over a piece of bread. The holes their beaks made resembled targets, and the way they ate reminded me of a family at a dinner table.

I examined them closely, wanting to be as much like other people as they were to each other. Having the same size, color and food as everyone else seemed such a comfort. Only if I packed my clothes, my conservative ones, and retired forever in Telkaif might such a life be possible. I had no hope of such nonsense occurring and wished I could just strip myself of the rules that held me apart from the rest of America.

I didn't want to move merely to make some sort of change. If only I could go away, really away—to foreign places with the blue lagoons, alphabet-shaped hotels and bathing suited tourists—I might discover a life outside of Detroit and Telkaif. Or I could quit college and work for an airline or cruise line that would take me away. Such jobs would be shameful of course. I'd have to sleep away from home and deal with men and Westerners, but it wasn't as though I'd do it forever. I'd quit once I spent a few nights at Acapulco's Pierre Marques or St. Thomas's Limetree Beach Resort, after I swam from one end of the sea to the other, went disco-hopping, ate papayas and drank coconut juice.

I looked at the ground and felt empty; my dreams did not match my nationality. I wanted excitement without jeopardizing my name or lifting a finger. I wanted a husband to go hunting for it and carry it back to me skewered on a spit, yet I felt threatened by marriage, suspecting the honeymoon lasted literally seven days. Then it was dishes, babies, fights and gaining weight.

Closing my eyes, I took a deep breath to relieve my melancholy. I had been content living on nothing but fables and rules for nineteen years but they no longer worked. When I looked at the parking lot again, the sight of a fat white-sea gull and the absence of the sixteen tiny birds surprised me.

I wondered whether the gull had swallowed the birds whole, tucked them beneath his wings, or scared them away to better enjoy his meal. Whatever his method might have been, it amused me. I observed him in admiration, imagining how powerful I would feel if I could unscrew the bolts around my wrists and ankles as easily as he'd made the birds vanish. Then I could take a vacation from convention and wander into the strange and new.

A yellow car pulled in and a man dressed in black leather and silver chains stepped out and opened his trunk. He brought out two garbage bags of empty bottles and cans.

"Morning," he said and went inside.

Before I followed I pressed myself to arrive at a definite decision, one that would help me start a life of my own. I'd visit Johnny soon. No, even sooner than soon. I'd go this Saturday. And if fear and circumstances got in my way, I'd light a match and burn them to ashes.

I was finally as impatient about seeing Johnny as the Arabian princess when she was about to reunite with the lover who'd fled her side after catching her in an intimate embrace with her female slave. I was gladdened by this impatience.

Chapter 8

My courage didn't last as long as I'd expected that week so I cancelled Saturday's plans and decided to visit Johnny after Christmas. At least this way I'd avoid the awkwardness of gift exchanges and wishing each other a happy New Year. I was more ready on the weekend of January 4th. To prepare for the occasion I searched for someone suitable to accompany me to the king's palace and present me to the handsome *amir.*

I couldn't go alone because that was shameful. It wasn't decent to take my sisters along, either, because they were married; older female relatives, especially those with husbands, are not supposed to encourage a young girl to become involved with a man unless he reveals his intention is marriage. No one will be beheaded of course for supporting a girl's decision to date as long as these relatives are discreet about it.

My only options were my two oldest nieces. My sisters and I chose Ingham, since she would mind her own business while Ashley was likely to eavesdrop and blurt out whatever she heard. Once that was taken care of, a restless wait ensued, one which, for me, resembled that of the prince who'd undergone many years of great hardship in his anticipation of possessing the Sea King's daughter. The besotted prince had fought wars and was turned into a bird by a sorceress, trials he endured to prove his love. A queen undid the witchcraft and on his way back to his kingdom his ship was wrecked. He survived to face yet other setbacks, but these troubles made his pleasure, when he attained his goal, all the greater. The story eased my agitation, assuring me that in the end I'd be repaid with joy, but that Sunday was so nerve-wracking I tried to speed it up as best as I could.

I decided to go in the late evening. I thought five or six hours of shopping would calm my fidgets so I took my niece to Spring Lane Mall, a three-story building where young Chaldean boys and girls, dressed in their best clothes and staying among their own sex, paraded themselves on Sunday afternoons.

"*Ha gahba,*" I heard Maysoon's voice call loudly.

I dropped the mustard suede shoe I was to try on, sure that people heard her. It would have been wiser to pretend I didn't know the girl who'd just shouted the word bitch in Arabic.

Wiggling her thick behind and noisily chewing a piece of gum, Maysoon approached. She kissed me on the cheeks and sprayed my nose with watermelon and rosemary scents. "Watcha doin' here?" she asked.

She always imitated street language when she was excited or wanted attention. I tried to answer when she leaned towards me and whispered, "There's this knockout guy that's been following me for an hour."

Her finger traced the braided gold chain around her neck while she looked to the exit where two Chaldean guys, each leaning against an artificial tree, were grinning at her. She looked at me again and said, "I'm so glad you're here. I hate shopping with my cousin. She's more annoying than long pubic hairs."

"Shhh," I begged, scanning the place again.

"Well, it's true," she continued. "She's such an idiot, I'm

always having to pluck her head out of her ass."

I regretted having come here rather than to Johnny's store. The embarrassment of shopping with Maysoon in the mall—aside from her bad reputation, she was half-naked—burned, particularly at three in the afternoon when those who were most handsome and important were arriving.

"Come on," Maysoon said as she grabbed my arm. "Let's get my cousin out of the damn coffee place."

Maysoon's eyes never left the men we encountered along the way, and neither did theirs from her bosom.

"Maysoon, you want to borrow my coat?" I couldn't resist. I prayed she'd say 'yes' and we'd be spared the agony of the stares.

"No, thanks." She blew a big bubble, then popped it. "When I seen it snow hard last night, I knew the mall was going to be jam packed with goodies today."

I couldn't believe my bad luck. The most important day of my life, and she was on the verge of ruining it. Not only must I worry about the problems she might create, but she was probably going to invite herself to my house for tea this evening, tell me of some sexual incident between her and Tony, and yet again plunge me into melancholy.

We entered the coffee shop and Maysoon dragged her cousin, still in line for cream and sugar, out. Then she rushed us to the soft ice cream booth. She ordered a vanilla and peach frozen yogurt in a wafer and as she scrounged in her purse for money, she asked if we'd like some as well.

"No, thank you," I said.

Her cousin, Naila, said no as well, but Ingham asked if she could have ice cream, and I hushed her up. I didn't want Maysoon to pay for my niece—out of politeness, she'd have to—and then I'd owe her patience, kindness, and worst of all, friendship.

Maysoon shook her head and bent to Ingham's ears. "Don't

listen to your aunt. Tell me which flavor you like."

I tried to protest but she immediately turned to the clerk behind the counter and ordered a second frozen yogurt. The lady asked if they wanted free toppings and Maysoon asked what sane person wouldn't.

She and Ingham pressed their foreheads against the window and examined the fruit, candies and nuts heaped in small silver containers. Giggling, they pointed to one then to another. My starving eyes were glued to the ice cream and colorful toppings.

My regime during the past four days had consisted of fat-free cereals and skim milk. I was desperate to taste something more solid, or at least different, but I feared a single bite would widen my appetite, and also my mind; it would make me think of what I'd be eating for dinner instead of what I should be saying to Johnny.

Maysoon and Ingham ate ice cream, Naila drank coffee, and I watched with envy. Then some Chaldean guy approached Maysoon and asked if she would take his beeper number.

"I'm spoken for," she said, licking the vanilla and peach swirl and crunching yellow and blue M&Ms.

He opened his arms wide as he shrugged. "So maybe I can speak louder."

Smirking, Maysoon ducked her mouth into the ice cream and walked away. I turned around expecting to see him sniggering, but he and his friend were watching her figure instead. Jealousy sizzled inside me even as I tried to convince myself that such men might want her as a girlfriend but never as a wife.

I tried to persuade Maysoon to leave the mall but she insisted we go into stores and try on spring clothes. I had no choice but to stay a few feet ahead of or behind her, especially when we came to the mall's intersection where most of the Chaldean guys hung out.

Another man drifted towards Maysoon, bundled in layers

of black leather and thick gold chains reaching to his pants' zipper. His hair was slicked back and he had a perfectly shaped goatee. He told Maysoon he wanted to get together because her thighs were creamy and fine and would be great for rubbing his backbone.

"No, thanks," she said. "I'd much rather chew on a *zibana*, fly."

He looked so angry I thought he was going to smack her with the five-pound trinket dangling between his legs. But he softened as he raised his head and backed away. "Hey, no problem. It's not my fault that you're *balait al-air.*"

We were speechless. It was extremely rare for a man to disrespect a girl by saying she performed oral sex.

"*Cuss ighteck! Gawad! Imhashis!*" Maysoon swore at his sister's private parts, called him a bastard and an inhaler of hashish. Before more vulgar remarks got tossed around, Naila and I grabbed Maysoon's wrists and pulled her away. I helped Naila calm Maysoon down and then took the first opportunity to excuse myself. I didn't care to disgrace myself further in front of hundreds of Chaldeans, half of whom were neighbors and acquaintances of my family.

As soon as I got home I dashed to my bedroom and telephoned the store while Ingham sat on the couch, eating salted cucumber slices and waiting my return.

"Azziz's Party Shoppe," a man said.

I hung up. This was not a prank. I'd been in the habit of making such a call for the past seven weeks in order to figure out Johnny's schedule. He and his sister operated this store while his other brothers worked at another, and I recorded the date, the hour, and sex of the person who answered.

At first I didn't get results because Johnny and his sister switched hours irregularly. But after four weeks I'd discovered that he worked every Sunday from morning until night. I made this latest call to make sure I wouldn't walk into the store and be faced with his cold and relentless sibling.

"Mervat, your sister's daughter has school tomorrow," my mother called from downstairs. "Hurry up."

I quickly reapplied lipstick and perfume and put on higher heels. Johnny was tall and I was short, and even though we'd already met I didn't want the difference in height to surprise him after eight months had passed and he might have eyes for someone else.

I tried to be simple about my clothes so my mother wouldn't suspect that my intention was to start dating Aunt Evelyn's son rather than drive Ingham home. Not having the nerve to look her in the eye while lying, I searched for the car keys in my purse as I said goodbye.

"Are you going to sit at your sister's awhile?" she asked as she placed fresh orange peels into a pot of tea.

I busied myself with tying the coat belt around my waist. "Maybe for a little bit."

Both Layla and Ikhbal knew my scheme, having outlined much of it, and were prepared to cover my tracks. The topic had not yet been introduced to Nameera, though. Layla thought it unnecessary for too many family members to get involved, and Ikhbal thought that unless it became definite, we should keep such rendezvous secret from everyone.

"What does she mean by definite?" I'd asked Layla.

"What else could she mean but marriage, Mervat?"

"Oh," I sighed, feeling tremendous pressure. If Johnny didn't eventually propose, it'd look as though I was tricked or used or wasn't good enough. I'd be forever burdened with a secret that weighed twenty times more than my first kiss. It was a good thing that intricate steps had been taken to make this occasion happen. Otherwise I'd have to run away and leave Johnny stranded.

I told Ingham I had to stop at a schoolmate's store so she wouldn't question the odd visit. Two blocks before reaching MacNaughton Street, I pulled into a restaurant and asked to use the restroom. I was nearly breathless as I babied my curls. I patted toilet paper against my lipstick so its shimmer wouldn't blind him and observed myself sideways in the mirror. If my stomach was not as flat as our kitchen's tile floor, I'd squeeze it against my ribs the entire time I stood at his counter.

"Are you going to pee or not?" Ingham asked.

"I will, but wait a minute." I continued looking into the mirror until she folded her arms and whimpered my name. Then I forced myself to use the lavatory.

When I came out, I observed the details of my lashes, nose, chin, and complexion. I examined the collar of my shirt and the skirt's hem beneath my coat. I wished the mirror was full-length so I could be certain my legs and feet didn't look funny. Measuring the ceiling with my eyes, I even considered stepping up on the sink. But that might crush the faucet, I thought, and involve me in reprimands, explanations and a much delayed departure.

"Are you done yet?" Ingham groaned. "Can we go now?"

I was so nervous that my niece's boredom and tiredness couldn't affect me. I did worry, though, that Johnny's store door would close soon if I didn't leave the mirror. "Yes, I'm done, and yes, we can go."

I tried to block all doubts by fueling my brain with gallons of thin air.

Gazing at the blue sign that read Azziz's Party Shoppe, I pressed my hand over my empty, upset stomach and rested my heavy, muddled head against the car window. The thin air in my brain had somehow dispersed so whatever I'd blocked out earlier was registering again. I wondered whether this risk would be worth it.

"Are we going down or not?" Ingham asked.

"We're going down." I remained seated.

It was all Maysoon and Sonia and my Uncle Sabir's green-eyed wife's fault. They broke rules and tempted me to follow in their *haram*—forbidden by God—footsteps. I should've been like Cousin Nagham, who didn't go to college and went to Hawaii for her honeymoon instead. She'd never had to impress any man because girls are empowered by the presence of their chaperones and the length of their flowery dresses in old-fashioned courting and are not supposed to show their true selves until the camera man turns off the lights and the wedding guests go home.

"Mervat?" Ingham cried.

I turned to my niece, who looked tired. I apologized for having been an intolerable turtle, opened the door, got out of the car and stepped into my story.

In a plain white T-shirt and black jeans, Johnny looked better than the two times I'd seen him before. The instant he flashed his smile I forgot, even questioned, the hell I'd put myself through to get this far.

"I thought you were never going to show up."

I didn't comment, baffled at how he could entertain such a silly notion. A man like him was impossible to reject, even by a sultana. He could be mistaken for a European model rather than a Chaldean immigrant. He obviously couldn't mean it, I concluded, but only said it to flatter me. Perhaps, though, he did mean it, and I'd wasted all this time watching Ahmad reach for Sonia's thighs and picturing Tony unbuttoning Maysoon's blouse instead of experiencing these pleasures myself.

But then I saw joy in his blue eyes, and I thought my decision to wait had been smart. He would appreciate and respect me now that I'd proven I didn't easily welcome a man into my life.

I introduced Johnny to my niece and told him how we'd spent the day at the mall. He said he wasn't very fond of the place because the Chaldean punks who lingered there on Sunday afternoons caused all sorts of trouble. Once police officers kicked a large group of them out for spraying each other with shaving cream, and another time a fight broke out when someone punched a guy for having hissed at his sister.

"Was it bad?" I asked.

"Of course. There was orange slush and blood splattered everywhere."

Ingham and I grimaced, and he laughed.

"That's disgusting," my niece said.

Johnny asked Ingham whether her aunt was going to get in trouble for introducing me to a man who told disgusting stories to little girls.

She frowned, hesitated, then frowned again. "No, I don't think so."

"I hope not. Otherwise, I won't see her for another year."

I blushed, lowered my head and felt him admiring my shyness. Shifting the discomfort, he asked us what we wanted to drink.

"A Yoo-Hoo," Ingham replied before I had a chance to stuff my purse into her mouth.

As he rang the bell nailed next to the lottery tickets, I glanced at Ingham disapprovingly for not having asked my permission before making her order. I didn't want to inconvenience him or seem ill-mannered. A customer, smelling of beer and tobacco, approached the register and bought two blue rolling papers. The stock boy came out of the backroom.

"What would you like to drink?" Johnny asked me.

"Nothing, thank you."

He tried to lure me into a Pepsi or lemonade, but I thanked him again and explained I wasn't thirsty. Since I couldn't be persuaded, Johnny told the stock boy to grab a Yoo-Hoo from the cooler.

My niece barely had a few sips before I sensed it was time to leave. The juice of conversation was leaking badly and my departure would be its best cork. Hanging around any longer would make me seem desperate.

"We'd better go now," I said, and Ingham, with the Yoo-Hoo pressed against her teeth, started towards the door. "I have to drop her off at home because she has school tomorrow."

Johnny didn't insist we stay, nor did he encourage me to come again. He simply thanked me for stopping by, smiled and nodded. Regretting I'd ever met or visited him, I also smiled and nodded as I followed Ingham. She was already outside and I went to reach for the door handle when Johnny saved me from the greatest disappointment of my life.

"Can I call you sometime?"

Not only was I grateful but his line impressed me. He was the first man who'd had enough class to want to call me rather than hand me his telephone number on a torn paper or a folded napkin.

"I can give you my work number."

He snatched a pen and pressed a register key to bring up a blank receipt.

Once he got the last zero he raised his eyes. They were so kind and reassuring that I feared little droplets of joy would spill to the surface if I didn't rush out of the store and expose them to the stars. I said goodbye and left quickly.

I couldn't react in front of Ingham so it wasn't until I dropped her off that I finally loosened the knot around my heart. For the entire drive home, I couldn't be still. Even when I rested my head on the pillow that night, I couldn't be still. Not only had my own personally engraved story begun, but it was going to be embellished with a splendid cast and unpredictable events.

Chapter 9

That encounter quickly gave birth to a romantic relationship. He telephoned the store early the next morning; we talked briefly but for the rest of the day I couldn't work properly. I did a horrible job stacking shrimp cocktail sauce and cereals. They seemed coated in margarine and constantly slipped through my fingers. I did an even worse job slicing cheese and meat. The customers requested thin and the machine, having no real supervision, cut it thick.

By the end of the week I was less excited about Johnny's phone calls and more worried about whether I could handle the burden of dating. I hadn't yet acquired the necessary tools of diplomacy and courage, like the Christian queen who was so brave that she secretly took her father's enemy, a Muslim prince of Baghdad, into her chamber and entertained and befriended him. She even protected him from her father's warriors when they came to cut off his head, permitting him to use his sword against them instead. I tried to focus on her to remember how small my troubles were, but that didn't qualm my fear.

"Does that mean you don't want Johnny to court you?"

Layla asked after I'd finished counting the pitfalls of dating. "That you'd rather read history books and travel brochures, press register keys and cuddle under your blanket, all alone, until someone appears in a flash from a genie's bottle, and proposes?"

I nudged my shoulders and pouted. "Yes, I'd rather do just that. I wish he'd stuff a handkerchief with gold, like in the old days you told me about, and come with his mother at six o'clock tomorrow morning."

She laughed. "No man asks for a girl's hand that early in the day, not even if her belly and ankles are swollen."

I pondered that a moment. "But if her belly was swollen, would he actually ask for her at all?"

"He might, if her father owned a rifle or her mother an axe." Then she grinned. "But don't get any wicked thoughts in your head, Mervat, and cause a scandal in our family. Babba can't afford to waste money on a rifle and Mamma has no place to hang an axe."

Her teasing turned my face the color of tomato paste. I knew as well as she that I would never disgrace my name, even though lately I was getting frustrated with the dividends of chastity. I was nineteen years old and had not yet had one decent suitor. Older women picked the homeliest girls for their sons, assuming their chunky hips and messy hair would guarantee they'd cook daily, clean constantly, and never answer back. Or they chose the youngest girls, imagining their innocence could also be easily molded into that of a maid's. It often angered me to know that, unlike girls who belonged to the strictest Chaldean families and were married off at age sixteen, dating was clearly in my path. If my parents were less liberal and didn't allow me a measure of freedom, I couldn't be picky about whom to marry. I'd just have to marry, period.

In the next few weeks, Johnny called me at work every

other day—as if a little more would have spoiled me or a little less upset me. Respectfully, he made no attempt to ask me out. My sisters and I were honored by his courtesy but Maysoon came over one evening and tempted me into wanting more than the sound of a man's voice flowing through plastic.

She greeted my mother in the kitchen and smothered her in kind words. It's disrespectful to compliment an elder instead of bowing shyly because it suggests the young person is either belittling their wisdom or not valuing their hardships. For other, more valid reasons, my mother disliked Maysoon.

"She's *wakieha*," she'd once said, when I'd pressed her to tell me why she refused to let me have tea at Maysoon's house.

I couldn't defend Maysoon by saying she wasn't naughty because she was. But I couldn't see what harm having tea in a naughty girl's home could do. My mother declared it would scar my reputation. Layla, on the other hand, softly said that my mother was exaggerating the situation a gallon or so, and then explained, "The most damage it could do is influence you."

"Being influenced is not that dangerous, is it?"

"No, not that dangerous. But when you don't yet have your personality shelved here accordingly—" she pointed her thumb at my heart, "—this could get pretty messy." And she pointed her thumb at my brain.

After Maysoon chatted about the neighbor's girls five houses down the block who, she said, never helped their mother chop cauliflower for *turshi* or walked on their carpet after their sandals had been worn in the rain, we went upstairs to my bedroom.

"Lock the door," she whispered.

"It doesn't lock."

"You think your brother will walk in on us?"

"No. He'd never come in without knocking."

"Oh good." I could see her disappointment.

"Anyway, Maysoon, my brother's married now," I reminded her with some irritation. "He usually visits us Tuesdays, Thursdays or Fridays. But never Wednesdays."

"Oh yeah." She sighed, remarking that no one could really blame her for forgetting Isaam had gotten married since she hadn't attended the wedding. What upset her more was that she hadn't been offered a copy of the videotape either.

"We mostly had close relatives at the reception," I stammered, feeling guilty for not having invited her and hoping she wouldn't end our acquaintance because of it. I'd have no one to entertain me with her kinds of stories.

"Didn't you have four or five hundred guests there?" she quizzed. "If not more."

"No, I doubt that many." I shook my head. "No, not that many at all."

Fanning her hands, she swore it didn't bother her that I, a friend and neighbor, neglected to include her in my family's happiness, as though we feared she would've jinxed it, or that we suspected she wouldn't pack enough money in the envelope to cover the cost of her plate. I told her she was crazy to think that way, that her speculations were far from the truth, and that–

"Don't get me wrong, Mervat," she interrupted. "I forgive you. It's just that for the past eight months or so, my heart's been itching to bring this subject up." She paused and blinked repeatedly. "Now I have, and that's that. I hadn't expected an apology, anyway."

Annoyed by the tint of mockery, my words were ready to race hers with worse slaps. She was clever enough to wheel herself out of the way of an ungracious confrontation and jokingly told me to shut up for now, to sit on the bed and to keep my eyes open.

"What for?" I asked.

"I want to show you something."

She took off her jacket and threw it on the floor, then hurriedly unbuttoned her red blouse.

"He gave it to me last night," she said.

I looked at the florescent-pink bra that hugged her plump breasts together. "How did he know your size?"

She broadened her chest in front of the mirror and gave a fanciful smile. "Dummy, I'm talking about this." She looked towards a bruise the size of a silver quarter.

I observed it, interested. "Does it hurt?"

"It's not a bullet, Mervat. It's only a hickey."

"Yes, I know," I said, when I really did not know. I was much more educated about bullets, which were occasionally heard in our neighborhood in the middle of the night, than I was about hickeys, which no one had dared flaunt in front of me before. I couldn't ask Maysoon about what, precisely, produced such a blemish for fear she'd snicker. It was normal and dignified for a girl to be naïve about a man's masculinity but when I was with Maysoon I felt childish.

She put on her blouse again, partially unbuttoned to show her cleavage. We were perched like kittens on my bed's apricot-colored blanket and I embraced the panda bear my brother had won two years ago at the state fair and she tucked the heart-shaped lavender pillow I'd sewn for Valentine's Day in eighth grade beneath her breasts.

She had a mischievous smile and my mind bubbled with curiosity. I knew how exotic the thoughts that danced in her head were. Now that I had a boyfriend, now that I was waking to the possibilities of love rather than listening in jealously, I wanted the stories of her exploits to slither from her wine-colored lips onto my thirsty imagination.

"Have you ever been kissed, Mervat?" she asked, her long nails circling the pillow's white-laced trimming.

Her bluntness caught me by surprise. Of course I had the option of lying and keeping my secrets as safe as the necklace I'd gotten for my First Communion was in the bank. But something prompted me to expose my private life as much as she did.

"I promise I won't tell anyone," she said.

I lowered my head and decided in favor of my flatly ironed reputation. "I've never kissed anyone, but what made you ask?"

She shrugged. "I don't know. I guess I wouldn't want to be the first to sully your virgin mind."

"Oh." I struggled to figure out the game she was playing. She was either tormenting me before lowering the blade of gossip, or she was excluding me from the fun because she resented my purity. "That's never stopped you before."

"Of course it has!" she sprang, startling me. "You think I've spit out all the kisses me and Tony ever had together?"

I was taken aback by her hostility. Was it common for a girl to lose all patience after she surrendered her virginity? "No, I don't think that."

She sighed in frustration as she lay on her back and looked at the ceiling. "My whole purpose in sharing what I do is that you benefit from it."

"Um-hum."

"But then I somehow end up feeling as though I've done you wrong, and that's not fair."

"Um-hum."

She fixed her eyes on mine. "Do you see what I mean?"

"Yes." I didn't like the way she treated me, nor did I understand it, but that evening I would've said anything to drag a few anecdotes of sin out of her.

She flipped over on her stomach and shuffled herself into a comfortable position. Her mischievous expression returned and she reached for the ivory ribbon on my nightgown, hanging between my breasts. "So tell me what you want to hear."

"I don't know." I was embarrassed she knew how anxious I was to hear about her and Tony.

"Fine, fine," she said. "I'll start with last night, before this gets too complicated and my blood hardens into wax."

She described the exact manner in which Tony had touched her chin and stroked her stomach, how he'd loved her thighs and enjoyed her fragrance. My arms and legs tingled as she twirled my nightgown ribbon.

"He especially loves my lips and ribs," she said proudly.

"Doesn't it embarrass you to be seen naked by him?"

She flung her head back and laughed out loud. She calmed down and looked at me with amusement. "*Ib-Mariam al-Athra*—in the name of the Virgin Mary—you're odd. How else do you think people have sex with each other?"

She'd completely misunderstood what I'd asked. I wanted to know how, despite the fat blinding proportions of her figure, she could lay naked in the hands of a man, particularly when she wasn't his wife. I couldn't clarify the question, though, because her feelings would be hurt and she'd never pour out her tales of the flesh again. Besides she was already engrossed in telling me how patient Tony was with her when they had sex.

"I mean, he always, always, lets me finish first."

I didn't know what she was talking about, but I was too mesmerized by her bliss and the slight caress of her fingertips against my nightgown to ask questions.

Maysoon's face became serious. "Do you have cashews?"

I blinked. "Huh?"

"Cashews. I'm dying for some."

"Oh." And before I left the room, she told me a Pepsi would make it even better.

"Okay," I obeyed, but I wondered how I was going to manage sneaking both food and drink into my bedroom since my mother disapproved of eating anywhere outside the kitchen. I tiptoed downstairs and hoped the freezer wouldn't be too loud, or the bag wouldn't crinkle, or the ice jiggle. As careful as my fingers and feet were, I was caught as I was heading upstairs.

"Where are you taking that?" my mother asked.

"To the mountain."

She scowled. "Does she serve you cashews and Pepsi in her bedroom when you go to her house?"

"I don't know. I never go to her house."

"If you did, you think she'd serve you anything, much less cashews and Pepsi in her bedroom?"

Without answering, I rolled my eyes and went upstairs. Maysoon was lying peacefully on the bed. I imagined Tony's eyes inspecting her thick curves as he slowly undressed, just before he joined her beneath the hotel's bed sheets, the ones I'd smell and wrap myself in when I'd one day sleep at the Hotel Solmar or the Buenaventura. For the first time I saw how he could be attracted to her: she was overweight and unsophisticated, but the idea of nestling beside her was cozy and serene.

The bed squeaked when I sat down and Maysoon's eyes opened. I offered her the bag of cashews and Pepsi. As she ate and drank eagerly, she informed me of the pimple in her ear which was caused by a bacteria in Tony's saliva. Then she lifted her skirt a few inches and showed me teeth marks all over her upper-thighs.

"He says he loves leaving a mark to remember him by," she said. "But I think he just wants to tell guys I have a vicious boyfriend."

"Aren't you afraid your mother or father will see?"

"I'm not afraid," she said casually, and continued to reveal more details. I was attentive at first but her chewing and talking and the heavy mixture of cashews and perfume put me under such a spell that I lost focus and started thinking about Johnny. I wanted him to stain my skin with bite marks so men would stay away. I wanted him to hurry and ask me on a date so I would stop trying on everyone else's stories and finally wear my own. And I wanted him to be so much a part of my life that I would be able to say "I'm not afraid" as casually as Maysoon had.

Chapter 10

The instant Johnny asked me out to dinner, I began starving. I figured four days of eating a plum for breakfast, a banana for lunch and a kiwi for supper would shave at least half an inch off my waist. Not only would I look thinner but I'd compensate for the food I absolutely had to have at the restaurant so that Johnny wouldn't know I dieted.

Our date was on Sunday and on Saturday I drove to Layla's apartment after work. She volunteered to do my upper-lip, as she normally did when a suitor was coming to inspect me or a party was going to take place. I loathed the process, which consisted of threads, water and pain—but it was as essential as going to the *hammam*—public bath—in Baghdad before and after sex. I couldn't possibly skip it.

Layla's little boy screamed happily and flounced in circles around me. I picked him up and hugged him, and while he drooled over my arms, Ashley came out and asked if I could take her to Meigher. She had to buy a white cardboard poster for a geography assignment. I didn't mind as long as I got to help her color Mexico pink and Brazil red, but Layla told the children to leave us alone.

Ashley complained about having a mean mother and my nephew started kicking his legs in the air. After I placed him back on the carpet, my sister took my arm, led me into the kitchen and verbally displayed today's menu.

"Mini-croissants, garlic bread, clotted cream–"

She named other things but I declined all offers. Instead I opened the refrigerator and grabbed a peach since she didn't have my fruit. I preferred to limit my appetite to three flavors or less so my hunger wouldn't stagger to other cravings, but I knew I needn't fret this time. My intent to impress Johnny outweighed all else.

Peach in hand, I sat across from Layla as she spread a teaspoon of butter over her croissant and added the pumpkin marmalade she'd made after last year's Halloween. I watched the butter crease and the croissant fold while she pressed it into her mouth. The marmalade overpowered my perfume. I envied my sister for being able to chew food as though it was a simple matter rather than an honor. When she had a second serving I found myself panting for her cheerful appetite.

Layla placed her sandwich on the table and went into the kitchen. "Do you want something cold, like milk or pop? Or would you prefer tea or cocoa?"

"Nothing, thank you."

"I have prune juice and *shaneena.*"

Yogurt juice sounded delicious, but I said, "No, thank you."

She accused me of being stubborn and said that a camel would have been a more delightful guest. I said I was insulted that she'd chosen a camel of all species to compare me to.

"You ought to be proud, Mervat," she corrected me while pouring herself a glass of prune juice. "In the olden days, in the Arabian tribes, owning a camel was as prestigious as owning a Mercedes."

"I thought a horse was more important."

Layla teasingly criticized Detroit's school system which

had failed to teach me about humps and hoofs.

"I didn't go to school in Detroit," I reminded her. To shelter me from the city's overindulgences and dangers, my father had snuck me into a better school, registering my name under my uncle's address in Madison Heights, six miles north of Seven Mile and John R. Then he'd taken responsibility for driving me every day.

"Then I accuse that school district of the same laziness," she said before explaining. "The horse, Mervat, isn't half as useful as a camel. A camel's long legs help it walk in the desert without sinking in the sand. And it can carry double the baggage that the horse can." She paused to drink some prune juice. "And oh, what a name a woman who dared ride a camel made for herself!"

"What name did a woman who rode a camel make for herself?" I asked eagerly.

"A most honorable name. She was said to be strong and brave."

I wanted to ask whether a woman was strong and brave before riding the camel or after. And if it was before, what prior incident had made her strong and brave to begin with. I also wanted to ask if my Uncle Sabir's green-eyed wife had accumulated all her defiance after she'd had an encounter with a camel, even though people granted her a name as ignoble as that of Talaal, *et-Tanbal*—the idle one, so nicknamed because he stayed home all day and did nothing. But these questions were as likely to be answered as the ones about Jesus' bread washing my intestines clean, so I kept quiet.

Layla was complaining about her husband canceling their dinner reservations for their wedding anniversary because his father was ill.

"He's been sick for three months and we've been visiting him regularly for three months. Then the one day when we finally plan on eating out, his cousin calls and wants to come over." She shook her head and sighed deeply. "My husband doesn't tell her we're going out because he's afraid if this news travels to his mother, it'll upset her. After all, how could her son think about eating steak and onions while his father sips bitter medicine?"

Layla suddenly stopped talking, wiped mucus with her bare fingers from her son's nose and carried it to the sink as though it was nothing but a dirty spoon. Washing her hands, she kept her head towards me and described her mother-in-law's insensitivity and conceit in an earlier incident.

"My in-laws had a doctor's appointment Wednesday, so they stopped in," she said. "I served them tea, cake, seeds and nuts. My father-in-law casually asked what I'd paid for the peanuts and I told him a dollar and nineteen cents. He was surprised because where he shops, they only cost ninety-nine cents."

She stopped talking again, scooped water into her palms and drank it. Then she dried her hands and mouth against her T-shirt as she returned to her seat.

"It outraged my mother-in-law that her husband implied her West Side—yes, she calls it *hers*—sold fresh peanuts at a cheaper price than did our East Side."

Something from the backyard interrupted Layla's story and prompted her to shout, "Ashley! Ashley!"

She snatched a robe from over the kitchen chair and sped outside before her daughter had a chance to modify whatever crime she'd committed. Through the window I noticed that the only damage my niece had done was to neglect her younger brother. I watched Layla stick her fingers inside her son's mouth and remove the pinecone kernels he was chewing. My nephew cried before he ran the opposite direction and Layla, wearing only slippers, a T-shirt and a thin robe, wrapped her arms around her chest and shivered.

"Mervat, come outside," she said, standing beside her son. "I must show you something."

It was too cold to leave the apartment but she was my favorite sister and I couldn't refuse. Using my arms for warmth, I sauntered out.

Layla pointed to a cage with a black and white rabbit. "One of Sermad's customers got him this as a late Christmas gift."

The last time I'd seen a rabbit was in a cartoon and I'd never imagined that in real life it was as large as five coconuts. His eyes were dark and big as black grapes and he had a lot of meat and fur. I wondered whether he felt sad or snug inside that cage. "Won't he get frost bites?"

"I doubt it. We took him out of the apartment so he'd get some fresh air," she said. "I don't want him to be as claustrophobic with me as I sometimes get with Sermad."

As though she'd made a most ordinary remark concerning her husband, Layla knelt to her son and twisted his curls. "Okay Robert, baby, listen. This is a rabbit."

"No—it's—not," Robert pronounced every syllable in slow motion.

"Then tell me, baby, what is it?"

"I—don't—know."

"Maybe it's a dog, a cat, a tooth brush–"

"No—it's—not."

"What is it then?"

"I—don't—know."

"If you don't know what it is, how do you know it's not a rabbit?" Ashley asked.

"It's—not—a—rab-bit."

"Then what is it?" Ashley insisted.

"It's—a—bun-ny."

While my sister and her daughter hugged their ribs with laughter, I studied my two-and-a-half-year-old nephew and admired his independence. I took him in my arms and kissed his cheeks, hoping his individuality could help unite my plurality—my beliefs that were split between Eastern culture and

Western liberty. Perhaps then, without having to come into contact with a camel, I too would be strong and brave.

Layla suggested we take the children inside and stand near the stove for ten minutes.

"We should," I said. "You're almost naked."

She viewed her body from shoulders to toe. "Instead of saying I'm nearly freezing?"

The way she made light of her clothes made me crave being a wife. A married woman had permission to flaunt her body without criticism. The problem was that my brother-in-laws created deterrence towards this institution. Lately my nieces' and nephews' capriciousness and my sisters' maltreatment at the hands of their in-laws weren't helping either.

Inside Layla was about to unseal more of her in-laws' wrong doings while she boiled a kettle when the telephone rang. It was Ikhbal, telling her that a friend had tattled about Salem betting on horses Thursday night. Layla asked how much money he'd squandered and Ikhbal told her a couple thousand.

"Oooh, *ya rabby.*" But before the Lord replied to Layla's summons, she delivered Ikhbal a dozen psychological and physical cures.

Meanwhile, I swung my legs and desperately waited for their conversation to end so I could discuss exactly how I ought to conduct myself with Johnny tomorrow night. A half hour passed before Layla hung up and repeated, word for word, what had been said between her and Ikhbal.

"I've already overhead everything," I said when her details began to tickle my patience.

"Oh, sorry. I forgot we have better things to discuss right now than our brother-in-law's gambling problem."

I blushed and bent my head.

"Please don't let your shyness rule over you, my precious sister," she said, dramatically. "Rather, tell me how passionately in love you are with Aunt Evelyn's gorgeous son."

"I'm not in love with him!"

"Of course you're not. We don't have girls in this house who'd ever dream of such feelings."

Her grin made me smile and I was going to go on when the telephone rang again. It was my mother wanting to know what time I planned on coming home and whether she should roast a chicken or bake a fish for Husnia's funeral Sunday afternoon.

"Mervat will be home in two or three hours," she said, "and for the funeral, it'll be easier to roast a chicken."

Although this was all my mother needed to know, they talked until my sister Nameera called. She wanted directions to the fortune teller's house, the one who didn't charge money for her services.

"She quit doing that long ago," Layla said. "Her husband got fed up seeing women eat watermelon seeds and drink Turkish coffee in his living room morning, day and night."

Ingham called afterward and asked to speak to Ashley. Then Robert started tapping my brother-in-law's calculator on the tabletop. Layla left to stop him as I grew edgier with frustration. It was nearly six o'clock, her husband was coming soon, and I still had to drive to Ikhbal's house so she could shape my eyebrows.

"I need you to do my upper-lip," I reminded her.

"Okay, just give me a minute," she said as she stooped over the carpet and yanked bits of pita bread from the nap.

Layla handed me a tissue and instructed me to wipe off my lipstick. She took advantage of those few seconds to get Robert out of his pants and shirt, yell at Ashley for staying on the phone too long, and to pick up the stuffed animals, the stack of diapers and the folded pajamas from the couch. With her chores finally done, she poured water into a saucer, brought a flowery cookie jar from above the refrigerator and searched through a pile of colored threads. She wrapped a cord of burgundy thread three times around her right hand, then grabbed the middle of the cord with her teeth and approached my face. I winced and fidgeted.

"Hold still," she lisped, as she tilted my chin upwards, "or your lip will get pinched and bleed."

I closed my eyes and held my breath. She dabbed water over my upper-lip to moisten it and reduce the pain, then pressed the thread against my skin and withdrew it systematically, tugging hairs from their roots so vigorously it made my eyes water and my nose sting. I begged her to stop.

Layla detached the thread from her teeth and pulled away from me. "I will not have you walk in the streets with half a mustache. So please, sit still."

I forced myself to concentrate on beach resorts and English term papers to distract myself. As soon as the thread nabbed my hairs I was squirming again.

"Please, Mervat, sit still."

"I am," I said, although I wasn't. I pleaded to dull some of the pain by adding water, but she said no, that the last tiny hairs could better be removed from dry skin.

"Be patient and swell up this area," she said. I nudged my tongue so she could detect the microscopic hairs and yank them out.

When she was done she stepped back a few feet and evaluated my upper-lip with the satisfaction of a painter surveying her work.

"I don't want to praise myself," she said, "so you look at it in the mirror yourself."

I went to the bathroom. It was flawless. I was genuinely happy with the results but I was too embarrassed to tell her.

She tucked her arms beneath her breasts and leaned against the door. "Do you like it?"

"I do." I couldn't thank her with words, so instead, I showed my appreciation with a large smile—one that faced the mirror, though.

Ikhbal plucked my brows afterward, and at home I waxed my legs and blotted my face with a mint-green mask Layla had given me. Then I took off my nightgown and stood in front of the mirror to examine my body. The plums, bananas and kiwis had not melted away enough bulges, and although I knew nylons would smooth surfaces, I scrounged the closet for an outfit that would best camouflage them tomorrow.

By the time I went to bed, I realized I'd made this event much too significant. I was simply Mervat going out with a liquor store owner and not Shahrazat, entering the King's palace as a one-night bride. I curled inside the sheets and I recalled Layla's voice lulling me to sleep:

"*Kan ma kan, fi qadim al-zaman,* a pretty and most clever girl named Shahrazat," she'd whispered into my ear late one night as my father sat on the couch across the room and sorted bills. "King Shahryar chose her for a bride, and–"

"Did he bring her two million servants and buy her gems the color of lemons and apples?" I'd interrupted.

"No, he wasn't that type," she said. "He liked marrying a different girl every night and having her beheaded in the morning."

"Oh," I sighed, disappointed. I pondered his behavior. "Was it because she made him mad?"

"No, Mervat, it was because he'd get bored with her."

"Bored," I'd echoed, thinking that men must be too violent and difficult to please.

"What are you teaching her?" my father growled. "Kings don't get bored! They have countries to run, wars to start, taxes to collect!"

"But Babba—"

"He despised women because his wife and his brother's wife were unfaithful daughters-of-dogs. They cheated on their husbands with servants, the exact men who scraped the castle's sinks and toilets," he said. "Beheading his brides was the king's revenge on all women."

Layla lowered her eyes and meditated a little. "Probably so, Babba."

"Do you think that's true?" I asked. This time, surely, she was convinced by father's version.

"It might be," she said, softly. "Although boredom, even for a king—a different king, perhaps—could have caused this behavior."

After my father returned to the utility bills, Layla described how Shahrazat was well aware of the king's marriage customs. When he chose her for a bride she realized she needed to use art to save herself and other innocent girls from death.

"And did she find one?" I'd asked.

"She did."

"What was it?"

"It was a variety of poetry, tragedies and comedies."

On their wedding night, Layla said, Shahrazat mesmerized the king with heroes and villains. She poured her heart into each word of the story, as lovingly as one did water onto roses, until the sun came up and the king fell sound asleep. In order to hear the remainder of the story, she was allowed to share his chamber once more.

"Then what happened?"

"Night after night, the beautiful lips of Shahrazat uttered mystery and passion and kept King Shahryar amused."

Shahrazat was able to keep the king's interest for a thousand and one nights, until, without realizing it, he fell madly in love with her. No longer needing to capture his attention with words, she finally ended her storytelling. Then together, they lived happily ever after.

I had for many years thereafter imagined Shahrazat's silk gowns and gold bracelets, her painted face and braided hair. I pictured the king lying on gleaming cloth and watching her lips go on and on. He must have monitored them as they smiled occasionally, pouted suddenly, and rested never.

It would be nice, I'd often thought, to stroll in Shahrazat's mind and explore the endless treasures that not only saved lives but gained her the love and devotion of a king. It would be nice—especially these days, especially tonight, when her talents would be most useful to me—for that to happen.

Chapter 11

Al-leeqa'—The meeting

I lost my balance getting out of bed the next morning. I felt dizzy. The room turned dark and it spun. Before I toured its dimensions a third time, I knelt to the ground and pressed my forehead against the carpet that smelled of dust and attar. I covered my face and took deep breaths until I regained my vision and most of my strength.

Eventually I managed to avoid tripping over nightstands and porcelain dolls by keeping my fingertips against the wall while walking to the bathroom. I stepped naked on the scale. My diet had eliminated two pounds and I was happy. The results had been worth the torture.

I was determined not to put anything in my mouth until Johnny and I were served our salads. That failed at the store when I felt unsteady twice—once while counting eight dollars a customer had given me in nickels and dimes, and a second time while mopping a kid's dropped Gatorade. Afraid I'd faint among the red ants and mustard stains, not to be found by Mathew until customers had stolen my father's money and cigarettes, I drank a quarter-bottle of grapefruit juice and felt better.

At home I nursed my appearance for hours but was far from satisfied. I considered rewashing my hair and redoing my makeup. I called Layla, who hours earlier had helped design each detail of my appearance for the night, to ask her opinion.

"It's six o'clock, Mervat," she said. "You cannot afford to be so picky right now."

"I think I can."

"You can't. You only have ten minutes left." We were both silent before she added, more softly. "Unless, of course, you purposely want him to wait in his car, in fifteen degree weather."

"I hadn't once thought of making him wait," I said, defensively. "But should I?"

"What kind of question is that?" she asked, again sounding astounded. "Of course you shouldn't."

"I look ugly, though."

She sighed and groaned. "Oh, Mervat, stop being so contrary. I know I can't see you over the phone, but I'm sure you look beautiful. It's nervousness, that's all."

I was quiet.

"Trust me, Mervat. It's nervousness, that's all."

"Yes, that's all."

After we hung up, I tried to convince myself that anxiety was the problem here and not lack of beauty. It didn't work. I wanted to hose the creams and powders off my flesh, tear my wardrobe into little pieces and feed them to the birds, but the clock was ticking too fast. I was trapped in a costume only servants would wear, yet I needed to be an elegant lady.

My mother had been sitting in the kitchen chopping vegetables. I didn't want her to notice me before I said goodbye and slammed the front door, so I tiptoed across the living room. The floor squeaked and the Chinese vase on top of the television rattled, and I knew I was going to be strip searched.

"Mervat," she bellowed.

"Yes, mother?" I answered loudly. I didn't dare enter the kitchen and have her read fraud on my already-anxious face.

"Come in here a minute. I want to talk to you."

That was not the voice of someone wanting to talk to me, but of one who was prepared to puff the sheet of lies off my face and pick out the truth with a pair of tweezers. I mulled over what to do but I was summoned again. I fanned the heat from my face, took a few gulps of air, and presented myself.

"Where are you going?" she questioned without lifting her eyes from the pungent vegetables that were now being seasoned with dried peppermint leaves.

My eyes darted in various directions except hers. "A classmate invited me to her birthday party."

She looked up. "What classmate?"

"You don't know her," I mumbled.

"What's her family name? Where does she live?"

"She's not Chaldean and she lives three miles away."

She stared at me in suspicion. I hoped a phone would ring so I could crawl into a caravan traveling to faraway lands. I'd have to suffer the consequences upon returning to Detroit, of course, but by that time so many real-life gypsies and sword-bearing warriors would have disrupted my boredom that I wouldn't mind the most drastic penalty.

"Do your sisters know about this classmate?" she asked.

"They do."

"And they approve?"

"They do."

She looked inside the large bowl of cucumbers, then asked me to bring her a slab of meat behind the carrots and parsley from the refrigerator. Under any other circumstances, I would have begged off, afraid I'd mute my perfume with the smell of blood. I risked the same end as the merchant who, on his wedding night, had gorged on a dish made with garlic and had forgotten to wash his hands afterward. When his bride embraced him and smelled the garlic on his skin, she was insulted by his lack of breeding and ordered his thumbs and big toes cut off. If Johnny detected an unpleasant odor, he wouldn't damage any of my body parts but he would cut our time short.

Still, I knew better than to disobey. I opened the refrigerator and was glad to find the meat partially frozen and held it two feet away from me as I delivered it to the kitchen table. I wondered if she was going to let on that she knew about my rendezvous and insist I cancel it. She didn't say a word as she unwrapped the meat from its plastic and slapped it a few times, just as she did watermelons before buying them. Then she raised her brows.

"I don't want you to come home later than ten o'clock," she warned formally. "Ten o'clock, Mervat."

Her permission choked me from head to toe as I fought to suppress my happiness. She might already suspect I was meeting a man, but I didn't want my heart to bloat any fuller and give her further proof of it.

Before my mother could discover how abnormally nice she had been, I quickly went into the bathroom, washed my hands, lotioned them and rushed out of the house. As I backed the car out of the driveway I saw the closed screen door and suddenly found myself in a panic I'd never experienced before. I was on my own, and I was caught between the possibility that this pretense of independence would lead to love, a suitable marriage, and abandoning temptation for the safety and familiarity of home.

I didn't come to my senses until I saw how late I was running. Only then did I drive away from my well-guarded shelter to mingle with the desert's sand storm.

Johnny met me at Farmer Jack's Shopping Center on the corner of Continental and Twelve Mile Road. He was in a red

Corvette with a black sunroof, and although the car itself didn't greatly impress me, his wealth absolutely startled me. There had been rumors of Aunt Evelyn's family fortune, but the extent of it had not been clear.

"Do you want to go anywhere in particular?" he asked after I got in the car.

"No, nowhere in particular."

"Then would you mind if I took you to the West Side? I'm not very familiar with this area."

"I don't mind. As long as I'm home before ten."

He looked at the clock, which read 6:36. "That might limit the possibilities, then."

"In what sense?"

"In the sense of skipping coffee and dessert."

"I guess I'll have to skip coffee and dessert."

"But in that case, I'll feel I've cheated you of a proper evening."

I wanted to tell him that in reality he could spare me unnecessary calories and fat grams if he abandoned restaurant plans altogether and took me to Baskin Robins for two-scoops of fat-free ice cream instead, but I thought it unwise to divulge strange preferences this soon. A much more rational time would be during our marriage.

The restaurant was extravagant and crowded. I scanned the room as the pretty, thin hostess in a navy dress and matching high-heels walked us to our table. I wanted to know whether any of the diners were Chaldean so I could keep myself hidden. In such circumstances a veil would be most useful: it greatly helped Farah, for instance, when his wife, Farha, was abducted by an old woman who planned to enroll her in the Khalifa's harem. Khalifahien were men who, after the Prophet Muhammad's death, were appointed in high-ranking religious positions to take over the preaching of the Mussulmen.

When Farah discovered his beloved was missing, he traveled from Iraq to Damascus to recover her by dressing as a girl, painting his eyes with kohl and twitching his hips like a female past the guards at the gate and into the castle.

Since I did not have a veil (although even if I did, I wouldn't have taken the chance of ruining my hair by wearing it), I prayed to God that no one would spot me. Being caught with a man by a family friend or relative would be so disastrous it would discourage me from ever going out with him again. But aside from a Chinese couple, there were only Americans and Italians sitting at the dimly lighted tables and booths, all eating pasta and drinking wine. I relaxed a little and felt ashamed of asking anything of God out of desperation when He was well aware of the numerous times I criticized Him.

"Your waitress will be with you in a few minutes," the hostess said, handing us two huge menus.

As I scanned the entrees, I panicked at having to choose among tortellini with creamed mushrooms, carbonara, fish Milanese, veal Florentine and chicken Marsala. These dishes were not only foreign to my yogurt/bagels/fruits/skim milk regime, but I balked at the hazards to my figure—layers of Parmesan and mozzarella cheese, cupfuls of meat, bacon, batter and buckets of olive oil. And each meal included a garden salad, a bowl of soup, a portion of spaghetti and bread sticks and butter.

I tried to make a choice before the waitress appeared and coaxed Johnny into ordering an appetizer because I knew if I indulged on a night when I wasn't already feeling bloated, I wouldn't forgive myself for months. Vegetable lasagna was the fastest meal to nibble on I decided as I closed the menu.

Once Johnny decided on the chicken Marsala, we were both quiet. I felt shyer by the moment. I'd been so consumed with my appearance and my diet that I'd forgotten there would be talking as well, and I hadn't a notion of what to say that wouldn't change his opinion of me. So I remained mute, allowing him, who surely had ample experience, to start a conversation.

Johnny took a sip of water, appeared on stage and created a tiny dialogue before he drew the curtains open on the first act of the evening's drama. That was when I was introduced to an intriguing twentieth century American citizen—the character of his half-brother, Nabiel.

"You have a half-brother?" I was a bit amazed. I had never met a Chaldean family who didn't have children from the same mother and father.

"Two half-brothers and two real sisters," he said. "My father's first wife died in a fire at the age of twenty."

"What kind of fire?"

"She was baking bread and while she was gathering a finished batch into her apron, some flames caught her dress."

"Oh." I couldn't utter another word, worried about what would sound appropriate.

I visualized the flames girdling her skirt as Johnny explained how his father married his deceased wife's first cousin within a year so he'd have a relative rather than a stranger to raise the children while he worked in a village outside of Telkaif. Three years later, he moved his family to Baghdad, and fifteen years afterwards he immigrated to America.

These things saddened me terribly. I wanted to know how his father replaced the woman he'd shared years of quarrels and harmony with and who'd given birth to two of his children, but I thought it better to ask about this from my sagacious sister.

During dinner Johnny told me his half-brother Nabiel had been one of Baghdad's famous scoundrels. Once he visited his aunt's house in Mosul. She'd welcomed him, despite his reputation, and when Nabiel claimed he was hungry she cooked him two eggs, over-easy, salted and peppered. While she was frying the eggs, he stole her sewing machine and disappeared for days. On another occasion, sitting on the second level of a public bus, Nabiel had casually unzipped his pants and urinated over a bald man's head sticking out the window. And one day, he'd gone into a bicycle shop and, while the owner was busy dealing with customers, took off into the streets with a brand new bicycle. The owner, like the rest of Baghdad's business-men, knew exactly who Nabiel was, so he went to his father's office to complain.

"Your father must have been very upset," I said.

"My father was used to it. The poor man offered my broth-er money, work and vacations just to keep him from misbehav-ing. But Nabiel loved being bad. He absolutely loved it."

Listening to his voice and seeing the expression on his face, it seemed as though Johnny was bragging about his half-broth-er's wrongdoings. I pictured the three brothers sitting on a couch, bottles of beer at one hand and steamy, lemony chick peas at the other as they recalled details of Nabiel's thefts and trickery. They must have patted him on the back and kissed the sandals on his feet for being the devil himself. I couldn't blame them. I too would have applauded Nabiel, but it wouldn't have been for being a devil. It'd be for having the choice to be bad without facing eternal public humiliation and disgracing the family name.

Later in the evening, Johnny's talk turned to himself, but it wasn't personal. He told me about his weekly schedule at work and the gym, his interests in football and sports cars. To divert his attention from my full plate, I asked him about his hobbies. I couldn't take another bite, my mind racing to calculate the calo-ries and fat I'd had so far. When my watch read 9:18, I happily placed my fork on the table and asked him to take me home.

Before I got out of the car he asked if I'd had a good time.

"Yes, thank you."

"Will you trust me to take you out again?"

I found it difficult to say yes when I didn't want to show

how much I liked him.

"Well?"

"Yes," I forced myself to say, knowing it would be impolite and risky to keep silent.

"You say it with hesitation, but I won't complain. Compared to how long it took you to visit the store, this is progress."

I wanted never to show my face to him again, but he went on to salvage my pride. "It's too bad not all girls are as decent as you."

My stomach was as stocked with food as our store but my heart was famished. It had been for years. All that seemed over now. His words were my reward for having starved myself of food for years and from men all my life. They confirmed that being a good girl led to happiness.

I thanked him once more before closing the car door. We waved goodbye, backed out of the parking lot, and drove our separate ways. I was too anxious to think and it was not until I was home that I could relive the night.

I cuddled into bed with the dress I'd worn pressed against my nose to make sure that when I woke I'd know the evening had been as real as my apricot-colored blanket.

Chapter 12

The next few days were spent in a pool of analysis. My sisters and I pried apart each aspect of the night: Johnny's regret that I passed up coffee and dessert, his praise of my virtue, his ease in talking about his reckless brother. Through our intricate evaluation, we (and especially they) fathomed Johnny as being confident and *dama ghafeef,* buoyant. But after getting a good laugh out of his pranks, my sisters were understandably skeptical of the half-brother.

"I didn't know Nabiel had such tales hidden in his pockets," Layla said in my room, where she and Ikhbal had steered me after a supper of stuffed zucchini. I only had a burnt pita bread (I'd heard a rumor that the longer grain was toasted, the fewer calories it contained).

"Maybe that's why he's never mentioned," Ikhbal said.

"No one even sees him," Layla commented.

"Men like him don't go to weddings and funerals, Layla," Ikhbal said. "They hang out in coffee shops, casinos and jails."

My eyes and mouth widened in horror.

"Are you disappointed that the man you adore is related to a criminal?" Layla jested.

"I don't adore him and he is not related to a criminal."

She and Ikhbal grinned and eyed each other knowingly.

"I don't! And he's not!" I cried, frustrated.

Although they didn't disagree I found it impossible to calm my temper and was relieved when my mother called them downstairs. Their teasing hadn't bothered me, but their speculations that I liked Johnny were embarrassing; that he had a crook for a brother worried me. Only boys were meant to like girls, never vice versa, and if Johnny had inherited any of his family's mildewed traits then he could be a terrible threat. He might lie, lead me on, and without conscience toss me aside to pursue a prettier, younger, thinner, wealthier girl.

After all, it had happened to the shoemaker's wife. Her husband sailed a boat across the Nile to escape her and the sultan in the new land liked him so much he offered his daughter as a bride. I thought about that story until I admitted it had no real comparison to my situation. The shoemaker escaped his wife because she treated him miserably. When he failed to buy her *kanifa* with her favorite sugar cane honey, she beat him. Then she took him to court and accused him of having ruthlessly abused her. Not knowing it was a hoax, the judge pitied her and sentenced her husband to a hundred lashes on the soles of his feet.

I dwelled on such gloomy stories until night when I resolutely put them out of my mind and went to bed with the dress I'd worn to the restaurant once again hugged to my chest so I wouldn't forget Johnny's blue eyes, smile and the place he'd assumed in my life. I was about to establish a grown-up role in the community without having to endure, the way my sisters did, the difficulties of their lying, poor, arrogant husbands.

The next night, I watched Ikhbal's children while she went to a party with her husband. I paged Johnny after I put the kids to sleep, thinking it would be a good chance to talk without worrying about my mother constantly picking up the kitchen extension or that I'd be heard in my parents' connecting bedroom. The last thing I needed was for her to fulfill her role as a Middle Eastern mother and mercilessly scold me while I was still on the telephone. Her disapproval would be only a little less severe than the Christian woman who'd made her daughter wear mourning clothes in memory of having lost her virginity to a Muslim, but it would be just as humiliating.

"When can I see you again?" Johnny asked before we'd said three words.

"I don't know."

"Let's figure it out. When do you leave work tomorrow?"

"I'm closing with my father tomorrow because my brother and his wife are going to a baptism party."

"What time do you close?"

"Eleven o'clock."

"You have breaks between your classes, don't you?"

"Yes."

He cleared his throat. "How long are they?"

"I have an hour between history and algebra."

"I can meet you then and we'll have breakfast or lunch together."

His offer disturbed me. I kept quiet because I could neither agree nor disagree. He sensed my distress and asked with amusement whether I needed a few days to think it over.

"No, I don't need a few days to think it over," I said seriously. "If you pick me up at school and my classmates see us, I'll be the talk of the cafeteria."

There was an odd silence that scared me. I couldn't tell whether he was angry, hurt, annoyed or indifferent at my diffidence. And when he burst into laughter I was baffled. I waited for him to stop but when he didn't I asked him what was so funny. He gabbled some explanation but it was so broken I couldn't paste it together.

"What are you laughing at?" I demanded.

"At you, of course."

I kept quiet. Gradually the laughter ceased.

"Mervat?" he asked, restraining himself.

"Yes."

"Are you upset?"

I did not respond.

"Are you?"

"No. But it's not fair to ridicule me."

"Oh, but it is fair for you to torment me?" he said. As I attempted to defend myself, he trampled my words. "Ever since I met you you've done nothing but make it impossible to see you."

I explained that I couldn't sneak out of the house without my mother suspecting I was getting out of hand and tightening the handcuffs on my curfew. Not having friends to cover my tracks meant I was lying on very low fuel. I also pointed out that in our old-fashioned kinship the phone was supposed to be an adequate and convenient form of day-to-day courting.

After I finished my speech, there was a stiff pause between us, long enough for me to begin condemning myself for what I'd said.

"Maybe the problem is that you don't want to go out with me."

"I do!" I hated him for sabotaging my willpower by making me confess.

He laughed sarcastically. "Yet you want to substitute the phone with seeing each other?"

"I don't want that."

Again there was a pause. I was afraid he'd get tired and want to sweep me out of his life, so I tucked my pride in my bra cup, the way my mother did her money and handkerchiefs, and gave in. "When do you want to see me?"

I felt his heart blossom before he replied, "Right now."

"Seriously, Johnny."

"Yes, seriously."

I smiled and I offered the best alternative I could come up with.

"Wednesday afternoon would be best." My classes ended at two o'clock and I didn't have to work afterwards.

That morning I packed a bottle of perfume and hair spray, bobby pins, barrettes and a brush into my school bag and told my mother not to expect me at my usual two-thirty because I was going to the library. She didn't even turn her head from the liver and onion breakfast she was frying for my father as she nodded and shooed me away. Her permission had been gained so easily that I considered having all my rendezvous in daylight.

Later in the afternoon, after I'd taken four pages of notes on Ireland's famine and had solved a pageful of quadratic equations, I drove to a Coney Island three blocks from college. We had agreed to meet there so none of my classmates would see and report me to whomever was reporting on my Miss Chastity impression. I scanned the parking lot as I turned in and found Johnny at the far left, in a red sports car—a different one than the last. I couldn't identify the car's make, but I didn't need to polish the thin snow off its trunk to recognize it was new and expensive. His wealth seemed as wide as a palace's garden and the risk I was taking became a bit more worth it—getting caught would be a small sacrifice. Although that didn't mean I was going to stop using caution.

I scurried into his car in the hopes that no one would see me and we drove to a nearby restaurant. I focused on the Lean Variety section of the menu, ordered a turkey-breast salad without mayonnaise and gave him the excuse that most dairy products didn't sit well with me. Johnny demanded I eat a whole meal instead but I shook my head and insisted on salad. After the waitress slipped the yellow pad in her pocket and walked away, he chided my shyness, thinking it was the reason for my lack of appetite. He claimed it cost the restaurant its profit as well as starvation and spontaneity on my part.

"I didn't order a salad because I'm shy," I said.

"I think shyness had a little to do with it. But don't bother defending yourself, Mervat, because I know you are shy—regardless of what you say or order."

"Maybe I am. Would you prefer I was bold and forward?"

"Never!" he said. "I don't want to spoil your shyness. Of course, I don't. I just want to adjust it when it's in my company so I can get a peek into your worse half."

"That would be an achievement," I mumbled.

He looked at me speculatively. "Do you mean to tell me you don't have a bad side?"

"I'm sure I have a bad side. The only thing is I don't know exactly what it is yet." I clasped my napkin and with my index finger drew a horizontal line over it. Then I added, "Maybe you've been sent to help me discover it."

"Why? Do I look like Lucifer?"

"Who's Lucifer?"

"*Al shaytan.*"

"*Al shaytan?*"

"Yes," he said, narrowing his eyes. "The leader of the angels who rebelled against God."

I counted how many millions of miles away he was from being the devil. How could he be anything but a part of Eden, when I had already roamed a bit of paradise with him? And if he ever did differ with God, I was convinced that his reasons would be understandable. Or that maybe God would actually be in the wrong.

After lunch (of which I had four bites of lettuce, one of turkey and two of tomato), Johnny suggested we take a walk in the park. This put my guards up. It was only our second time out and I wondered if he already wanted more than food and conversation.

"Mervat, do you want to go to the park?" he repeated.

I kept my eyes straight ahead. "I don't know where I want to go."

"Obviously you don't like parks, so I'll make some other suggestions. How about a church or a mosque?"

I looked out the window.

"Okay, how about Macomb College's cafeteria?"

I tried not to laugh, and once he saw my mood change again, he teased me until in the end he somehow made me go along with the idea of the park.

"Isn't it too cold to be walking?" I asked, still trying to save myself from a mistake.

"Don't worry, we're going to keep our clothes on."

"Seriously, Johnny," I cried, blushing.

"Yes, seriously."

Without more arguing he walked to the playground and climbed the monkey bars. He invited me to do the same.

"I can't," I said, sizing up the poles which looked as complicated as a space shuttle. "I'm not good at these things."

He extended his hand towards me. "It's not as dangerous as it looks."

"I know it's not dangerous, but it looks difficult."

"Yeah, but what's not difficult in life, Mervat? If you ask me, you're a hundred times worse when it comes to being difficult. And I'm still here."

His point stopped my complaining. I took a deep breath and climbed beside him. We sat quietly on the cold bars and watched the pine trees. They didn't have a single judgment against us, and their discretion reached out to embrace us. And since neither good nor evil eyes were scrutinizing us, I felt a wave of a sweet, a most unimaginable, freedom that had nothing to do with choosing where to go or what to say. My body blended with all that was around me and it felt lighter than after a week of starvation: I was disconnected from diets, my sisters' marital problems, Chaldean laws and our Detroit neighborhood.

"I love parks," Johnny said, looking around the area as though it were a historical sight. "All of them. They're basic but they remind me of sports and goofing off and elementary school."

"Elementary school?" I said in surprise, recalling how alienated I'd been from my US-born classmates. "I hated grade school."

"How can you hate anything that involves being a kid—playing nearly all day long and never getting into real trouble?"

"I hardly played when I was little."

"What did you do after school and on weekends?"

"I listened to stories."

"What stories?"

"All stories."

He looked at me a while but his mind seemed to be on something else. "And you never got into trouble?"

"If you're talking about stealing students' pens and erasers and disrespecting teachers, then no. I avoided these things."

"That's impossible," he said. "Even if you didn't look for trouble, how were you able to keep away from it?"

I watched the sky, the uneven clouds and their sporadic movement towards the east. "I wasn't. It managed to sneak into my mother's womb and choose the weaker gender and an old-fashioned birth place like Iraq. Then it brought me here to America, where everyone was raised to have a do-as-you-like attitude."

"That wasn't trouble, Mervat. That was life."

"It looked like trouble to me." To lighten the mood before he thought me too philosophical or somber, I added, "Maybe I wasn't wearing my glasses."

He laughed and we joked about how simple Calvin Klein made life look as we sat on the monkey bars until the wind worked through our gloves and we rushed back to the car. Johnny turned up the heat and glanced at my shivering.

"Put your hands inside your coat. Your body heat will help until the car warms up."

I did and I lifted my knees to my chest to gather as much warmth as possible. I was beginning to relax when I suddenly felt a tingle in my hair. Except for the trees rustling in the wind, everything—from the air vent to the car's engine to my nerves—fell silent. The silence continued until Johnny's gloved hand began to move loose strands of hair from my face, causing my nerves to reawaken.

I didn't know how to react. Half of me was weakening to his touch as the other half struggled to stop him, but before I reached a decision, his lips met mine. His smell was so redolent and taste so sweet that I was more hypnotized than by any favorite food or travel pictures or character from my sister's stories. Still, I knew I had to control the temptation and like a good girl end the kiss soon.

That night, with my wrists snugged against my nose, I fell asleep inhaling the fragrances of wool, leather, perfumes and skin. I felt as safe about my future as when I was a child hurrying home from school for The Brady Bunch and a hot meal. A romantic, lively, handsome man had swept me off my feet, and I was going to turn all the other heroes and fables out of my mind and make him my very dearest lullaby.

Chapter 13

Al-Nus—The Middle

January was miraculous. It blotted out the drab family problems, school and work problems and landed me in heaven. My fears of falling into my sisters' housewife traps or remaining a Detroit resident were melting away. I no longer felt that my only options in life were to wash dishes, fry meat and vegetables and yell at rowdy children, be forever called *binit* and live in a dowdy suburb, or dream I was the model on the cover of Apple Vacations, holding onto a happy man and floating on a yellow innertube.

Johnny didn't resemble my brothers-in-law. He had a power to lift even strangers to another plane on first meeting. I'd sensed this from the very beginning, but I saw it when we went to the park again and a policeman gave us each a violation ticket.

"See that," he pointed to a sign that said No Park Entrance After Sundown. "You should've read it before you came here."

Johnny shrugged and spoke abrasively to the policeman, even cussing him mildly when his back was turned.

"Johnny, be careful," I whispered. "You're upsetting him."

He looked at me. "He's upsetting me!"

I admired his courage, but I was also scared it'd get us handcuffs and mug shots. After the cop drove away, Johnny asked for my ticket.

"Don't worry," he said. "I'll take care of it."

"But he said if we wanted to dispute it we'd have to go to court and . . ."

"You don't have to do anything," he interrupted with an assurance I'd only seen in the movies. "I'll take care of it."

Since I didn't want any evidence of being in the park at night, I was more grateful than curious about his ability to wipe these tickets off the records. He offered me what God offered others: protection. And if he could address a policeman with such confidence, he could teach me to do the same with life.

By early February I felt there were the customary ululations lurking in the air. Then one day, Johnny's gallantry slipped on icy pavement, jolted off track and fell hard on my feelings. Although he was in charge, it was partly my fault. I had sparked an idea while drunk on sweet and sour pork and black forest cake and he took it literally.

It started when we'd gone to a Chinese restaurant and then a 24-hour diner. Johnny surprised me by bringing his five-year-old niece along. The minute I saw the little girl, dressed in blue ribbons and a purple dress and staring at me shyly, I was flattered by the trust he was showing. Introducing me to a family member, even to one barely out of diapers, was the nicest compliment he could pay. I was more than a temporary companion; I was almost his fiancée.

Johnny read the menu and said we had to order at least eleven different combination platters because Brittany wanted to take doggy bags home to feed his six cockatiels and his macaw.

"They like rice," she said in English, twisting her arms together and squirming inside the booth. "But Uncle said they can't eat egg rolls."

Johnny told me that she had chosen a Chinese restaurant because she was afraid the birds might choke on French fries and hamburgers.

"She's adorable," I said, feeling fortunate that this chunky little girl was with us. I was in full pre-menstrual wildness. Now I could hide my appetite behind hers, taking full advantage of my gluttony without him suspecting I was a sewer disguised as a lady.

Of course, we didn't pick eleven platters, but we did manage to order four: sweet and sour pork, beef chow mein, Kung Pao chicken and vegetable fried rice. Within seconds, an old woman brought a basket of hot rolls and a plate of butter to our table. I took one bite and immediately unbuttoned my discipline and went to the playground.

I had fun dipping fried chips into my won-ton soup, pouring orange sauce on the spring roll, slurping oily noodles, eating battered pork and salted peanuts, languishing in the minced fresh ginger and the green onions that were mixed with soy sauce and chicken cubes. By the time I was half way through the meal, I'd lost complete sight of myself and of Johnny.

Luckily, his niece's attitude towards the food was no less enthusiastic than mine. She spared no egg noodle, grain of rice or ginger slice on her dish. Johnny must have watched us closely because as soon as we finished everything but the soy sauce he offered us combination platter #12, sherried beef with spinach.

Although I wanted more in compensation for a month's starvation, my limits had to start here. Brittany's giggles and baby-fat couldn't divert the shame I'd feel in devouring another meal, and besides, the old woman had already served us fortune cookies and the check.

"Okay, we won't order another meal," Johnny said. "But

we'll have to go somewhere else for dessert."

Had I been sure that my skirt seam wouldn't tear as it had with the jinxer Hassina's neighbor, I would've knelt on the ground and kissed his feet. Perhaps he sensed that once the sun came up tomorrow I'd likely get my period and do nothing for the next three-and-a-half weeks but lust after food. Maybe, like me, he too had heard about girls wanting to eat more before their periods without the usual guilt over the consequences. I'd read in some women's magazine that a female's system burned off two or three times as many calories just before her period than on an average day. That made me feel better, not that, even if the data was false, I had any choice on whether or not to gorge on comfort foods during such times.

Johnny paid for a quart of fried rice to give to the birds and drove us to a diner. We ordered a slice of black forest cake for me, a slice of chocolate mousse pie for him and two-scoops of strawberry ice cream for Brittany. It was delicious but left me light-headed. When I told Johnny, he laughed and asked if he should carry me to the car. I blushed and told him he shouldn't joke like that in front of a child. Then Brittany, placing the back of her hand on her ponytail, impersonated me.

"I feel light too," she whimpered.

Johnny said it would be impossible to lift both of us and asked Brittany's help. "I'll carry Mervat, and you carry me."

She looked at him in confusion, and I laughed in an uncon-trollable way that suggested I had not laughed in years. Johnny swore he was serious as he placed his hand around my waist, but I jerked away. I did not want him to touch my waist given the amount of food I just ate.

"What's the matter?" he asked.

"Nothing."

And like a drunkard, I staggered to the car.

By the time Johnny drove me to my car, I was heavy and

exhausted. He tried to kiss me good night but I refused.

"It's not nice for your niece to see such things," I said, when, really, I worried that my lumps and bumps would disgust him.

"Her parents have three television sets—with cable."

"Oh, but Johnny, it's not a good idea."

"It's not a bad one, either."

I forced a smile and rested my head against the window so he wouldn't see me rolling my eyes. He asked if he could give me a box of treasure that might change my mind.

"What?" I asked, laughing. "Are you Aladdin now?"

"Aladdin won a kiss that way?"

"Sort of. He won the princess of his dreams with fruit-shaped diamonds and sapphires."

"Where did he find them?" Brittany questioned.

"From the bottom of a cave," I said. "They were hanging from trees just like fruit."

"Could he eat them too?"

"No, that he couldn't do," I said and asked if they wanted to hear the story in its precious details. Johnny said he preferred not, that he'd rather give me treasures like Aladdin and receive a single kiss in return. I said I didn't want treasure, but that a queen-sized bed in a large overpriced hotel room would be fine right about now.

"You wouldn't mind that?" he asked.

"Of course I wouldn't," I said, looking towards the sky, where the stars crowded and flattered each other. Their distance made me feel my weight, that my body itself, was tiny.

I felt Johnny's warm breath. "You're so beautiful, Mervat."

It was an uncomfortable compliment given how ugly I felt. He told me I was beautiful again, I think in expectation of a kiss. My lips felt fat and smelled of too many different spices and foods but I didn't want to deny him entirely so I gave him my cheek.

Johnny sighed before he gave me a peck. "For your meanness today, I have to see you tomorrow."

"Tomorrow? Tomorrow is too soon."

"No. Promise you'll see me tomorrow."

"But tomorrow is too soon—"

"Promise me, Mervat, tomorrow."

"Yes, yes, I promise you tomorrow."

And before my skirt burst, I raced home like a fox and changed clothes.

I couldn't keep my promise to Johnny the next day because I was sick with cramps. I took aspirin and slept a lot until I revived and was skinny again. Only then did I agree to go out.

That day Johnny had to close the store at eight. Claiming he didn't want to waste time, he asked me to meet him there. At 7:49 he was counting the register trays as I walked between the aisles and looked at the canned food. The rich colors and nutritional data on the labels saddened me more than usual. I grieved over the fact that my appetite would have to be forever squashed to avoid a double chin and the neglect of men.

To stop these dark thoughts, I went behind the counter and stood beside Johnny. He offered me a cherry licorice while he turned the register off. I shook my head but he begged me to take a bite.

"I can't," I said. "Right now, I'm as stuffed as your register."

He glanced at the large stack of money. "Do you think this could make me rich?"

"Yes, I do." I regarded the size of the store and recalled the extravagance of his two cars. "I think you're very established for your age, Johnny."

He looked at me briefly and ignored my compliment, placing the register tray under a pile of paper bags. I waited for him in the candy aisle as he made sure everything was in order.

Then he turned off the lights and set the burglar alarm.

In the car, Johnny told me that one night he'd taken some garbage to the dumpster and found a few cases of beer beneath a pile of dirty cardboard. To catch the culprit he waited across the street where his car wouldn't be recognized among the trees and bushes. A few minutes later a blue Chevy drove up and two Puerto Ricans got out and shuffled through the garbage for a case of beer, cheering over their booty before leaving quickly.

Johnny said it didn't take a genius to figure out his Puerto Rican stock boy was behind the theft. First he cussed him and then he fired him.

"Did he give you any trouble afterwards?" I asked.

"He wouldn't dare. I would've had Nabiel glue his nose to a donkey's ass." Then he added to himself, "Yes, Nabiel could be counted on for that."

As he talked more about the theft I noticed we were turning into Wendy's.

"Do you mind if we get food here?" he asked.

"Of course not," I said. "I'm not that hungry, though."

"But you're going to eat, right?"

"Yes, I'll eat."

He ordered a large salad with ranch dressing and I asked for a plain baked potato with extra salt and pepper. Johnny said he'd once been so addicted to baked potatoes with toppings that for one week straight he'd driven back and forth to Wendy's—three times a day—and had gained five pounds. He lost the weight by going to the gym and eating salad.

"I didn't know how ugly five extra pounds could look until they were mixed with my blood."

"But you're so tall and muscular, I'm sure it didn't show."

"It did, and I hated it." He paid the girl behind the window five dollars as she handed him the food. "Looks are very important, Mervat," he informed me while waiting for the change.

That was my theory as well, but hearing it from him was

dreadful. When we married I wouldn't be able to taste my own wedding cake much less my Arabic cooking. From the sound of it, he'd be the type of husband who'd expect me to be gorgeous and fit for life, and if I wasn't he'd get bored. Like the Muslim queen whose king neglected her for a pretty slave, I'd be humiliated by my own husband.

Perhaps I was exaggerating the situation, I thought. Islam allowed men a multitude of lovers and wives. Christianity didn't. So Johnny might dislike my being fat but he'd never abandon me because of it. Besides, keeping my looks might not be as difficult as I imagined. Any girl who had such a prize of a man would have enough sense to maintain herself, even if she was pregnant with twins or nursing an eighteen-month-old baby.

"Make sure she didn't mess up our order," Johnny said and while he drove I busied myself checking the contents of the bag. He hadn't said where we were going but I assumed it was to a parking lot where we could eat in privacy. The girl at Wendy's had included all the essentials but my eyes remained on the bag until we came to a stop. Johnny shifted the clutch into park and turned off the engine.

Curling a strand of hair around my ear I lifted my eyes towards the building in front of us and read the sign in stupefaction. "You think we can park some place else, Johnny?" I asked, feeling awkward about eating a potato near a hotel that advertised rooms by the hour.

He was as baffled as I was by his choice of where to park. "Mervat, we're going inside."

The entire world suddenly paused as it kicked my hopes and dreams. Not soap and water, bleach or rubbing alcohol, Jesus' bread or a *leefa* could scrub his presumption away and restore my regard for him of five minutes ago. I burned with indignation.

"Take me home right now, please," I said in the harshest,

most imperious voice I'd ever used in my life.

He switched the clutch in reverse and answered coldly, "Okay."

He drove back to his store and parked beside my car. I clasped the handle and leaned against the window as he sat back and masked his eyes with his arm. I concentrated on the vent noise to distract myself from the rage of just having my name murdered and the worry that there was no bringing it back to life.

When I cooled off, I turned to him: his eyes were half-closed and his cheeks flushed as he looked at me cautiously. He must know, I thought with some satisfaction, that my anger could destroy his loftiness with one well-aimed, good old-fashioned spit.

"Are you tired?" I asked.

"What?"

For the first time since we'd met I looked him in the eye. "Are you tired?"

"Yes, very."

I continued to look at him a while. "Then why did you ask to see me today?"

He blinked in surprise and I could feel my face harden. Scorn without animosity is an enormous weapon in the battle of love, and I wanted him to see exactly how badly he'd behaved.

"How could you take me to a place like that, Johnny?"

"It's not what you think—"

"It's exactly what I think!"

"It's not!" he protested violently. "My friends and I often get a room here. We don't do anything but sit around eating pizza and watching TV."

"I'm not your friend."

"Still, my intentions were no different."

Astonished at his excuse, I watched him with disapproval. He raised his seat. "Honest, Mervat. Even my friends' friends do that kind of thing. They bring cards, a VCR, some movies, video games—"

"Johnny, I don't care what your friends do," I interrupted. "Don't you understand? I've never been to a place like that before."

He winced. I turned to look at the traffic in the street. I wanted to go home and weep. I'd been living under the idea that two people should start clean, with respect, in order to end clean, in marriage. I sensed this was the beginning of the end.

Johnny moved towards me. "Mervat, look at me."

I refused. He'd injured my pride and honor, and I would never forgive him for it. He edged closer and braced my hands together. I leaned away from his easy apology.

"Put your arms around me," he whispered.

If I bowed to his request, I'd let him think this transgression was minor as a child's prank on the playground. I should be firm and . . .

"Put your arms around me," he repeated, his forehead touching mine.

The closeness hypnotized me. My willpower was about to collapse. How could I refuse when I felt like an instrument in his hand? He said those words again, and twice more until my hands left my lap and with much hesitation crawled over his broad chest. But they managed to quickly return to my lap.

"Mervat, put your arms around me."

He said it in such a demanding, tender tone that I ached to be kissed. But I still struggled. With his hands around my waist, the blocks of my careful discipline started tipping.

"Mervat, put your arms around me."

It was the last time he had to say it. In tiny slow motions, my arms went around his neck. My wrists felt his pulse and my chest his heart-beat; I was filled with fear—fear of making a most regrettable mistake.

The instant he kissed me I forgot what he'd done earlier

and discovered a weakness I didn't know I had. It was then that I first stepped over the boundaries of my family's ideas of a proper girl's feelings and behavior and drifted into a world where situations were based on the desires of the heart.

Chapter 14

I awoke the next morning feeling rocks filling my skull. What Johnny had done last night was becoming so grossly magnified that I wanted to scream at myself for not treating it as seriously as the fisherman's daughter had her husband's mistake. He was a perfume merchant and one day, while he was at work, a woman came to the shop and offered to sell him a one-of-a-kind bottle of perfume in exchange for a single kiss. He agreed to the bargain, but while her lips were on his cheek, she bit him and left teeth marks. Furious that he'd been unfaithful, his wife punched him and almost broke his jaw. Something like that, I thought, would have been an appropriate punishment for Johnny.

I tossed and turned as the evening replayed itself, jumping from the bright hotel sign to the pardoning kissing. I was scared I was losing him, along with the belief that my virtue was the key to an easy and prosperous life. Marriage might not have occurred to him. Maybe his sister knew it when we met and she'd tried to protect me. I don't know why I assumed he'd want me for a wife. I lived in Detroit; I wasn't a doctor or lawyer; I lacked confidence. He liked my looks but he wouldn't marry me based on them alone.

To avoid facing my sisters with last night's story, I thought of hiding beneath my blanket and claiming I had strep throat. I could lie to them when it came to my health, but I couldn't when it concerned my honor. If I told them the truth they'd have no mercy towards Johnny and I wasn't prepared for that. Ikhbal would advise I cut off all contact with him. Layla's suggestion would probably be to punish him with coldness until he learned his lesson. And Nameera would have absolutely no comment, since it would be too embarrassing to tell three separate people and she'd never be given an opportunity to add her voice to the chorus.

But when Ikhbal came over that afternoon, I threw away my plan of feigning illness. I knew if I didn't I'd have more to answer for than a criminal to a judge. She, my mother and I sat around the kitchen table and they ate fried curried cauliflower, eggplant and potatoes with beef cubes, minced parsley and juicy tomatoes. Despite the aroma, I didn't want any. I was too anxious and could not feel pleasure.

"He thinks I don't know he wants money again," Ikhabl said about her brother-in-law's collect phone call from Baghdad, the fourth since September. "His wife greets me for an hour, she gives me kisses on the phone, says Salem is her husband's favorite, his truest brother. The whole babble irks me. It's tedious and it's all done at our expense."

"Tell her that a collect phone call is double the price of a regular one," my mother advised. "Don't just chew your lips and pretend you're grateful to hear her voice."

Ikhbal sighed. "I'm sure they know the cost is outrageous and I'm sure they don't care. Their main concern is for us to give them three thousand dollars so they can emigrate all seven of their family to Greece or Spain—whichever is easiest—before their oldest turns eighteen and is drafted into Saddam's army."

"Yes, well don't give them anything," my mother said, "not one red cent. From what your uncle says they can afford to travel the world with the dinars they carry in their purses alone."

"I told them we have debts right now, that in this country we have more bills than we do wild cucumbers. I didn't mention the gambling, of course, so they won't accuse me of disgracing my husband's name overseas."

"You did well," my mother praised. "Your uncle also said they paint their house every year and that they have a gardener who grows grapes and pears in their never-spoken-of acres of land. So don't give them anything, not one red cent."

"I won't, but I'm worried that they'll call Salem at the gas station and with a honey-coated word here and a syrupy compliment there, they'll have his wallet vacuumed right out of his pocket."

For the first time I wanted to switch problems with my sister. Hers sounded so trivial that I suddenly hated life. If girls had to be patient first in courtship while being humiliated and burdened by men's insensitivity, and then be maids to their husbands and children, the world was unjustly cruel.

The talk in the kitchen and my mental grumbling was interrupted by a loud shatter in the bathroom. Ikhbal, after her initial scream, shouted at whoever had done the damage and so did my mother, who sent me to investigate the scene and clean it up. I found Raed near the toilet with a statue of the Virgin Mary cracked in half on the floor.

"Look at what you've done!"

He flattened himself against the wall and stopped breathing. I didn't want him to suffocate and then get blamed for it so I told him to run to the kitchen and bring me a broom and dustpan. He darted out and I stooped down to pick up the broken ceramic.

Staring at the Virgin Mary's face, I wondered what sort of power she possessed that made older women kneel and pray to her. I couldn't see it, but that day I gently closed the bathroom door and whispered a negotiation: if she mended the damage Johnny did last night and we could be back to where we'd been before, I'd go to the Chaldean church every Sunday for the next three months.

I'd barely finished my end of the bargain when I started feeling guilty for having requested anything from her. Aside from being Jesus' mother, I wasn't really certain what made her special, but then I thought that not all people who made deals with saints and prophets were acquainted with them. Take, for example, the Chaldeans in Iraq who take food and blankets to the city of Mosul one day in April to honor Saint George. It is obvious that, for most people, the real reasons they make the pilgrimage is to dance and have fun or to lose weight.

The Chaldeans attend Mass in the morning that day and gather in a large field afterwards. It is customary for each family to share whatever is in their pots with others before eating supper themselves. In that field, I'd been told, is a hill almost as straight as a math book where children of all ages compete to climb the highest before faltering due to thirst, heat, and exhaustion. Older people climb it as well but for different reasons.

"What reasons?" I'd asked Layla. "To build muscles?"

"I don't think so, Mervat, although it is excellent exercise," she'd replied. "They normally make an oath to climb the hill so many times—say, for instance, ten or thirty—in order for one of their deepest desires to come true."

"And do they?" I'd asked anxiously, imagining the magic the hill could produce.

"Sometimes yes, and sometimes no. It all depends on the person's faith."

"Oh." Although my sister had once defined faith as one's belief in God, I still didn't understand the word. "Tell me, what sorts of things do they desire?"

"Oh, I don't know. I suppose anything from passing a final

exam with high grades to marrying someone suitable to receiving a visa to America. People never speak of their desires, you know."

"Why not?"

"Because it is a secret between them and God."

"Will He get mad if you tell?"

"No, He won't get mad, but you might be disappointed."

"But why would I be disappointed?"

"Because what sounds true to you might sound silly to others." Her face glowed as she added, "But it never sounds silly to God."

"Never ever?"

"Never ever."

I looked at my sister in wonder. She not only knew Iraq well, but she knew God too. And I wondered why, although we lived in the same house and slept in the same bed, He wandered in her presence and not mine.

My mother and Ikhbal grieved over the twenty-dollar Virgin Mary for a few minutes and scolded Raed for his negligence a dozen times. They attempted to paste the pieces back together but gave up the job because it was too messy and complicated. They decided to leave the pieces in a kitchen drawer until Isaam came over and fixed it, as he did the windows and sinks.

Then they went back to spouse, money and in-law troubles again. I was bored and I wanted to go to Layla and tell her about last night's shame. I was sure she'd be able to erase whatever graffiti had been scribbled across my name. She'd also convince me that losing the man of my dreams wasn't a tragedy, but before I could get up my mother poured everyone a fresh cup of tea and a new subject was opened. This time Sermad was the main topic. It was rumored, Ikhbal said, that Layla's husband had his eye on a young waitress who worked at a famous Lebanese restaurant in Dearborn.

"He tips this girl forty or fifty dollars when the bill hardly comes to a hundred," Ikbahl said. I hoped, for Layla's sake, she was exaggerating.

Also circulating in our Putris family newsletter was the story that Sermad liked the blond clerk who worked at the corner gas station. "He buys three dollars' worth at a time so he can see her sooner."

My mother tightened her jaw and shook her head. "I've told her a thousand times to pay attention to her family and stop worrying about what her mother-in-law said or did."

Ikhbal sipped her tea. "She is sleeping, and I don't know if she'll ever wake up. Or if she even wants to."

My temper was about to boil. It was unfair to go on about Layla's husband when there was no solution. Layla couldn't undo the bolts holding the jamb and have a house without a door. Such conduct would not only affect her own heart and welfare, it would impoverish her family name in the Chaldean community—not to mention what it would do to my own marriageability. No man would want to wed a girl whose sister was divorced. And no girl would want to see her divorced sister struggle with unnecessary loneliness, either.

While Ikhbal was wiping more of Sermad's flaws onto my mother's apron, her glance fell on my teacup and she asked why I hadn't touched it. I looked blankly at the tea in front of me.

"She cannot answer you, Ikhbal," my mother said before I had a chance to respond. "She's in a daze because last night she was out with the so-called friend whom her sisters approve of."

They stared at me so intently I thought they were patrolling my thoughts, which mostly consisted of the hotel's neon lights and the kiss. To avoid their scrutiny I told them they were being ridiculous, claimed I had homework to finish, and went to my room.

I lay on my bed and let my mind drift. I wondered how Johnny thought of me before and how he thought of me now, whether he'd ever call again, whether my reputation was ruined even though nothing but fuming and one kiss had actually taken place. I hated what happened. Before last night my reputation was as clear as water. Now I felt a permanent stain on the fabric of my pride.

I called Layla and with much hesitation told her what had happened. She listened without criticism. When my confession was over it took her a while to articulate her advice. She didn't condemn Johnny or tell me to break up with him, but she did suggest I keep my distance until he could prove his intentions.

"How can he?" I asked.

"He could."

"If by chance," I began, reluctantly, "I'd said a very foolish thing when we went out with his niece, and he thought I meant it, is he still in the wrong?"

She asked what I'd said and I recited my story of Aladdin and the large hotel room.

"I thought he knew me well enough to know when I was flirting." I stopped and remembered the quantity of food and his easy air of expertise. "I guess I was stupid. Very, very stupid."

"You sound half against him and half defending him."

"I am not defending him."

"You aren't?"

"No, I am not."

"Good. I don't want to race too far ahead and come up with absurd assumptions about why Johnny did what he did. After all, the man might have meant well."

"Meant well?"

"He might have been testing you."

"Testing me?"

"Maybe he thought if–"

"He couldn't run his fingers beneath my skirt to test me!" I interrupted angrily. "No one takes a girl he plans on marrying to a hotel. No one. We've done nothing but kiss so far. He has seen nothing of my body but my neck." I paused to inhale a little air before I blurted out more blame—half came from the bottom of my heart and the other half from the pride of my anger. "He's the worst man I've ever met and I never should've dated him to begin with!"

"That's better," she said. "As long as you realize he didn't do this on account of your tongue having slipped backwards, you have nothing to cry about."

"That doesn't matter. I feel humiliated anyway."

"You can feel whatever you want, Mervat. I can't stop you from that. But don't analyze. True feelings can't really hurt you, but gloomy thoughts certainly can."

I'm not sure why but her words calmed me. Had I known how to show her how much I loved her, I would've thanked her for somehow easing the burden I'd carried through the night. She sensed my calm. "I don't think this means Johnny is evil. He might just be stupid, like you."

"I thought men were smart."

"I don't know about that. I've met smarter women."

I kept quiet.

"Are you still surprised, Mervat?"

"I'm surprised, yes. He seemed good and smart and classy."

"Let's slow down a little. We've talked and we've specu-lated, but it's not official yet that he's stupid."

I felt better. My sister, an extraordinary soul, had once again succeeded. Later that night the mood was dampened, however, when he didn't call. Despite Layla's soothing encouragement, I went to bed crying into my pillow.

Two days later I no longer expected the phone to ring or our courting to continue. I should have known better anyway. My sisters were doomed in their marriages and since we were blood-related, why should I be privileged with a husband who wasn't arrogant or poor, didn't gamble or put his mother before his wife?

I ought to be smart and remain single, I concluded. Then I changed my mind. Spinsterhood would suit me only if I had a career, and that required years of schooling and dedication, not to mention an interest in a specific (and of course respectable) profession. I was trapped in limbo and I wondered how long I was going to be there so I could pack enough clothes.

Chapter 15

Life returned to Johnny-less routine by the third day, and this led me to being impatient and full of melancholy towards life. After all, the world was unrelenting by nature, duping people into the concept of goodness but refusing to give proof. It asked for our day-to-day patience and gratitude when the last time it'd given us anything was thousands of years ago. He didn't even live past the age of thirty-three.

I kept my composure around my family and aimed my anger at classmates and customers. When the Middle Eastern students in the cafeteria discussed politics and gossiped, I found their voices and giggling annoying and sat elsewhere, pretending to be engrossed in homework. In the afternoon, when a young boy at the store dropped his corned beef and cheese sandwich after paying for it, I wanted to scold him rather than replace his purchase.

I became less temperamental when the store slowed down at two that afternoon but only because I thought I had a chance to sit on my stool and open my history book. I had a lot of reading to catch up on after wasting time thinking about Johnny. However, a multitude of distractions ensued—beer salesmen and undecided lunch-buyers and telephone surveyors—and I'd hardly scanned a few pages on the Vietnam War before I put the book back in my school bag. How could I concentrate on the assignment when abandonment was as fresh as the yogurt my mother made last night?

My mood grew darker in the evening when the telephone rang continuously. My mother asked me to bring home a pound of turkey, a quarter pound of ham and ten slices of Provolone. Ikhbal wanted me to cut out a Winkelman's coupon from today's newspaper and drop it off when my shift was over. Layla asked if I could watch her children for a couple of hours the next night because she wanted to go congratulate one of her husband's relatives on his new home. My brother presented me with a complaint and a command: "You lost the beer and wine price list and I want you to find it!"

By night, all I wanted was to go home and build a tent for myself in the darkest corner of the basement. There I could try to figure out what I'd done wrong, why Allah brought my head down in shame. Perhaps the piles of clouds He lived behind shrouded his sight, and thunder and airplanes impaired His hearing. Surely that was why He couldn't establish my innocence and grant me success in love.

I scrubbed the meat slicer, swept the floor and wiped the counters down while my father worked in his office and Mathew dumped empty bottles and filled the coolers. I was rinsing a few spoons and knives in the sink when the telephone rang. My father told me to answer and I hurried over, nearly tripping over the cord.

"Putris' Party Store."

There was a soft "hello" and then a pause.

"Who is this?" I was in no mood for pranksters, secret admirers or a delinquent relative who wanted to make me guess his identity.

"We don't talk for two days and you've forgotten my

voice?" he asked. "That's not a very good sign, Mervat."

The sound of my name on his lips paralyzed every joint in my body, as had our first kiss.

"Don't tell me you still don't recognize me."

"I recognize you," I said carefully so he wouldn't detect my shakiness.

"Do you think you might be nicer if you didn't?"

"No, I don't think so," I said, gently.

"Oh, please don't be kind with me today, or else I'll have to keep beating myself up for having upset you the other night."

Tears formed in my eyes, ready to wash away whatever bitterness remained since he'd said my name seconds earlier.

"Are your father or brother nearby?"

"No."

"It feels as though they are."

"I wasn't expecting you to call, Johnny," I said to justify my awkwardness.

"You weren't?"

"No."

"Why not?"

His question caught me by surprise. I had padded my heart with feathers and cotton so the pangs would bounce off it rather than settling in. I needn't have bothered. The ordeal hadn't meant he was going to hurt me. It was a simple misunderstanding.

"I hope you're glad I called."

"Yes, I'm glad."

"Because, you know, I've been thinking a lot these past few days and I have many plans for us."

My eyes were blurring and my heart dancing. I had some fine tuning of my senses to do so I could act like a human instead of a robot.

"Are you going to hire me as your cashier?"

"I wouldn't mind hiring you," he said, seriously, "but I'm

afraid it'd have to be for a higher rank."

"A stock boy, maybe?"

He laughed. "Never!"

"There aren't any other jobs in a party store."

"Of course there are. You can, for instance, spend the day sitting on my lap and feeding me grapes. Black and green ones—with no seeds or dents or discolorations. Grapes are the favorite snack of kings, you know."

"If you're going to be a king, and I'll be feeding you grapes, then that would make me your concubine."

"What, queens can't feed their husband grapes?"

The lights in the store dimmed and I heard the chains on the front door rattle. My father called out my name, then Mathew's. It was time to close and I felt stifled by impatience and frustration. I needed this lover's talk to cradle my heart and make up for all the anguish, but my father was approaching the counter and there was no room for romance and pampering. I whispered we had to hang up and promised I'd page him from school tomorrow.

When I got off the phone, the tension of the last few days dissolved immediately and I felt drowsy. I was so glad we were back together that rather than remembering the oath I'd made to the splintered Virgin Mary, I renounced any mistrust I had of marriage and began waiting restlessly for a proposal.

I couldn't pay attention to lectures or focus on the inventory list the next day as I imagined Johnny as the hero Saint George was for a young princess. The comparison was a little off, I admit, since Saint George saved many lives whereas Johnny was only saving me from boredom and a dull marriage, but my heart said it was reasonable.

The fable told of a king and queen who lived happily in a small village until one day a dragon roosted in their river. Whenever he was hungry he devoured the fish and drank the water so roughly that he plugged the village pipes, affecting the people, crops and animals in a most disturbing way.

"Did he kill the village?" I asked.

"Practically," Layla had replied and then went on. "So the king and his people decided that whenever the dragon stopped the water, they'd throw him one of their young girls to satisfy his appetite until they found a more permanent solution."

"That's disgusting."

"It was," she agreed, "and it was useless too, because he ate all the little girls but was still hungry."

"So they fed him frogs and grasshoppers?"

"Impossible. That would have been a speck of sugar to his huge stomach. His next prey had to be the king's daughter."

"That would be the princess herself!"

"That would," Layla agreed. "Now this girl was so noble that although she wept as she said goodbye to her parents, she didn't object when her turn came. But a miracle happened while the villagers were escorting her to the river. A strange man on a horse appeared and offered to save her life by killing the dragon."

"Was the strange man tall and handsome?"

"I'm not sure what he looked like, but I know he was a strong believer in Christ."

"Oh," was all I could say to such a vague description. I begged her to go on.

After the king gave him permission to help, Saint George lured the dragon to shore and stabbed him with his sword until he died. The king was so overjoyed that he wanted to reward Saint George with gold and treasure but the gifts were modestly declined. So the king granted him the princess herself as a bride and was surprised to see even that offer received the same humble response.

"Saint George desired only that a church be built where he'd fought the dragon, so the poor would have a place to pray and obtain help."

"That's a boring desire."

Layla shook her head slightly and calmly explained how honorable it was to refuse material wealth in order to perform God's will.

"Then it can't be fun to perform God's will!"

Smiling her usual smile, she caressed my forehead. "Oh, Mervat."

Her expression confused me, but I was still determined not to follow God's will, not if it meant going into battle with a dragon only to be rewarded an incensed alter and an extra-large bell.

Johnny and I went to the movies after we made up, and this time I was the one who upset him. All went well until we left the theater. In the car, his hands were everywhere at once, touching what I allowed through many layers of clothing and saying prettier things to me than what had dripped from Shahrazat's lips. It was perfectly exciting until my mind waltzed into the room, made a few disturbing points and generated a tempest.

"You're making me do things I don't want to do!" I said, disentangling myself from his arms.

His eyes narrowed and his face flushed. He pressed himself against his door, creating a distance. "I think it's best we go home now."

My heart fell ten stories. "What?"

"I think it's better we go home."

"Why?"

"I'm not in the mood to stay here anymore."

"What is it?" I begged. "Did I say something wrong?"

"No. I just think we should go home."

"But Johnny . . ."

"Mervat, I don't feel like staying!"

I couldn't say anything. He was serious and I had to hurry

and melt the ice. He straightened and reached for the ignition.

"No, please wait." I grabbed his arm and looked into his eyes. "I'm sorry, Johnny. I didn't mean to offend you."

He turned his face away.

"Please, Johnny, don't be mad. I didn't mean what you thought."

He acted as if I wasn't even there, which didn't stop me from kissing his cheeks and pleading. "Please, don't be mad. Please."

My ardor eventually wore him down and Johnny's red heart started working again.

"I'm sorry," I whispered as I breathed his fragrance in deeply. "I didn't want you to think I was bad."

His hands tightly pressed against my hips. "Oh, but I know you are bad."

I stiffened. The idea of an experienced man thinking I was bad was stimulating. All along I'd thought he liked me for being good. I didn't know he could see the other side and approve. I also didn't know I could show unprompted affection to a man and be proud of it.

The next time Johnny asked me out I told him my mother was getting too suspicious and I preferred we waited until Valentine's Day. He sympathized with the difficulties in sneaking out for his sake, but pressed me to meet him briefly.

"Even if it's for half an hour, I need to see you."

He sounded uneasy. I was curious about what was on his mind so I agreed, even though I suffered my mother's scorn for it—including an "I'm going to tell your father!" warning. I drove to his store and found him busy counting the register.

"I should've come later."

"You should have come sooner," he said. "It would've made me feel better."

"What's making you feel bad?"

"Me. Only me."

I wanted to ask more but he told me to hold still while he set the burglar alarm. He turned off the lights and locked the door, and then we drove to an apartment complex where he parked between a large gray van and a brown dumpster.

"This spot suits me perfectly today," he said. "I can blend in with the garbage and no one will notice. It would be a great hiding place."

Before I asked for an explanation he opened his arms. "Come here," he said. "I want to feel better."

I leaned against his chest and allowed my long curls to cover his shirt, like the *abayat,* long black veils, of the Arab women's skirts and dresses.

"Why couldn't they be like Aunt Najeeba and wear red suits and black shoes?" I asked Layla once when she was describing various customs Iraqi immigrants had not packed into their suitcases and brought to Detroit.

"Some could, if they wanted to," she replied.

Layla explained that besides being worn by strict Muslims, long veils were often chosen as a form of comfort so a female could avoid being harassed by men or so she wouldn't have to think about her clothes while she endured long market lines and crowded *souks.*

"But don't the veils make them trip and fall? Don't they choke or suffocate them?"

Layla looked at me in amusement. "Mervat, I doubt that a veil could trip, choke or suffocate a woman. I'm sure her vanity could do a much better job of that."

"What's vanity?"

"It's a type of pollution."

"What's pollution?"

"Something that humans cooked up centuries ago."

"I don't feel well, Mervat," Johnny murmured into my ear. I raised my head and looked at him. "What's the matter?"

He regarded me gravely, then winced and turned his face away. "I'm sick. I'm very, very sick."

I was scared, thinking of doctors and deadly diseases, but questions risked answers I wasn't sure I wanted to hear. "Do you have a—a sort of a—a virus, or—well, I mean—"

His smile spared me. "As of right now, my health is fine."

I was relieved and he went on to recount how an American girl he'd dated told him she had AIDS shortly after they'd broken up. He was bedridden for months after and his family prayed the whole time, even after the doctor's test results.

"Then one day, I get a letter in the mail from her, telling me she'd lied," he said. "That was her way of revenge."

Men had permission to enjoy the pleasure of women to no avail before they got married. Women were expected to enjoy housework, schoolwork, and job-related work. I pictured how awful it would be to marry a man who gave me a disease after I'd spent my youth ensuring my heart and body were clean of dangerous emotions, impure thoughts, and excess fat.

"Did you like that true life story?" he asked wearily. He didn't give me a chance to answer before he laughed harshly. He seemed upset and worn out all at once. I wanted to cheer him up but it was getting late and I pushed him to tell me what was bothering him.

"I have a secret no one is supposed to know," I said.

"I promise this secret will never leave my lips."

He cleared his throat and pressed his arm against his forehead.

"If I were to tell you my secret, would you trust me?"

He laughed. "What kind of secret could you possibly have?"

"What do you mean?"

"I mean, you and secrets couldn't have met."

"What does that mean?"

"Never mind, but go on, tell me your secret."

I hesitated. Half of me feared that what I had to say was scandalous enough to hurt my reputation, and the other half worried he'd make such a mockery it would lose value. If word spread and somehow Maysoon heard that I'd once allowed a Muslim to kiss me, she'd think I wasn't any better than her.

Laughing for no apparent reason, Johnny started playing with the zipper at the back of my dress. He asked me to tell him quickly before he fell asleep on my bosom. "And if I'm tempted to do something more to them," he regarded my breasts, "you'll regret not telling me now."

"How can you speak to me like that?"

"How can I not?" he asked, sliding his hands along my waist. "You're my girlfriend."

"That's no excuse for not respecting me."

"I'm complimenting you, baby. That's how people who like each other talk." His hands cupped my ribs, almost touching my breasts. Then they went beneath my skirt. "And this is what they do."

I wrestled to move his fingers away.

"If you don't tell me your secret right now," he threatened while he tugged at my sleeves and I started to protest, "then you'll go home naked and your mother will be furious."

"I'll just tell her that Aunt Evelyn's barbaric son did this to me."

"Go ahead. If you even try to bring my mother's name into this I'll tell her what you did to me."

"Me?" I cried. "What did I do to you?"

The blue of his eyes dissolved into the brownness of mine. "You made me fall in love with you."

His words stripped me of all strengths, but he grew abruptly serious.

"I'm dealing, Mervat."

I waited.

"I'm dealing drugs."

It took time to absorb what he said and when I did he transformed before my eyes. I tried sitting up but a mannequin could have moved more easily. I smoothed my dress and patted my hair into place as I grappled with the blankness I felt. I went to ask him to drive me home and forget he ever knew me when I heard him say, "I'm just kidding, you know."

I turned in fury.

"How could you do that to me?" I struck his chest with both fists. He sat imperviously until my anger dissipated and, exhausted, I leaned my head against him and took long deep breaths. I told him to share the big secret this time without any fabrications so I wouldn't die of unnecessary worry.

"It's no big deal," he said, even though he made me swear never to repeat it. "I was playing with you." He pointed his index finger against my forehead. "This thing is so innocent and delicate that it makes fooling you fun."

"What you did was cruel, Johnny, and you're going to pay for it." I gently touched his shirt. "Now tell me the truth and stop torturing me."

He prepared his speech by sighing. "My brother and I have been paying some guys to smuggle cigarettes from Ohio, and we suspect the police have caught onto us."

"Can you go to jail for this?"

"No. We have good attorneys. But once we're caught, we'll probably have to pay a large fine, our tobacco license will be suspended for a while and the two thousand dollars we make each month will end."

I laughed. "That's it? That's what's bothering you?"

"Two thousand dollars a month for doing nothing is a lot of money, Mervat. We basically get it free."

I shook my head and told him I refused to hear another word on the subject. "Who cares about two thousand dollars?

I don't!"

"Okay, okay," he laughed. "Now tell me your secret."

I covered my face and spoke rapidly. "I went out with a Muslim once."

I peeked between my fingers to see his reaction. It was surprisingly indifferent.

"So? I've gone out with *abdat* before."

"You've what?" I asked. Although dating a Muslim was forbidden, it was much more common than dating a black person.

"Of course, they weren't ordinary *abdat,*" he explained. "These girls were absolutely gorgeous."

Seeing he was feeling a lot better, I kissed him with all my might. "So these lips have been with *abdat* before?"

He looked at me adoringly and I laughed at how I'd magnified my secret, as worthless as a gumball, and had criticized him, a full-grown man whose reputation didn't matter, for being with a black woman.

"I led such an untamed life when I was younger," he smiled to himself. "I'd walk out from the bar every night with two or three girls, and we'd go—"

"Shhhh," I smothered his mouth with my hands, then my lips. "God, Johnny, you scared me," I said. "You really, really scared me."

He wrapped his arms tight around my body and kissed my head. If we came this close to breaking up again, I thought, I probably wouldn't survive. I hoped he'd hurry up and make me his wife.

Chapter 16

I took the liberty, the very next day, of telling Layla about the cigarettes. Although I'd taken an oath not to, I really didn't feel as though I'd betrayed his secret. Layla, my mentor from birth, didn't count. She molded many of my perceptions of the worlds of Baghdad and the United States as well as my opinions on social and romantic matters. Our beings were undivided. We were like a slice of homemade pie, she the solid crust and I the moist pudding.

That week I shopped at Spring Lane Mall for Johnny's Valentine's Day gift. Skipping over the expensive cologne, heavy sweaters, gold pens and leather wallets, I decided on a box of Godivas. I figured a simple present wouldn't *it-tali'ayna*—bring out his eyes—an old Arabic saying meaning to evoke one's arrogance or venom by being too nice. In the same spirit, I bought a Valentine's card that was as vague about its sentiments as I was about the upcoming change in my life.

I shoved the items beneath my bed so they wouldn't accidentally fall into my mother's hands. She was already at least partially aware of me dating, but any unquestionable evidence would have put her in a frenzy. It's quite customary for a Middle Eastern mother to go mad and beat her hands on her chest if her daughter's honor, even vaguely, is in question.

Take, for example, Princess Sulaima. A man snuck into her chamber, earned her love and her virginity, and shared her bed for a month until her mother discovered their naughtiness. When she saw Sulaima's face unusually exhausted, she wasted no time in grabbing her daughter's nightgown and plunging her fingers between the girl's thighs and into her private area (a section of the story which always made me blush and caused an uncomfortable tingling). Discovering that her young one's virginity had been broken, the queen flew into a rage, shook Sulaima furiously and called her all sorts of vulgar names. Then she asked the guards to find the man who'd done this so she could have him beheaded.

Of course, in this country and time my mother couldn't put an animal, let alone a daughter, to death. But she could grind in a lifetime of guilt and shame without being penalized or exiled.

Once the gift and card were taken care of, I tried on half my clothes for the dinner plans Johnny probably had. I also wondered what he'd picked out for me, whether it would be quiet enough to be worn in front of Maysoon and the Middle Eastern students or so significant or private that I'd have to hide it. I suspected it would be the latter.

I lay on my apricot-colored blanket, crossed my right leg over the left and swung it leisurely as I replayed for myself the story of how we met: Aunt Evelyn and the wedding invitation and Johnny behind the cash register, straight and blue eyed; his arrival at the reception in an olive-green suit, coolly prepared to welcome me into his life.

Stretching my arms over the pillows, I thought about how everything that followed was painted in lovely, nameless colors. It was like being in a never-ending amusement park and never getting tired, sick or fat.

The next time we spoke, however, he didn't mention Valentine's Day, speaking only of the gym, his bird, a stalking customer and his lazy stock boy. I prolonged the talk to help him remember we were supposed to go out but it didn't work. After that I didn't hear from him again.

"He doesn't want me anymore," I cried to Layla.

"Mervat, *iyouni*—my eyes—you shouldn't jump to such conclusions . . ."

"I'm not!" I interrupted harshly. "He doesn't want me anymore. I can feel it."

Layla succeeded in calming me down for about an hour. I leapt at every telephone ring. He must have a surprise, one which had cost him a lot of money and preparation, I told myself. Or maybe his mother planned to call mine that morning to come over and request my hand in marriage. Telling me he loved me and confiding in me must, I assured myself, mean our future was secure. He wouldn't dare vanish and blot my happiness out of existence.

"Or do you think he would do just that?" I asked Layla for the thirtieth time. My face was becoming pale and my stomach bubbling with worry.

"I don't know, Mervat," she answered. "His behavior is strange, but there must be an explanation for it."

"You think so?"

"I'm sure there is. There must be."

"Yes, there must be."

But the fact that there was an explanation, whatever it was, didn't mend my heart. Especially not when February fourteenth was a day away and I was still hoping for an invitation or a telephone call from his mother. By night I gave up. I no longer wanted to fool myself. Ignoring me on Valentine's Day was the most effective way of letting me know he'd lost interest. After all, I was forced to admit, he tried to abandon me once before. That he had eventually contacted me again was mere pity.

"I don't know if it's fair to generalize his actions the way you're doing," Layla said when I expounded my over-worked hypothesis. I had, for the fifth time, stopped at her house for tea and support.

"Aren't his reasons obvious?" I asked.

"Not necessarily, no."

"Can't you see what he's implying?"

She shrugged. "Not exactly, no."

"You're just tricking me so I won't throw myself out the window."

"On the contrary. I'd be tricking you if I pretended to know what's going on in his head right now."

I looked at her skeptically and turned away.

"Honestly, Mervat, I don't know what Johnny is thinking. I'm not a mind reader." She shifted my chin so our eyes would meet. "And you're definitely not, either."

Unable to get her to admit the truth even when things were at their worst, I left, still feeling unsettled, and drove to work with a headache. I was grateful to be at the store Valentine's night where I'd be occupied selling beer and chips instead of moping around. For the next few days I busied myself with school work and shelving gum, but my optimism petered out by the third day.

Studying and wiping up soda stains no longer functioned as distraction. I ransacked each word and every step I'd taken with Johnny, reviewing the material with the same diligence I did my lecture notes. I came to the conclusion that he'd grown weary of my curfews and lack of experience, or that he found someone prettier and skinnier, wealthier and more educated. Maybe he was disgusted that I'd been with a Muslim or thought I'd judged him for being with *abdat*.

I was as much a fool as the old monk who set his cane down one day and rested on his mattress, dreaming what possessions he could get from the jars of fresh honey shelved over his bed post. He'd sell the jars and with the proceeds he'd buy twice as many jars and sell them again. Then he'd buy lambs, raise them, slaughter them and sell the meat and wool. Then he'd buy cows, milk them, make cheese, butter, yogurt, and eventually market the beef. With that money, he'd buy a farm, work its fields and grow rich from its crops.

Later he'd marry a princess who would bear him a boy. The boy would be raised with wealth and education. But there the monk's dreams took a darker turn. One day the boy would behave badly and, carried away in his fantasy, the monk actually grabbed his cane and struck him repeatedly. There was a loud shatter. The monk opened his eyes to see all the jars of honey broken.

In this trail of gloom I discovered so many new faults in myself that I wanted to strangle my ignorance, my diet schemes and rules. There were so many of them—rules, and more rules, technical and confining. Maybe then I could prevent future mistakes and I wouldn't once again, like the old monk, outstrip myself on one hand and on the other shatter my own prosperity.

I visited Layla after class and asked her whether all men get tired of women so quickly. She chided me for breaking my promise to stop this constant over analysis and busy myself in more productive activities.

"Just remember we don't know what happened."

"But we do know."

"No, Mervat, we don't."

"I know. Don't ask me to excuse him now or I'll start building up my hopes again."

Robert interrupted us by smacking the television with his mother's sandal. Layla yelled and chased him away before going into the kitchen. She was there so long that my thoughts had plenty of time to unsettle what was left of my sanity. If only I hadn't told him my secret or been so serious when he joked about dealing drugs. I shouldn't have so much as blinked at his *abdat* lovers or accused him of making me do things I didn't want to. I should've lived up to his needs. A man like Johnny deserved the most amendable and beautiful girl he could find.

Layla came back with a large plate of baked pita bread with tomatoes and feta cheese. She placed the food on the table and told me to try it but I only threw my head back on the pillow.

Layla sighed as she sat on the edge of the couch and caressed my hair. "The poor man might be ill or in serious trouble and here you are being unreasonable because he overlooked Valentine's Day."

"He could've called," I said, sniveling. "He doesn't want me."

She pressed her finger against the tip of my nose and told me to stop acting like a child and sit up. "I want to tell you a small something."

I wiped my runny nose with the back of my hand, took a deep breath and obeyed.

"I know that Johnny not calling you seems tragic right now," she said gravely. "But I think that the problem he told you about last week might have—well, somehow—multiplied."

This scared me.

"I think the nicest thing a girl who cares about a man could do is ask about his welfare," she said. "So, in case my instincts are right, and God forbid, he is sick or in trouble, why don't you do just that?"

"What if your instincts are wrong?"

"If they're wrong then at least you'll have made a good impression."

I looked at her with doubt and she looked at me with compassion. She won.

"I'll do it," I agreed, when what I really wanted to say was, 'what do I have to gain by leaving him with a good impression?'

But Layla's advice pleased me more than I could admit because it offered Johnny and me a second chance. I struggled with my pride through the night as I persuaded myself that to call a man who was obviously avoiding me was a gesture of goodwill and not a means of humiliating myself.

By morning I couldn't stand the thought of being without him. I would be at the mercy of unfavorable suitors, reputation-threatening meetings and a college degree with no probable career.

I dialed his store, prepared to be sympathetic to whatever excuses he handed me. Regardless of how badly I wanted him I had to keep my composure if it came to the worst. I didn't expect someone else would answer the phone.

"Azziz Party Shoppe," a man with a heavy accent said. I presumed it was his older brother.

"Can I speak to Johnny, please?"

"Johnny is not here. He is on vacation."

I was startled by this information but then a feeling of relief washed over me. He might have left the country, but he hadn't left me!

The man asked if I wanted to leave a message but after thanking him I told him I'd call another day.

"I can take down your name, if you don't mind."

"No, thank you. I'll just call another time."

"You are sure? I can write it down on paper. I have a marker here." I sensed his smirk as he meddled in his brother's affairs and I wondered if I was speaking to the famous scoundrel Nabiel.

"Yes, I'm sure, thank you."

Only then did he relinquish the quest for my name and I hung up. Breathless with excitement, I called Layla to share the news but happy as she claimed to be, I could tell she was unimpressed. When I accused her of this she said I was correct; her heart fell a bit short of enthusiasm because her mind wanted to know why Johnny had gone on vacation without telling me first.

"I'm pretty sure it's not a real vacation," I said. "He might have had an emergency of some kind."

She kept quiet.

"I think it's more of a business trip, though," I tried. "If it was family, his older brother would've gone, don't you think?"

"Maybe."

I couldn't understand her coldness, but I was so drunk with joy I didn't really bother trying.

That Sunday afternoon, I decided to celebrate not-having-been-dumped-on-Valentine's Day by going to the mall with Ingham and Ashley. It was below zero outside and the streets were covered with four inches of snow; the mall was very crowded with Chaldeans who, possessed of prying eyes, made our visit exciting. My two nieces and I enjoyed ourselves making fun of skimpy leopard-skin dresses and shiny silver blouses. I tried on three-inch high heels, they put on big feathered hats, and we all laughed at each other's costumes.

As I was wandering inside one of the department stores, a Chaldean man, grinning behind a thick zebra-striped mustache, approached.

"Yau've boutifool eyez."

I frowned at the pock marks on his skin and the odors of fried potatoes and onions lodged in his leather coat. "Excuse me, what did you say?"

"Yau've boutifool eyez," he repeated. "What'z yaur naime?"

I was going to shove him away with my bulky purse but all that changed when he smiled. His teeth were so awful that, oddly enough, I managed to suspend my annoyance and had to struggle to stifle my giggles.

"Come on," he wheedled. "Tell me yaur naime."

"Sorry. No."

"Come on, yau foggot yaur naime."

"Sorry. No."

"Come on, yau foggot yaur naime?"

I hung the blouse I was holding on its rack and called Ashley and Ingham. They emerged from the huddled clothes, hands over their mouths and their eyes twinkling. I grabbed them and started out of the store. The man followed us.

"Tell me, yau foggot yaur naime, huh? Yau've zat bad habit, huh?"

"On occasion, yes."

"Anacasia?" he pronounced with admiration. "Oh, yaur naime is as boutifool as yaur eyez."

My nieces and I burst into laughter as we hurried away towards the frozen yogurt booth. I was helping the girls choose among the toppings when I noticed Johnny in a nearby telephone booth. I went so numb I couldn't respond to Ashley's dilemma over the M&Ms or crushed peanuts.

"That's four-dollars, sixty-five cents," the clerk said impatiently.

I shook away my discomposure, stepping to the side of the line. My eyes remained on Johnny. I found myself in everyone else's path so I took my frozen yogurt and walked towards him.

"Should I get some napkins?" Ashley shouted.

I said nothing and continued. When I was a few feet away, Johnny saw me and flushed the color of pomegranates. He stumbled over his words as he tried to rush the conversation, then he hung up and gave me an awkward smile.

"Your brother said you were on vacation," I said without greeting him.

His blush deepened. "I told him to say that. I assumed they'd all be my friends. You usually page me, so I didn't expect you to call. I planned on getting hold of you, but–"

"Johnny, where have you been?" I interrupted, softly.

"Nowhere in particular. Just catching up on work, and ummm—" He glanced around. "Do you want to take a walk?"

Strolling in the mall with a man was hazardous to my reputation and I was expected to say no, but I found myself quietly accompanying him.

"I've been worried sick about you," I said.

"You were?"

"Of course I was." I stopped and faced him. "Did you think I wouldn't be? You disappear without a word and I'm left imagining a hundred things that could've gone wrong with your business—or us."

He stood speechless before me. I waited.

"Would you like me to buy you ice cream?" he asked.

I raised the frozen yogurt in my hand.

"Oh," he sighed, rubbing his forehead. Then he started walking again. "You want to go someplace else?"

"What do you mean?"

"Out of this mall, maybe?"

"I can't. I have my nieces with me."

He turned to look for Ashley and Ingham, who were sitting on a bench and licking their spoons. He didn't say anything after that.

"Can you please tell me what you're doing here?" I asked, surprised I was forcing this encounter along.

"I'm supposed to meet a friend," he said uneasily.

"Oh." Why ask me to go someplace else then? I didn't want to corner him into more explanations, which were probably mostly lies anyway.

Realizing he couldn't soothe my doubts, I figured it was time to leave. "I'm glad to see you're not ill or hurt."

He nodded, and I hurriedly called Ashley and Ingham to my side. He didn't try to persuade me to stay, and I walked out of the mall in bafflement and fear. None of his fairy tale charms had been what they seemed. It was as though I'd woken from a dream and, like Ala al-Din's wife, had fallen into the hands of a Moorish magician.

After marrying Ala al-Din, the princess had lived in luxury and splendor, until one day she woke to the discovery that nothing she owned was real. It had been acquired by her husband through a magic lamp, and in the same fashion, everything had disappeared; the palace, the princess and her in-laws had all been carried off from Baghdad and brought to the wilds of Morocco.

If I were lucky, perhaps, as Ala Al-Din ultimately rescued his wife and his happiness, Johnny would also be able to sort this mess of deceit and dark moods out and replace it with a safe haven instead. Otherwise, my heart would surely die of thirst. Now that it had a sip of love, it would never be able to substitute wine for water.

Chapter 17

Al-tahkieq—The Investigation

There was an assembly in my room Sunday night: two adults, Layla and Ikhbal, and one adolescent, me. My rank was that of compliant listener and theirs of professional speculators. They eyed each other knowingly, kept silent periodically, and in the end surmised that Johnny was linked to illegal matters bigger than he'd confessed to. Last of all they cautioned me to keep my distance. His business could put me in real danger, they said. Men like him were followed and targeted.

"Men like what?" I asked.

"Men like him," Ikhbal stressed. "Men who are involved."

"But I don't know what he's doing."

"We don't know, either," Layla said, "so we won't label him—at least not until anything is proven."

"Of course," Ikhbal added, giving an amiable performance. "No one's name deserves to be twisted without evidence. That sort of thing is *haram.*"

Layla looked at me apologetically. "In the meantime, we don't think it's wise for you to see him."

They watched my reaction carefully. I dropped my eyes to

the carpet.

"If he wants to continue talking to you, then he can do it over the phone," Ikhbal said. "He'll understand."

"He'd probably prefer it that way," Layla said.

"Who says he'll ever call me again anyway?"

"He will," she said with confidence.

There would have been more ordinances handed out if our mother hadn't called us. She complained that we'd left her alone with the children when she had turnip stew on the stove and chicken necks in the oven. The meeting adjourned.

"Won't you come down with us?" Ikhbal asked.

"Later."

She nodded. They looked at me sympathetically and, acting as if things were normal, Ikhbal assigned Layla the task of chopping salad and washing dirty dishes.

Layla slapped Ikhbal's arm. "And how will the older servant contribute to our dinner?"

"I'll pour the olive oil and lemon juice into the bowl. And while you're standing over the sink, I'll tell you how Suaad saw a price tag hanging out of her cousin's party dress when they were fixing their rouge in the bathroom."

"Really?"

"Her cousin was so furious at being caught that she spread rumors about Suaad's husband being a drunkard."

"You're kidding."

"I'm not."

"Is he really a drunkard?"

"Oh, please," Ikhbal cried. "He's too cheap to buy a can of beer, much less hard liquor."

They laughed and started towards the door. Before they left Layla paused. I was hoping she'd whisper an assurance or two, something like "don't worry, Mervat. Johnny will call first thing tomorrow" or "you have my whole hearted permission to see him once he does call" would have been nice. But she only told me to come downstairs once I'd had enough time to my-self. Otherwise, Ikhbal added, her youngest and dearest sister would end up lamenting over nothing and become the leader of all the teenage *ghoulat* female monsters.

I forced myself to smile so I wouldn't hurt her feelings. After they were gone I wondered why they'd given me more attention the day I'd gotten my first period than they did when I was on the verge of breaking up with the rich, handsome man I adored.

When Johnny called me at work the next day, I immedi-ately forgot the words "involved," "dangerous," and "distant," and agreed to see him. He asked me to drive to the west side because he was feeling too ill to travel the long miles east. The idea of accommodating him after the negligence and lies felt cheap. Such a feeling was temporary, of course, and before I had time to think about it I gave in.

My sisters urged me to cancel but I was too determined to listen. When they saw they'd failed to influence me, they told me to proceed with caution. Remain in public, they said, avoid secluded restaurants, and be home by nine.

"And don't promise him anything," Ikhbal ordered. "Not anything."

"I won't." Of course I had no clue what she meant, but at that point I would have acquiesced to a million hazy commands just to see him.

Their advice given, I rushed out of the house, my blood tasting the spices of excitement and panic. Never had I been so intractable about a decision I'd made on my own and in de-fiance of my sisters. Hopefully the consequences wouldn't re-semble those of the *kalander,* homeless man, whose calamities were his own making.

The *kalander* had once been a king and his passion for sail-ing landed him near a palace made of brass, where he met ten men with blind left eyes. The king asked the reason behind their affliction, and they swore that, for his own safety, he should be kept unaware of it. His curiosity so needled him that he insisted on knowing and, furthermore, in following their footsteps. So they gave him directions to the lavish palace. Forty girls lived there and they not only welcomed the king but entertained him for an entire year.

The situation changed when the girls left to visit their parents. They gave the king the palace keys and told him that while they were gone he was free to explore any room but the one behind the copper door. If he disobeyed he'd never see them again and evil would hound him forever. The king agreed but shortly before their return, temptation proved too much. He unlocked the prohibited door and the same punishment the other men had suffered befell him. After that, and for the rest of his days, he wandered the roads of Baghdad a homeless man.

In my case, however, I'd risk having a homeless heart if I didn't cater to my curiosity.

We met at a shopping center off the Munravia Exit. I was so eager for explanations that I got into his Corvette bubbling with questions. Before I had a chance to buckle my seat belt he brought out a red rose with lots of thorns.

"Happy Valentine's Day."

"Thank you," I said, simultaneously smiling and gritting my teeth. His gift felt like charity but I pretended to admire it.

The mood was ruined and I was quiet as he talked about the weather. I responded to his remarks despite their insignificance and wondered when he'd get to something of substance. His chat went on, and without consulting me, he drove to his house, suggesting we hang out and watch television before dinner.

"No one's home right now," he added. "They're at some party, so they'll be gone for hours."

This was impertinent. Did he think I was the kind of girl he could invite into his home, unchaperoned and relying on him to get back to my own car? Did he think I was a Maysoon? I wished I'd listened to my sisters' advice and cancelled.

I contemplated what I gambled by accepting, but there was no time for indecision. Johnny had already gotten out of the car and opened my door.

"Come on. I want to show you my pets."

My heart beat rapidly and my thoughts scattered.

He extended his hand to mine. "Let's go in, Mervat. The birds are beautiful. It'll be worth your while."

I took a deep breath and prepared to yield. I concentrated on the cracks in the pavement so I wouldn't have to think about what I was doing. When I heard his keys rattle in the door I considered changing my mind and keeping to my straight-lined world. The door opened before I could turn back.

He went inside and I followed slowly. There was a faint curry smell in the dark kitchen, blended with the scent of laundry detergent and bird feathers. He turned on the lights. I didn't see any of what I'd smelled, though I noticed a china plate of dried fruit on the table. I was tempted to take one but I didn't have the courage and I didn't want to give the impression I was either hungry or presumptuous. Besides, I didn't want to start snacking between meals.

Johnny led me to the living room. We sat on the couch and, for the next twenty minutes, he flipped through some fifty-four television channels. I was so anxious to speed up my visit that when I heard chirping coming from beyond the kitchen, I gently drew the remote control away from his hand.

"I thought you wanted me to see your birds."

"I did, but after the football game is over."

"What football game?"

"The one starting in five minutes."

"Oh, but seriously, Johnny!" I cried.

"Yes, seriously."

I complained about his joking until my protests yanked him to his feet.

"How about I kiss you all the way to the next room, then?"

"No." Not after the rose. "Johnny, stop. If I don't leave soon I'll get a headache."

"Fine, fine, your majesty," he gave in.

The room he took me to contained a wooden chair in the corner and a birdcage in front of a curtained window. The six birds were gray and white with orange ears and yellow feathers on their heads.

"Did I underestimate how beautiful they were?" he asked with the admiration he normally showed me.

I wondered what it was that mesmerized him. They stood on bars, twitched their heads, ate, drank and chirped, but did nothing else. Still, they'd won his affection, probably faster than I had.

Johnny tapped on the cage and smiled at them. "They're so innocent."

They were just that, I thought, but I couldn't respond. Jealousy wobbled in my chest. They had no limits with food and water, yet they weren't gluttons. They didn't need make-up, elaborate clothes or jewelry to earn approval. I wanted to pluck out their feathers and take a peek into their blissful brains and tiny hearts to examine what it was that made them so simple and content, yet glorious.

"Do you want to see my macaw?"

"Yes, I do, but please, for my sake, hurry. I dread the thought of running into your family."

"Okay, just wait a minute."

I walked to the mantel and looked at the various family and religious portraits. Most intriguing was one of the Virgin Mary made of colored sequins. The background was burgundy, her veil green and her face gold. I wished she could open her luminous mouth and tell me how she'd been chosen to occupy a place in Jesus' life while the rest of us had to settle for the Bible or church.

Desperate as she knew I was, she refused to speak. Maybe it was against the laws of heaven for deities to associate with common people. I wondered how many sinful thoughts I'd have to pay for before my worthiness approached divine expectations.

I shook off these impracticalities when I heard Johnny behind me. I was startled by the dazzling bird on his shoulder, its tail as long as a tree branch and beak as big as a tangerine. The bird was radiant. It lit up the room and my psychoanalysis of God: like Saint Rita, a powerful shaft of sunlight found its way through a solid brick wall to splinter my triviality.

"Can I pet him?" I asked.

"You can try, but he'll bite you."

"Does he bite you?"

"Sometimes." The bird pecked at a small stain on his white T-shirt. "He's tasting the spaghetti I had for lunch."

"Why don't you feed him?"

"Don't worry about him. I guarantee he's licking my shirt out of greed, not hunger."

I examined the macaw closely, with something like awe. "Can he speak?"

"He can say my name and my brother's." Johnny tried to get him to do it but the bird only sneezed a few times and lifted his wings, which were clipped. He looked too huge to fly but Johnny assured me he could.

"If he flew away, would he know how to come back?"

"No, he'd just die out there," he said. "He's used to the tropics."

I imagined what would happen if I allowed my wings to grow and then had enough gumption to use them. I'd journey into deserts with Bedouins and camels, jungles with banana trees and gorillas, the savannah with elephants and lions. The problem was that once I flew away I most likely wouldn't find my way back home. Or worse, I wouldn't want to.

"He's the smallest macaw," Johnny said. "A Bolivian Scarlet."

"What's Bolivian?"

"Bolivia is a country in South America."

"He's foreign?"

He laughed. "If you want to call him that."

I recalled the brochures of the deluxe hotels and palm beaches. "Mexico is in South America too, isn't it?"

"It's in Central America." He followed the macaw's eyes. "I went there with friends a few years ago."

"You've traveled?" I asked in surprise. "Why didn't you ever tell me?"

"I didn't know you wanted to know."

Forgetting all about his family coming home, I begged him to describe Mexico: the people and their way of life, its beaches and mountains. He said it was hot, filled with Mexicans, had lots of buses and taxis and pretty, turbulent waters. On his way back to the US, he said, immigration officials gave him trouble because his two-week visa had expired and so he stayed another four days.

His version of Mexico wasn't as elaborate as my sister's, but it didn't stop my envy. "You're very fortunate, Johnny."

He shook his head. "No, I'm not. Right, my friend?" The macaw fluffed its colors and maintained its gaze at nothing at all.

I asked again if I could pet him and Johnny said I could try. Its eyes instantly and firmly met mine, making me gasp and jerk my hand away.

"He senses the direction of the wind," Johnny said proudly.

"So he won't let me touch him?"

"Nothing could touch him. Not unless he wanted it to."

I wanted to scrape out a spoonful of the macaw's bone

marrow and make a potion with it. I would gulp it down in the hopes of assuming the bird's vigilant self-preservation. No evil eye, no massacre of my reputation, no separation from Johnny would dare lay a finger on me and threaten me with hell.

We went to a restaurant for dinner, but Johnny was restless and we left before our meals arrived. We went back to the shopping center because he wanted to switch cars. I wondered about his fidgetiness as he played with the radio buttons.

"Nice car," he said. "Very roomy and comfortable." He squinted at the dashboard. "How many miles?"

"I don't know."

He knocked twice on the window. "Strong. Are they bullet proof?"

"Johnny, enough," I said mildly. "I don't care about the car. What I want to hear is why you ignored me last week."

He quit fussing and relaxed a little in his seat. "I'm sorry, but I can't tell you anything."

"Why not?"

"It's better you don't know."

"No, it's not." I raised my voice. "I probably already do."

He frowned so fixedly I was breathless. "Yes, you probably do."

I cringed. I regretted having had wrung it out of him.

"I tried telling you, Mervat," he explained, "but you reacted so strongly I had to lie. I couldn't handle losing you."

I didn't speak. Shock had taken my voice and my reason and left only silence.

"Are you upset?" he asked after a while.

"Oh no, Johnny. I'm very happy."

I heard him chuckle and I looked at him sharply. There was no use speaking my mind, I figured. Neither scorn nor sympathy could rebuild the married life he'd just broken.

"This is not just street level, Mervat," he said, "I'm in so much danger it wouldn't surprise me to see her explode into a trillion pieces right now."

He was referring to his Corvette, and the idea stupefied me. I'd taken his predicament much too lightly, convinced my sisters were jumping to conclusions.

"Nobody was supposed to know," he said, rubbing his forehead. "You're the only girl I've ever told."

This didn't pacify my heart's soreness, and I wondered if time would dissolve this feeling, like sugar in hot tea. Than again, despite its invisibility, the taste always remained.

"How long have you been involved?" I brought myself to ask.

"Five years."

Five years and I couldn't smell it on him! He used his handsomeness and his family name well. Or I must have been a terrific idiot.

"How could someone like you do something like this? It's usually the poor or weak who slip into it, isn't it?"

"I had a few bad friends, and they persuaded me. They were so young and so powerful that laws were changed on their behalf alone. Girls worshiped them. The world seemed opened to them."

"Umm-humm."

I sounded knowledgeable when I knew nothing. By listening attentively to peoples' stories and using great caution, I'd assumed I could understand life's capriciousness, avoid its storms and be spoiled by the sun. I was about to enter a hurricane.

"It's not like I grew up wanting this," he said. "I got carried away and before I knew it it became my life."

"It just doesn't seem like you."

"It's not me!" he protested. "I wasn't born into it. It wasn't my goal. It might seem like I chose it, but I didn't!"

This baffled me but I didn't want to upset him anymore

than I already had.

"If I could've, I would've been a boxer or a football player. That would've suited me. That's what I really wanted."

"If I could, I'd travel the world," I said softly. "The whole world."

"That's impossible," he said.

I was taken aback by his belittling tone. His dreams were no more practical than mine. "What makes you say that?"

"Parents, culture, gender, money, love," he pointed out. "Too many obstacles."

"Oh." I regretted mentioning my stupid dream. I looked like a nitwit, going to college full-time yet wanting to vacation for a living.

"What does it matter what we want to be?" he asked with sarcasm. "None of it counts anyway."

"What have you done, Johnny, to turn them against you?"

"I asked to get out. But they won't let me."

"And what has it taken for you to hate it enough to think of getting out?"

"You." He looked directly into my eyes. "I want to get out because I want you."

This made me wince. I pressed my head to the window. I grieved for him. Johnny softly touched my hair and tried to kiss me. I did nothing to stop him even though I knew I should. Our infatuation was terminated; he could be jailed or killed tomorrow, and his hands had dealt narcotics and blood money. As soon as his lips touched mine I forgot the dangers and dirt. The promises I'd made my sisters were broken and my only thought now was to be in his arms forever. I was so determined to keep whatever it was I felt with him that I ignored what he hurled at me next.

It was past eleven o'clock when Johnny ended the last remaining of formalities between us.

"Mervat," he whispered, stroking my hand and drawing

me towards him. "Make me feel better, Mervat."

At first I didn't understand. He drew my head past his throat, past his shoulders. "Mervat–"

"Johnny, I can't."

"Just do it."

"But I can't."

"Mervat, please . . ."

"But Johnny . . ."

"Just shut up and do it!"

I drew away. His face was still and focused.

"What?" he asked.

I didn't understand and he must have felt sorry because his voice and expression softened. "Okay, then unbutton your shirt for me."

I obeyed, as he watched and slid my bra straps over my shoulder. "Mervat—"

"I can't, Johnny."

"Why not?"

"I'll feel naked!"

He studied me in amusement, as though I was a toy or extraterrestrial curiosity. "Then of course you absolutely mustn't."

His big arms enfolded me and he caressed my cheeks and neck with his lips. "You are so beautiful, Mervat."

But neither my beauty nor his had been generous to us.

"I can't wait until this mess is over, so I can make you feel good again."

Like Ala al-Din, I thought, did for his wife . . .

"I promise I'll make you feel good again."

Before we parted Johnny explained that for his safety, he wouldn't be able to leave his house and we might not see each other for a long time. I said I understood, even though I didn't, and we kissed goodbye.

Driving home that night I realized I'd reached a strange aloofness from my old self. Whom had Johnny transformed me into? There I was with the whole of his failings and I still believed our story would continue on a lovely path. I really and truly didn't want it any other way.

Chapter 18

Al-hafla . . . The Party

Easter was approaching, and we were baking *keleicha,* a famous holiday treat. My mother was stationed beside the oven with the task of glazing the raw *keleicha* with egg and milk before sliding the tray into the heat and pulling it out when its crust turned golden. My sisters took this opportunity to cross-examine me.

"What if he's caught by the FBI and sent to prison?" Ikhbal asked. I'd told her and Layla Johnny's big secret, though I hadn't yet gone through with the break-up they assumed would accompany it.

I pressed a cup rim into a flattened sheet of dough to form the small circles which Layla would stuff with crushed walnuts, sugar and cardamom. "I don't think it would be so terrible to wait for him."

She patted the dough. "You don't mind wasting your youth on someone whose occupation is *haram?* On a drug dealer?"

I knew his occupation was forbidden by God, but it was the first time the phrase "drug dealer" was used so bluntly to describe him.

"I'm only twenty years old," I said, busying my hands with

the cup and dough, "and I doubt that he'd be committed until the world came to an end."

"He might be, if the judge was Babba," Layla said.

I smiled halfheartedly but Ikhbal warned us that the problem wasn't funny. "You have to take into account that men like Johnny don't have a conscience or a future."

My eyes stung with tears. I wanted to knot the dough, shatter the cup and hide in my room.

"You think you could at least stay away from him until his situation improves?" Layla tried to lift me up.

I was incapable of saying yes, and this angered Ikhbal. With narrow eyes and tight lips she rolled the dough until it became as round as a wheel. She spread melted dates over it and wrapped it into a burrito-style sandwich. "Mamma and Babba won't approve," she said. "And they'll blame us for having allowed you to court him."

I lowered my eyes in shame.

"Mamma and Babba are not the main problem here, Ikhbal," said Layla.

"Oh, then what is?"

"Mervat, of course. It's not fair for her to go through such torture at her age."

"But for God's sake that's a given." And she turned to me. "Listen, Mervat, won't you care if Mamma and Babba don't approve?"

When I didn't answer immediately her face became grim.

"Yes, I'd care," I said before she threw me into the hot oven with the *keleicha.* "But he's getting out. He promised."

She scoffed at my blindness. "You honestly have no idea who this man is, do you? His bosses are his god. He can't squash a spider or eat a celery stick without them knowing it. They know his past and his present, and they determine his destiny."

"What she says is true, Mervat," Layla affirmed, killing any misgivings I had about Ikhbal's intentions.

By night their talk had checked whatever dreams I had left. And before I had to face worse truths, I thought it best to excuse myself from his life, as swiftly as my great-great Aunt Ammo did when three days after her wedding she discovered that her husband Jamal had a wife he hadn't divorced.

But that opportunity never presented itself because Johnny disappeared for two weeks and I had yet another change of heart. I missed him, especially when I imagined the loneliness and boredom he must have felt from being incarcerated in his house during these long winter days. Since he was probably depending on my loyalty and patience to help him through I didn't want to betray him by splitting up with him. Besides, his business wasn't my concern. If he treated me well, I could play deaf and mute. I'd sacrifice my security for whatever came of being with him.

Then one day my family and I went to a Chaldean Easter party and my dream-saga of fighting for Johnny began to disintegrate as gradually as rose petals fall from the flower.

The day started well. I'd bought a short violet dress and crystal earrings, and that evening brought out my curls with lots of gel and sprayed on a few ounces of Calvin Klein perfume.

I was happy at the admiring stares and soft whistles I got from the young men at the party. They were sincere and convincing enough to brace my self-esteem until I could see Johnny again. Soon enough I found myself gawking over the enormous olives, humus, tabbouleh and tropical drinks everyone else was indulging in. I was eager for dinner because I'd kept myself to three food groups (pretzels, orange juice and red apples) in the past days, but as the waiters began serving chicken and shish-kabobs, I noticed Johnny sitting at the next table and my appetite evaporated.

"He told me he couldn't leave the house and yet there he is," I said to Layla. "He lied."

"Don't be silly, Mervat. Yes, he's wearing a suit and sitting in a banquet hall, but that doesn't mean he's been liberated by the mob."

"I know it doesn't," I said, jabbing my fork into the pickled cabbage. "What I don't understand is how it's safe for him to eat kabobs in front of six hundred people when it's too risky to use the phone."

Layla slowly unfolded her napkin and placed it in her lap. "He is doing you a favor, I hope you know."

I took some parsley and tore it into tiny pieces. "He is the biggest ass I ever met."

"Good, then you now have reasons enough to forget all about him." And bringing a fork of rice to her mouth, she casually looked in Johnny's direction. "His sister and brother are here too."

The sight of Johnny's siblings, tucked behind the balloon and wedding arrangements, made me uncomfortable. I couldn't touch my food so my meal was distributed among the rest of the family, and by the time dinner was over the men's joking steadily massaged my heart until I relaxed.

I went to the restroom during dessert, and on my way back I glanced over at Johnny's chair. It was empty. I grazed the crowd with my eyes and in the middle of what should have been a private gesture, I realized that his sister and brother were watching me. For the first time in my life I was introduced to the evil-eye.

Embarrassed and frightened, I stumbled back to my table. I was furious with myself for allowing them to see my anxiety. It proved I was Johnny's girlfriend when he had assured me that no one knew about us—not even his half-brother, Nabiel, whom he was closest to. I was flattered because in the Middle Eastern community the harder a man works at keeping a romance secret, the more serious he is. Secrecy doesn't just show he cares about the girl's name enough to protect it, it also implies he might marry her.

With one glance my display of worry had succeeded in ruining all that wonderful and necessary secrecy. Another unspoken rule a good Chaldean girl follows is that any demonstration of zeal or passion can become a curse.

"They caught me looking for him," I said to Layla when she returned from the dance floor, "and now they know everything."

She handed me a fork and told me to stop crying and taste the black grapes and watermelon. "You haven't eaten one bite since you saw him, and Babba paid fifty dollars for you to come to this party."

"I can't eat," I objected. "I know they don't like me and they'll do whatever it takes to convince him I'm not good enough."

Layla inspected my face as if she hadn't seen it in decades. "Are you trying to make me laugh, or do you mean that?"

"You might as well laugh." I didn't want her to see how steadfast I was about waiting for Johnny to get his life together and marry me.

Johnny and I didn't speak or look at each other during the party. This was discrete, but the way he watched me was as clear to me as Uncle Sabir's green-eyed wife's adultery was to the village. My affection and designs for the future expanded.

I waited for a call the next morning but none came and I blamed his brother and sister. I tried to hide my uncertainties from Layla, who would have chided me, but by the third day I couldn't help it. Living with myself, by myself, was excruciating. Besides, whatever reproaches she pitched couldn't possibly compare to my own.

Before she served the tea she told me a story about her mother-in-law having forgotten to dust her raw potato chops in corn starch and blaming her son's un-subservient wives for it.

"She told her daughter, who later told us, that we didn't offer to buy the potatoes or stuff them," Layla said. "But when I asked my mother-in-law if she'd said this, she said the only complaint she'd made was that potatoes are not as good as they used to be—during Muhammad's era is what I believe she meant."

"Is her daughter lying?"

"Of course not. My mother-in-law just wants to make out that we're no good and deny it in the same face."

She was about to go on but I begged her not to.

"What's the matter?" she asked. "Did Johnny call?"

"No. That's the matter."

She sighed. "Don't you think that might also be the solution?"

"Not really, no."

"Do you have a better option?"

"I don't have anything. But I know if he's gone, I won't even have that."

She laughed lightly. "Mervat, you're getting your priorities all tangled up . . ."

"I have nothing without him."

"Don't be ridiculous," she said, her tone intentionally careless. "He's terrible, though, isn't he? We should call Aunt Evelyn and have her punish her son for being incredibly pretty yet extremely poisonous."

"If I were to call Aunt Evelyn, the only thing I'd have her do is make Johnny call me."

"As if that would do any good. All you'll get is a few more pointless dates because in the end he cannot take you for a wife."

"But why?"

"Because you're too damn innocent and his brother knows that too damn well. Don't think that Johnny slipped because of his friends. The only person who could influence him like that

178

is his half-brother."

"What does it matter who influenced him?"

"It matters a lot. Johnny wants to protect his brother and his family name. And they want to protect themselves. So you see, he cannot marry a stranger."

"I thought you said we were third cousins?"

"That's not what I mean. He must choose from his own kind. It's less complicated and more prosperous to join a family who's already familiar with the business."

"But if I know what he is and I accept it, what difference does it make?"

"It makes a difference to them and it makes a difference to us. His work is a little more dirty than our family is accustomed to."

"But he's trying to get out."

"And that's as far as it'll get—him trying, them refusing."

"The worst that could happen is he's arrested."

"The mob won't be so kind. Don't mistake this man for the bums that sell rolling paper and plastic bags on the streets. Men like him work with millions of dollars and mobsters have no mercy for men with millions."

"He promised he was going to fix everything."

"For whose sake—yours?"

I didn't answer but my face said it before I looked away.

"Don't you see that's all the more reason why he can't be with you?" she pleaded. "I bet the thought of leaving the business never crossed his mind until you came along."

"That's not fair. His being where he is now is all an accident."

"Whatever it was or wasn't, he will not walk away from it. He can't afford to."

"Yet he can afford to lose me?"

She raised her brows. "It's better to risk a broken heart than a broken neck."

"You don't understand. I can't leave him."

"Then be thankful if he leaves you."

I tried to be thankful but I couldn't fake it. I was crushed. I was about to miss the express train traveling from Boredom Town to Fabulous Land. I hurried to Layla's house, hoping her connections with God could delay the departure time and get me a seat.

She served me a plate of Spanish cheese, Saltines, tea biscuits and a jar of grape jam. I reminded her of my diet, pushed the plate away, and asked for the answers she'd guaranteed earlier.

"It's very simple," she said, placing a slice of cheese on a cracker. "Call him."

"That's not so simple."

"It's simpler than depending on him to do it."

"I'm not really depending on him to do it."

"Yes you are." She bit into the cracker and swept crumbs off her thighs. "Curiosity is making you sick. It's better to stick your finger down your throat, vomit and feel healthy again."

"Gross."

"Maybe, but it's a solution."

"I don't want to chase after him."

"That's hardly chasing."

"And I don't want to be barked at, either. The worst is hearing him make up silly excuses just because he feels sorry for me. I don't want him to court me out of pity."

She dipped a spoon into the jam and shrugged. "Alright, then don't do it."

"Oh." I'd expected her to persuade me further, and when she didn't I tried to get her to talk about him more by hinting that the idea made sense. "It's not easy to say we've broken up when he might call me anytime."

"That's why you should confront him," she said. "And if

he confirms it, then be glad because you won't have to wonder anymore."

"Won't I come out of this mess with more dignity if I just ignore it?"

"I'm sorry, Mervat, but you in particular don't know how to ignore it. You will dwell on it until your brain hatches pigeons."

I couldn't defend my strength of will because I hadn't become acquainted with it yet. I wasn't like the saints or clever Sharazad or my Uncle Sabir's daring green-eyed wife. Up to now, wanting to shave my legs in fifth grade was the closest I'd ever gotten to showing courage.

"Azziz's Party Shoppe."

"Hi, Johnny," I said, sounding as casual as I had while rehearsing in the mirror.

There was a pause and I went onto the next line in my script. "How've you been?"

"Who is this?" he asked.

"Are you busy right now?" He recognized my voice as well as he did his own mother's.

"Who is this?" he repeated.

I forced myself to make light of his inquiry. "You honestly don't know who this is?"

"Can I put you on hold?"

Before I replied he placed the phone down and waited on a customer. My mind and nerves were in shambles as I listened to the register and a rustle of paper. There was grumbling about wrong change.

"What, you didn't go to school, man?" a man asked with irritation.

"No, actually, I didn't," Johnny answered. I could feel the tension in his voice.

"Are you sure this place is licensed?"

Despite my own predicament, I couldn't help smiling as I thought how exhausting it must be to break up with a girlfriend while being harassed by customers. Johnny tossed a few remarks at the shopper but they were flustered and ineffectual. His uneasiness was so obvious that I knew what the outcome would be. He wasn't going to get out of the business or keep his promise or give me a life different from my sisters.' I was getting pushed out, and although my heart was stubborn about it, I was ready for the rejection that I knew would drop me into a void.

"Hello," he said again, breathlessly.

"Johnny, are you busy?"

"Yes."

I paused. It was almost over now. A few more seconds and we'd be done and I'd begin paying for the joy I'd found last spring. All along I'd thought it was gratis, a complimentary gift from the King and Queen of Virtue themselves. I hung on to my dignity when everything else was falling away. "Okay, Johnny, I understand."

"What do you mean?"

"Johnny, I understand," I emphasized, harboring a certain satisfaction at his bafflement yet feeling bitter that there was no turning back.

I could tell he wanted me to probe, demand an explanation, plead for a reconciliation. But since he'd chosen the coldest way to force me out of his life—surely afraid I'd bawl and cling—I was going to walk away with pride.

"I think it's best I let you get back to work."

He was silent.

"Goodbye, Johnny." I spoke like a soldier, barring any chance of accidentally saying a word that might mollify his distress or increase mine. If he could be this cold, the least I could do was pretend to be unmoved.

"Yes, goodbye."

I knew these were the last words I'd ever hear him say, so I stayed on the line a moment. He stayed on as well; I didn't know why. It was too late to stitch up the heart he'd torn. Before either of us could change our mind, I hung up.

I didn't cry. I was so impressed with myself, suddenly strong in battle, that I thought this deliverance should, like Shahrazad's stories, be written in gold letters by scribes. I lightly stretched the telephone cord and spun my finger around it, then opened the top drawer of my dresser and took out my travel brochures. Costa Rica, Punta Cana, Antigua, Waikiki.

"That's impossible," he'd said. "Parents, culture, gender, money, love . . . Too many obstacles."

But becoming a boxer or football player was as effortless as reading a bedtime story, I thought. I sighed, laid on my back and stared at the ceiling. He hadn't chosen his path, but I still had a chance at mine. I could travel the world and show him— or myself—that it was possible. I could become a stewardess or a cruise director and live in the air or on the sea, where the turbulence would keep my memories in check. I talked like that to myself until midnight, when I remembered the limits of my gender and culture and the man I had just lost. Then I flung the brochures off of the ground as ambition lost out to sorrow. I promptly spent the following months in a state of depression.

Chapter 19

My depression was obedient in the beginning. Half of it was regulated by my ego while the other cut a quarter of my fat and calorie intake, got a spiral perm, bought two very expensive party dresses, stayed up all night tearing at my blanket's loose threads and changed routes to and from college so I'd pass MacNaughton Street and Azziz's Party Shoppe.

When my depression occasionally misbehaved—causing me to raise my voice to my parents, be bitter towards my sisters or almost cry in front of customers—I pressed it forcibly to my stomach. I didn't intend to fool people into believing I was happy. I simply figured they didn't need to witness my weakness when at any minute Johnny might reappear and escort it out the door.

But ultimately it developed a mind of its own. It hated anything that didn't have to do with Johnny. Because fat-free yogurt, professors, school books, deli meats, travel brochures and all the other things that cluttered my life didn't carry his name or convey his stories, I lived for night. Then I could tuck my head beneath my blanket and, until he could appear with either a good old-fashioned life or an exhilarating modern one, lose myself in the romantic events of my first story.

Johnny didn't reappear. He was too ashamed to show his face, I convinced myself, and he was going to wait for circumstances to bring us together. Or perhaps his siblings forbade him to see me. I ought to be like Saad, the ice cream salesman, and drink myself back onto his arms.

Saad wanted to marry a girl named Layla but her family didn't approve because he wasn't their social equal. So he drank *arak* to work up his courage, forced his way into her home and tried to stand up to her family. Layla's brothers beat him badly and threw him out, but he got drunk a second time, went knocking on Layla's door and was abused and kicked out again. Saad then got even drunker and camped for days with the fish and frogs by a stream beside Layla's home. The people of the town, disapproving of the unjust interference between the lovers, forced Layla's family to consent to the marriage and made Saad a happy man.

A man could push himself into a girl's life without loss of dignity. I couldn't, but I could make myself available by going to the mall, Arabic parties and festivities. Since none were going on in May, I would hold my breath until summer. Within a week of reaching this decision, a coincidence brought Johnny and me together at an engagement party. Only Ikhbal, her husband and her in-laws were invited but she'd taken me along as a change of atmosphere.

"*Mashalla,* he is handsome," Ikhbal said, looking across the banquet hall. This was only the second time she had seen Johnny.

My hands in my lap, I kept quiet. At first I was surprised and pleased to see him at the party, hoping he'd fly to my salvation. After an hour dejection set in. There was no hint he'd try to approach me or a single glance in my direction.

"Look at Azhar," Ikhbal said as she watched the newly engaged couple dancing slowly by themselves. Azhar was wearing a tiara. The way she moved her feet and held her head, I believe she thought she was wearing Queen Victoria's crown.

I patted the utensils wrapped in the cloth napkin in front of me. "Has he looked this way at all?"

Ikhbal craned her neck. "I can't tell, Mervat."

That meant he hadn't. I was crushed. Forty days of mourning hadn't ended and he might as well be dressed in red.

"His back is turned anyway," she said.

He could have switched chairs with his brother and had a clear view but Nabiel had claimed that privilege instead.

"Aren't you going to eat anything?" Ikhbal asked.

I shook my head wearily. "I'm full."

Ikhbal attempted to entertain me with gossip; the girl in green was said to have been in love with an Italian but was forced last month to marry a Chaldean. The mustached man in a gray suit had a child by an American, and the middle-aged woman dressed in gold sequins had her daughter-in-law thrown out of the house when she asked her to bring a bottle of Diet Verners.

I asked Ikhbal what time it was.

"Ten to twelve."

Only an hour before Johnny and I would again be separated. I stretched my heart like a rubber band but he went on dancing the *depka,* eating and drinking and talking among friends as though we'd never met. As though he'd never said "I've fallen in love with you" or "I will make you feel good again."

"They were watching you like hawks during the last two *depkas,*" Ikhbal said in the car. We sat in the back seat while her husband and father-in-law were in the front.

I had sensed their last-minute gazes and was annoyed that Nabiel had his nose in what was not his business. Ikhbal told me that while I was in the circle of the *depka* they watched me like I was a fifty karat diamond.

If that was what they thought why not gather me to themselves where they could keep me safe?

"I don't think he ever liked me," I said to Layla after I recited the details of the engagement party and had two sips of cardamom tea. "I think I hallucinated the whole thing."

"I don't think you think that at all."

I stroked my fingernail against the cup's rim. "If what we had was special, why wasn't it worth being kind to me?"

"Let's be realistic, Mervat. You can decorate a brick up with pearls, but its harshness won't become smooth."

"So this is realistic?" I asked, sarcastically. "This is the dating kingdom?"

She occupied herself with slowly picking up breadcrumbs from the table.

"I shouldn't complain. Lots of Middle Eastern girls would sell their gold to have the man of their dreams at their feet hinting he'll marry them and then say goodbye."

"Mervat, you cannot condemn all relationships based on this incident alone."

"I will not give anyone a chance to break my heart again."

Her eyes down, she folded the edge of the tablecloth upwards. "Maybe you won't have to go through this again. One day you might receive an ideal suitor and get married in the blink of an eye."

"How reassuring!" I laughed. "And then I'll really live happily ever after."

"Why not? There are as many ways to fall in love and marry as there are people in the world. I mean, dating is only a few hundred years old, if even. Given the divorce rate and the emotional troubles in the process itself, it hasn't proven to be the most successful way to meet, anyway. Before dating, for tens of thousands of years, people were matched or fell in love without one glance or a single word—just by familiarity."

"I will never marry like that," I said stubbornly.

"Why?"

"I just won't."

"Why not?" she insisted.

"Because that's how Ikhbal got married, and Nameera and even you!"

I wondered if I'd gone too far.

"What is it that frightens you about our marriages?"

If I said anything a gush of rage would follow.

"Tell me, Mervat, what's so wrong with our marriages?"

"Everything!" I burst out. "Absolutely everything. None of your husbands deserved you. And they still don't."

"What, or should I ask who, led you to that belief?"

"I have eyes. I can see. All you do is complain about your husband, and it's no different with Ikhbal and Nameera. I hate it. I don't ever want to be a part of such misery. I don't want you to be a part of it."

Layla sighed deeply. "What gave you the impression that we're what you claim we are?"

"This," I opened my arms, looking around her apartment. "Every day there are fights. Money, in-laws, kids—money, in-laws, kids—money, in-laws, kids! It's no life!"

She leaned back and folded her arms. "If marriage offends you so much, why did you want to be Johnny's wife?"

"It wouldn't have been like that with him."

"You think his looks would've stopped you from fighting about money, in-laws and kids?"

I said nothing.

"Our husbands have many little flaws, but Johnny has one big one, yet you were willing to forgive him and, had he asked you to, fight for him."

I looked away in shame.

"As unbearable as my life might seem sometimes, Sermad is as much a part of it as you are. He and I don't have the same blood but we might as well have."

I didn't know where to hide my face.

"But don't think I'm encouraging you to marry the way we did," she continued, saving me, as she always did, from chagrin. "For God's sakes, you give up so easily. Those who have practiced dating since its beginning haven't mastered it yet you expect to in the first try?"

She was right, but that didn't help me feel better.

"If I were in your shoes, Mervat, I'd put this subject aside for now. I'd first go and figure out how to make the world do what I want it to. We live in a country where you could do just that."

I did not feel I lived in this country. My thousands-year-old customs were so overpowering they guided my thoughts, words and actions. Changing that was a strenuous, if not impossible, task. All I wanted the world to do was bring Johnny back. Anything else—a career or travel or dating—would only make life more puzzling and insecure.

The world didn't yield to me, though. It did bring me into contact with Johnny at the mall three Sundays in a row, but only briefly and unsatisfactorily. Whenever I crossed paths with him I either lifted my chin and pretended not to notice, or I turned and walked the other direction.

I badly wanted him back, but on my terms. He had to pay for my humiliation and misery by tasting my coldness, my rejection, and that was the cause of our fourth encounter at the mall.

I was with Ashley and Ingham paying twenty-five dollars for a pair of shoes when I noticed Johnny standing beside me. He was wearing sunglasses and staring straight ahead as though considering whether to buy socks. A thick resentment built inside me. I was flustered, unable to differentiate between a wise or stupid decision as I grabbed my purchase and ordered my niece to follow. On the way I passed Nabiel near the adjacent beauty salon. He was enjoying what he'd just seen. I shut myself in a bathroom and panted with anger.

Ashley and Ingham worriedly asked what the matter was.

"I have a stomach ache."

"Are you going to be okay?" Ingham asked.

I nodded, hating how I'd handled things. I knew I was going to be the exact opposite of okay and I wanted to cut my wrists over it.

"Mervat, stop crying. There's nothing you can do now," Layla said. "He'll approach you again."

"He thinks I hate him."

"He wouldn't be wrong if he did."

I curled on her sofa and fixed my eyes on the ceiling lamp. "I can't help it," I said. "I know it's too late for him to keep his promise, but part of me wants to hurt him."

The other part, I added silently, wanted to run off with him to a village in Mexico and live safely away from the mob and its threats and our families' criticisms.

Johnny stopped going to the mall after that. I doubled my drives past MacNaughton Street. I wanted to know whether he had been killed or arrested or if he was just not interested anymore. It must have been the last reason because his red sports car, always parked in the front of the store, confirmed he was alive and still catered to by Aunt Evelyn.

Determined to fix things, I started attending whatever West Side party was held for charity or to honor a Saint or Iraqi holiday my family agreed to. Johnny was never there. I went to the State Fair twice during the weekend and once on a Thursday, searching for him between the Ferris wheels and octopus rides. I lingered among the games and patiently watched clown shows and school bands.

In the midst of my quest I spotted Ahmad, Sonia, Tony and Maysoon. They weren't paired off but I was sure they'd find a way, if they hadn't already, of getting together. Imad was there as well with the three brothers who lived on my block and he had fun harassing and stalking me.

"Oooh Najah, you're so pretty," he'd say to one of his male friends whenever I passed by. "Please, will you go out with me? Please, I'm so in love with you."

And all four would laugh.

Their teasing didn't annoy me because I was absorbed in the corn dogs, popcorn, French fries, and Johnny's absence. He wasn't there, yet I was determined to find him. When the Fair week was over I began to look forward to the Chaldean Festival in Oak Park.

It started at six and my sisters and I arrived soon after. We were huddled near an apple tree with relatives we hadn't seen in months when I noticed Brittany a few feet away. I looked around, hoping to see her uncle Johnny nearby, but saw Johnny's sister instead. She was standing with a group of women. Our eyes met and before I looked away she grabbed the girl to her left, who looked so much like her. She must have been the cousin I'd mistaken her for the day we met. She whispered something to her and the girl inspected me as though I was a visible germ.

I was raging with indignation. In Middle Eastern culture, it is taboo to publicize a girl's personal affairs because it could jeopardize her marriageability. Yet Johnny's sister dared expose my name as casually as she would jiggle her wrist bracelets!

"I wouldn't be surprised if she announced my business to Aunt Evelyn," I said to Layla after we came home from the park. "She's just low enough."

"She does have *eyoun al-didjaj.*"

If she had the eyes of a chicken, as my sister claimed (and everyone knows a chicken can be scolded and booted a thousand times without giving up), then I'd have to twist her neck to save my name. I fretted with the couch's pillow ruffles. "I don't trust her. She hates me enough to spread lies."

"Telling her cousin doesn't equal telling the entire world, Mervat." Layla placed her finger on her forehead and thought. "But we must be cautious."

I was hurt to think that Johnny hadn't protected my name enough to stop his siblings from using it. If they thought I went out with men casually or was just any girl to him, it was because he hadn't defended me. He'd managed to cheapen my character.

"I think his sister's mouth needs professional cementing," she said and extended her hand to me. "Give me Johnny's number. I'm going to call him."

"You're what?"

"What is his number, Mervat?"

I was perplexed. Contacting him was an attractive thought but I didn't want to use his sister's spite as an excuse.

"Is that really necessary?"

"It is."

My heart was beating rapidly. A door was going to open between Johnny and me, and I didn't know whether he'd take advantage of it or slam it shut. Looking at Layla's impatient face, I reluctantly cited the number and she dialed. I knelt on the carpet and listened to the silence in the room.

"Can I speak to Johnny, please?" Layla asked. I wished I'd kept my mouth shut but I envied Layla for getting to speak to him. A few seconds later she went on. "Hi, Johnny, this is Layla, Mervat's sister."

The rest of the conversation was in Arabic and lasted twenty minutes. My face was sweating and my knees shaking as I imagined the outcome of this talk. If Johnny contacted me tomorrow I'd be drinking milk and honey for the rest of my life. If he didn't, my diet would consist of grapefruit and hot peppers.

When Layla hung up, I slowly lifted my head, afraid of what she'd tell me, and saw a big smile on her face.

"He talks like a gentleman," she said.

"What did he say?"

"He said 'my sister actually did that?'"

"What else did he say?"

"I was busy discussing his sister's misconduct when he asked, almost interrupting me, 'who was Mervat at the festival with?'"

My heart quickened.

"Later he asked 'which day did you say Mervat went to the festival?'" Layla laughed. "I don't think he heard a word I said, engrossed as he was in pronouncing Mervat, but he did promise his sister wouldn't bother you again."

I closed my eyes and sighed as his kisses drifted into my memory. I missed him terribly and was willing to help him salvage what we'd had. I went to public Middle Eastern events even more, passing MacNaughton Street daily. Then Chaldean Day at Boblo Island's Theme Park in Canada cycled around and shattered my hopes.

Johnny's sister was there, jinxing me. My family and I were standing in line for the roller coaster and she was with a girl at a nearby children's ride. When she saw me, she automatically leaned to the girl, exchanging comments as they looked me up and down.

My blood itself demanded retaliation. I grabbed Isaam's arm before he stepped forward in line. "That's Aunt Evelyn's daughter," I pointed my finger at her. "Do you know her?"

He looked in that direction and squinted.

"Right there," I pointed more clearly.

He focused hard. "No, I don't. Why do you ask?"

"I was just wondering."

I was content. Her mouth and eyes opened in horror, a

mouse in a trap. She feared I'd spread a rumor about her or disclosed her family's secret. That I'd had the audacity to do so with a male relative must have piqued her, but I wasn't done.

My skin burning in irritation, I collected quarters and dimes from my brother and Ikhbal and went to a telephone booth. I called Layla and told her what had happened. "Her mouth is not cemented yet," I said. "What should I do?"

"Is Johnny there too?" she asked.

"I haven't seen him."

"If you do, pull him aside and tell him about it."

I was quiet, not knowing if I'd have the courage to do so.

"Mervat?"

"Okay, I'll tell him." I was so angry I wasn't going to resist even the most torturous advice, but first I asked Ikhbal's permission. She agreed and as soon as I saw Johnny I approached him.

"Can I speak with you, please?"

The older woman who was walking with him stared oddly as we stepped aside.

"My sister asked you to stop your sister from talking about me," I said, solidly. "Why didn't you?"

"I tried but she says she has nothing against you . . ."

"I've caught her doing it!" I interrupted. "Twice!"

Speechless with shame, he looked at me for a moment. "I'll talk to her again."

"Please do." I trudged off feeling resentful towards everything, not the least of which was Johnny's empty promises.

The day at Boblo was supposed to last until ten, when the boats made their last crossings from Canada to Detroit, but it started raining after four and people hid inside restaurants or beneath rooftops. The rain didn't slow and everyone left their shelters and got drenched on their way to the boats.

We waited our turn for an available boat, every part of me, from my hair roots to my toenails, freezing. The sweetness between Johnny and me had been replaced with sourness. He was cruel to me months ago and knowing he wasn't going to do anything to foster our courtship, I had repaid him well today.

After half an hour we were seated inside a boat, crowded because the top deck was roofless and no one would sit there. People shared food and clutched onto each other whenever the boat rocked and the river splashed the windows. I watched the storm and I wondered what would happen if the boat collapsed and the water swallowed me. Only me. In order not to grieve others' deaths during my own, and for my death to be recorded in the encyclopedia under "Ill-Fated," everyone else had to survive.

My end would be written in thick books and compared to the weaver of Baghdad who worked day and night yet remained very poor. God had stubbornly preordained him to this fate. Even when a princess, thinking he'd stumble upon the riches in cleaning a goose for supper, gave him a bird whose belly she'd filled with forty dinars, he failed to notice his own luck and sold it cheaply. The princess gave him another goose and he sold it as well. Finally, the king took pity and offered him a bag of treasure but on his way out of the palace the weaver tripped, fell on his head and died. God then spoke to the king. "It's not you who can make a poor man rich or a dead man live."

If I had to depend on God to give me purpose, I thought as the Boblo boat was nearly lifted off the waters by the winds on the wild river, then I was in a predicament.

Chapter 20

In June, a suitor came to see me. By then I was sleeping a hundred inconsecutive minutes a night, counting the number of loops in my blanket's stitching, clipping individual split-ends and plucking hair from my calves and thighs with tweezers. I was also eating four hundred calories and two grams of fat a day. People called me skinny, and at first my mind swelled with pride. Later I was angry because my weight granted me only size zero dresses, criticism from my sisters and praise from strangers. It did not bring Johnny back.

I told my mother not to welcome the suitor, but she ignored me, which was justifiable since I'd gotten my associate's degree and turned twenty. Middle Eastern families, except for those whose daughters are too young to marry or whose daughters want to attain a wider education, don't refuse a suitor's company. A refusal would insinuate the girl had a lover.

So I consented. Aside from offending my sense of what was seemly, I secretly desired a suitor's visit. If he was tolerable, maybe I'd accept his proposal. I never saw Johnny after Boblo so I was hopeless, bored and lonely, and like my Uncle Sabir, I would've married a cow.

"*Al-Salaam aleikum.*" My father greeted the guests with the Arabic words 'may peace be with you.'

"*Wa aleikum al-salaam,*" they returned.

Two men in suits and a woman in a black dress with yellow print entered our house. My parents, Ikhbal and Layla took them to the living room as I went into the kitchen and prepared trays of tea and *knafee*—shredded wheat stuffed with cheese. I was about to slice the walnut cake when I saw Ikhbal's hands hovering over mine.

"Let me do that," she said, either suspecting I'd ruin the cake or wanting me to sit across from the suitor so he could begin his inspection—from the bobby pins holding my hair in place to the #214 L'Oreal Cherie painted on my toe nails.

I handed her the knife, returned to the living room and sat on the couch beside Layla. The woman, who must have been the suitor's mother, examined me as closely as she would a gold chain before buying it. She gave a ghastly smirk. "Is this your youngest daughter?"

Everyone's eyes fell on me and my mother's face beamed proudly, attempting to make the customer hallucinate that the chicken sitting on the couch was as fat as a turkey and fancy as a quail.

"She is my youngest child, yes."

Her eyes wide, the woman saluted me. I wasn't certain whether she approved of me or thought my appearance too fashionable for a wife. With a knee-length skirt and a short-sleeved blouse, my clothes were neither modern nor conservative. If she planned on having me share her house she might have preferred ankle and wrist-length clothing.

Eventually their inspection ended and everyone rummaged for a topic to discuss. First they talked about last night's rain and Michigan's finicky weather, then I-75 North's traffic and I-75 South's construction. Then someone mentioned a crime that happened on Detroit's East Side a week ago. A thief had entered a Chaldean liquor store at nine in the morning and fled with a few bottles of beer. When the owner chased him into an alley, the thief's friend, waiting in a car, shot the Chaldean three times in the stomach.

There was a minute of silence before the suitor's mother mentioned the speculation that the man who'd been shot was "involved." Johnny's name surged into my heart. For the first time since breaking up I admitted Johnny's decision to leave me and stay in the business was politically wise. I forgave him and blamed the Other One.

"We also heard that," my mother said, "but it might be a rumor. Nowadays no one really knows a truth from a lie."

The woman shrugged. "You have to wonder, though, why a man with a wife and three children would run after a thief, a black man, just because of two beers?"

"Not necessarily," her husband said. "Maybe he was upset, and reacted. Maybe the killer was—excuse my language—a son of a whore. God only knows."

His profanity was odd given this was his first and most formal encounter with us. Nonetheless the company agreed with him. I found myself loathing God for having life's many secrets and not sharing any of them with me. It would greatly assist His so-called children—which I assumed included me and Johnny—in creating better lives. His stinginess and game playing annoyed me and I couldn't wait until I died so I could lash out at Him in person. I doubted I qualified for heaven, but surely He visited hell every now and then.

I was about to further disfigure God's image when my mother ordered me to go to the kitchen and bring the tea. I was happy she'd interrupted me from such wicked thoughts. It was enough that they took over whenever I was alone.

I was pouring tea when Ikhbal appeared. "What do you think?"

"He has no lips."

She laughed without making a sound.

"It's true," I said. "His mouth stretches like a necklace around his jaw, but he doesn't have lips."

"Shhh," she warned, grabbing the dessert plates. "If we keep this up, they'll think us rude and they'll never call back."

"Hmmm," I said, with the feigned delight of having just swallowed a cookie. "That's the sweetest threat I ever heard."

"Shhh," she insisted and started towards the living room. "Now pick up the tray and go before me."

I served the tea, starting with the woman, then her husband, her son, and then my family. Ikhbal followed with dessert. The room fell silent and, knowing they were scrutinizing me the way tourists did pyramids, I kept my eyes on the carpet. I didn't stumble, but I did notice that the suitor's left sock had a hole in it.

As soon as we took our seats the company returned to the subject which had been interrupted by the tour of the pyramids. They were discussing the changes in Chaldeans after they immigrated from Iraq to America. The new land provoked us foreigners, they said, to think only of work and money.

"It's the bills that confuse a man between wanting to work and not wanting to work," my father said. "I like spending time with my family, but my six-foot loan officer and the liquor store down the block has my hands and feet tied like a sheep's."

"No freedom!" the suitor's father said. "It's always competition! Competition! Competition!"

My sisters and I bent our heads and smiled as the man continued, "And ooof, the bank! They're a conspiracy. My oldest son bought a forty-five thousand dollar house and his payment is $535.40 a month. Now, why do you think the forty cents? Why not point zero, zero?"

My father bit into the *knafee*. "Terrible, terrible."

"A penny," the suitor's father declared. "Once the bank sent me a bill for one penny."

"I hear people in Mexico are better off," my father said, I believe to prevent us from starting to giggle. "There, if the police stop you for speeding you ask him how much was I going, officer?" He rubbed his thumb and fingers together. "And he'll say a hundred pesos, mister. And the whole deal is over."

The man huffed. "Here in America—you can't even fart around your ass."

My sisters and I could no longer keep ourselves from laughing. Instead of reprimanding us, my parents and everyone else laughed as well.

"Life in Iraq was simple, yet complicated," my mother said. "True, we had no worries but when we decided to emigrate we had to be as cautious as convicts."

"At Baghdad's airport, people couldn't bid their loved ones goodbye." The suitor made his first statement; I gave him credit for having a manly voice. "If anyone wept, the officials suspected someone was fleeing and interrogated them."

"Or canceled their trip," his father added.

"We've been out of Iraq for some twenty years," my mother said, "but we can't forget the conditions there. America, despite its horrendous bills and work schedules, provides the best future for us and our children."

"And that's exactly why I keep my green card in the bank," the suitor's father said.

My sisters and I knew we couldn't laugh this time. He had chosen his words seriously and we had to treat them that way. The discussion moved to less interesting topics: relatives I'd never heard of, unfamiliar towns and cities, various political situations. My head began to ache.

I thought of Johnny and hated the luck that led me to be looked at by strangers this way. As soon as we met I'd hoped he would be able to trace a ring of flowers around my future, the way the prince did with the fisherman's daughter. She had lived a hard life with her stepmother and two stepsisters, but things improved one day when she went to a henna party to decorate a bride-to-be's feet and palms and she accidentally dropped her golden shoe in a river. The next day a prince found it. He cherished the shoe's tiny fragility so much that he wanted to marry its owner. So his mother, the queen, searched for the girl and when she finally found her, she married her to her son and they all lived happily ever after. That could've been my ending had Johnny been a prince and not a drug dealer.

After the guests had drunk their Turkish coffee and gone, my family analyzed the suitor in detail: he was short, but fairly well built, had button-shaped eyes, but exquisite lashes, a flat nose but a masculine presence.

"He has a hole in his sock," I informed them in case they'd overlooked it. It indicated he was untidy and lacked respect for me.

Everyone ah'd and then laughed.

"A man's appearance is not as important as his character," my mother said. "He has two businesses as well as a reputable family name."

"Do you mean reputable from the father's side, or the mother's?" Layla asked. My mother looked mercilessly at her and Layla calmly went on to explain. "The father is no different than a *fallah,* plowman."

"The rest of his relatives are magnificent. His uncle played the lute in Iraq."

Layla turned to me. "It's settled. You are now engaged to the lute player's nephew, Mervat. Congratulations."

"Stop believing everything you hear, woman!" my father growled at my mother. "Last month a man told me he owned an ice cream factory in Baghdad. Five minutes later, I come to find out it was only a Popsicle wagon. For all we know, this lute player might be an ass-scratcher!"

And so it was decided the suitor wasn't suitable. The next

morning, knowing my depression wasn't going to lift, I was more irritable than usual; my niece ate a spoon of my yogurt, my mother carried a basket of laundry in front of me while I tried to walk to the bathroom, my father chewed too loudly while I had an orange for breakfast. I was so displeased with myself that by the time I left for work I cried twice as hard as other days.

"Can I have four slices of bologna?" an elderly woman asked, stretching her neck up so she could see me.

"You have to buy at least a quarter pound, ma'am."

I hoped this would make her go away. Since Mathew wasn't in yet I'd have to perform the messy job myself.

"I guess a quarter pound is fine," her voice jarred.

I cleared my throat. "How would you like it sliced?"

"I don't like it, well—make it thin, I suppose. But can I see the first slice to make sure it's right?"

Gritting my teeth, I washed and dried my hands. As I was about to take the bologna out of the cooler, my body froze. The new package was sealed in thick plastic, which meant more work and more resentment. I pealed the plastic with a knife and tilted the package over the sink to drain the liquid off. Specs of gelatin spilled on my shirt and jeans and a heavy dose of bologna smell rose.

I carried the package to the slicer and set the knob; a thin slice fell on my palm. Holding it up like a plate, I presented it to the woman. "Is this okay, ma'am?"

The woman looked at it carefully. I waited while another customer with long hair and pimples leaned impatiently against the counter.

"I suppose," she said querulously.

I weighed five slices together, estimating they'd add up to a quarter pound. The scale read .27 ounces and my heart dropped. "It's a little bit over," I said with hesitation and a simper, hoping she'd agree to the weight.

Her eyes rested on the scale for such a long time that I removed one slice, bringing it to just under a quarter pound. She relaxed. I rang up the bologna, along with a 2-liter Pepsi and a loaf of bread, and bagged them.

"Thank you." Hugging the bag against her chest with her bulky purse to her side, she started towards the door.

I wished I'd been kinder. She wasn't any fussier than my mother or sisters, but she was timid. I shouldn't have been so unsparing, I thought, but knew if I could replay the scene I wouldn't know how to treat her more kindly. I wondered why heroes and villains enchanted me, but real people didn't make sense.

"Gimme twelve lottery tickets," the next customer said.

The old woman quickly faded from my mind. "Which ones?"

"Make it four of each."

The thought of this man spending his hard-earned dollars on gambling annoyed me. He should have been sitting in a barber's shop getting his hair cut. Then I'd suggest, if I could, that he browse through the mall and purchase a jacket and a new pair of jeans to replace his oil-drenched clothes.

"Thank you." He laughed and looked up at me. "All losers. Maybe next time, huh?"

Once again, I wished I'd been nicer. Since Johnny left, my intolerance for the human race had quadrupled. Life offered nothing, and I hated anyone who demanded otherwise.

Once my shift ended I had the options of lying lifelessly in the car (another habit I'd picked up after Boblo) or on Layla's couch, which I'd been doing since Johnny and I went our separate ways. Unsure which would be more beneficial, I remained in the car. I parked in Hazelnut Plaza and surveyed the vacant stores as my tears went on duty. With the recent change of weather I was feeling hot and stuffy; the air conditioning was on, but I feared it would overheat the engine if I ran it too long or too high. I had to move the location of my grief.

I drove to Layla's apartment. With her children asleep and her husband visiting his bedridden father, she gave me her complete attention—not that, even with her multitude of responsibilities, she'd ever deprived me an ounce of it. She brought me a cup of tea, knelt beside me and comforted me as my thoughts raced their dark daily rounds. She listened as I inventoried my faults, accentuated my problems and took God's name in vain. I described how much I disliked this Unknown Creator and how eagerly I wished to break one of the Ten Commandments just to enrage Him.

"Are you going to kill someone?" Layla asked.

"Why someone else? Isn't suicide considered a sin?"

She looked at me fiercely. "Leave that subject alone, Mervat," she ordered. "You have too much going for you to speak, or even joke, about death."

"Me? What have I got? A degree the size of my pinky, a career slicing bologna, and Maysoon as my closest friend? Oh, but of course, she doesn't count. She's off limits."

"That's correct. She is off limits to you. But whose fault is that?"

"Who else's? You guys made her sound like a germ."

"And what did you do? You criticized her more than Mamma did, but all of a sudden she's this angel who could cure your depression?"

"That's not the point. I've only done what I've been taught."

"Then stop imitating us. Bake your own rules and beliefs. Don't just sit there and copy down our recipes."

I was astonished.

"Seriously, Mervat, don't listen to us. Yes, we're your family but we're not your brain and heart."

"*Now* you tell me. Now, when it's too late."

"I didn't know I was telling you to do otherwise."

"You once told me not to imitate. Only *once!* Why couldn't you have jammed that concept into my head?"

"Because I'm not a hammer! I am only human." She softened before she continued. "Besides, nothing is too late. You have youth and beauty and for what it's worth, a college degree."

"What it's worth is nothing. It's only an associate's degree. Without a bachelor's it's as useless as my youth and beauty. I might as well not have starved myself for years or taken a single class."

"Nothing is useless. It was all an experience."

"Not to me it isn't! I was only collecting good character traits, that's all. If not to please my family, then at least the Arabic community. But it turns out that no man cares how thin I am or how virtuous, and no company will hire me based on that tiny bit of education. I have no real experience or talent, or ambitions or interest."

"Neither does sixty percent of the world's work force," she said. "They're simply making a living."

"Then they're lucky, because compared to what I have, they're millionaires."

She gave up the argument and I relaxed. I shut my eyes, breathed deeply and rolled my head. When I'd gathered my wits a little, I came with one last retort. "I bet marriage would shut me up pretty good," I said. "The lute player's nephew isn't so bad, is he? I'm sure I can't do better, anyway."

"You amaze me sometimes, Mervat. You blame your sorrow on us, when you're the one who's constantly judging yourself. Then you go and assign magical powers to other people. You expect them to help you be happy and successful."

"I judge myself for my family's sake. To protect them from harm."

"That's not even fair. To take our advice is one thing, but to depend on it is burden—both to us and to you."

This was a vile sting, and to avoid more outbursts I covered my face and kept silent. Layla massaged my shoulders and begged me to forget everything that was even remotely sad.

Sniffling, I nodded my head, wiped a few tears and gathered my voice. "Even though it may sound like it, I'm not blaming you for my unhappiness."

"You don't have to explain . . ."

"I blame God," I clarified, before she got her hopes up that my faithlessness was mending. "The One I can't see, hear, touch or feel. I despise Him. He created me so that I could squirm and entertain Him."

"God doesn't need entertainment, Mervat."

"Of course He does! Anyone who's jobless does."

"Oh, I see. So if it's not your family who threw you into the fire, then it's God. You shouldn't be held accountable at all?"

"I didn't make myself. He made me."

"He made you to experience life, not damn it."

"Well, I can't help it that my experiences are damned."

"If you'd start living through your truest feelings instead of your scariest thoughts then they wouldn't be."

"That's just it. I can't live through my truest feelings, because I can't feel."

This caused her tongue to cease.

"It's true," I went on. "I cannot feel. How can I when the world wears a mask, disguising happiness as sorrow and sorrow as happiness? If it's not clear that what I'm looking at is good or bad, how can I decide what to feel?"

Her face filled with compassion, she remained quiet.

"Whatever good or bad belief I try to convince myself of, I can't seem to trust it. So I end up feeling nothing. And minute by minute, I feel less and less."

"Oh, Mervat . . ."

"And that feeling—that feeling of feeling nothing—hurts. It hurts worse than the break up."

With that, I was done with tantrums for the night although my crying continued to wear itself out. Layla drew my wet hair back and pressed my empty heart to her breast. The heat of my tears, her perfume and thick kitchen spices felt heavy but warm and I wanted to drown forever in the substance of them.

"You will heal, Mervat," she promised. "The second you open your heart, you will heal." And she stroked my head and cradled my body until I was sound asleep.

We went through this for many nights thereafter. Layla always played the role of *banj,* the drug which a female thief of Baghdad used on the chief of police and his forty men in order to rob them of their goods for her mother, or the powder a king slipped into a princess's drink to make her pass out so he could take her virginity.

Of course with Layla, the *banj* she seeped into me was with my consent. And instead of taking anything away from me, as it had the police chief and the princess, it gave me a sense of something wholesome, if temporary.

Chapter 21

July's heat and our bustling street deepened my depression. Seven Mile and John R wasn't a convenient area for acting as though the world had not come to an end. I substituted my mindless occupations by assuming the function of a telescope. I sat on the family room couch and, like a cat waiting for a mouse to come out of its hole, watched the neighbors make fools of themselves from behind our window.

They sat at their leisure on front porches drinking tea, eating sunflower seeds and watermelon. They enjoyed washing their cars and driveways during the afternoon and barbecuing after midnight. Their children jumped rope, played hopscotch and basketball. The whole scene was awful because they were happily intoxicated with such trifling matters.

While I belittled humanity, I philosophized what its purpose on earth was. It was truly an odd species, I thought, as I watched them laughing and ignoring their problems. One family's father was an alcoholic, another's a gambler; one had two unwed daughters over thirty, and one mother was an adulteress. I, on the other hand, was wracked with boredom.

Bigger issues, like death or illness in the family or the

store going bankrupt or our home being carried off by a torna-
do, would likely have me thrown into a coffin. But there was
no real reason to wait for my own bigger problems to come
along; if I wanted to steer clear of life's perils, I ought to hurry
up and hang myself. I wouldn't mind lying in an open casket,
reducing Johnny to guilt and having people say what a shame
it was this young pretty girl was lost to soil and worms. What
would please me even more would be if they questioned God's
life plan, condemned it and in a united decision overthrew it.

Then again, my death would make my family suffer tre-
mendously. They'd beat their faces in the funeral home the way
I'd heard described, and they'd wear black for years, growing
as frail as a cooped up butterfly. I wondered how long they
would suffer. Maybe only a matter of months. But was it fair to
torment them even for a day when they'd been good to me for
the past 7300 days?

As though these July thoughts weren't enough, Maysoon
came to my house one day and made matters uglier. She'd visited me often that summer, but feeling allergic to most human
beings I'd always found an excuse to avoid her. This time I
couldn't. She came unexpectedly and demanded we sit on the
front porch. This spooked me, not because of her reputation,
but because I couldn't tolerate front row seats to the world's
foul display.

"You've lost weight, girl," she said, yawning.

I pressed my chin against my chest and glanced at my
stomach and upper thighs. At least the break up was good for
something, I thought.

"You look yellow too."

"I'm sick," I lied so she wouldn't know that lack of sleep,
depression and excessive dieting were the real reasons for my
appearance.

She sat on the steps and cracked her neck. "Your poor itty
bitty stomach," she said. "It's probably dying for a blueberry

cheesecake, just like your thing is dying for a–"

"Maysoon!" I interrupted.

She took out a pack of gum and chewed, loudly, its smell dancing in my nose. It helped me recover my composure but then she knocked me down again. "Guess what? Me and Tony are getting engaged."

"What?" I was throttled with jealousy. The last person I would have suspected to marry was Maysoon. I'd always been sure that men didn't choose her type for long-term arrangements. Yet here she was, proving me wrong, even though she'd misbehaved atrociously throughout adolescence.

Maysoon blew a big bubble and popped it with her blood-red nail. "I'm going to have my ring customized. It'll be nicer that way, don't you think?"

I nodded, numbly.

"Hey, do you want to be a bridesmaid?"

"A bridesmaid?" I said airily, even though my nerves danced like a chicken who'd just lost its head. I'd never been so humiliated in my life. Not only had this slut managed to snatch a groom, but she expected me to be her bridesmaid, lift up her train and follow her down the aisle.

"Fuchsia. I'll have them all wearing fuchsia dresses, white shoes and a feather hair piece—a pink feather."

This was too real and unfair for me to handle. Maysoon was getting married, despite her naughtiness, and I with my old fashioned morals was not.

"I'm having the engagement party at the Victorian House. It holds 200 people, but I'm only inviting 150. It'll be too expensive otherwise, right?"

"Uh-huh."

She popped her gum harder while admiring a passing powder-blue convertible. Then she grinned and leaned her right leg forward so her plump thigh would be as noticeable as the sun. The car slowed down and a man sitting in the back whistled while the driver shouted, "Nice cinema!"

Maysoon accused them of being disgusting dogs who knew neither their mothers nor their fathers, who had no brains or testicles. She said if they dared pass our way again she'd throw her sandal at them and tell them to whip their cheeks with it so they'd learn some manners. I told her to calm down and not take them seriously.

"They're beasts! Didn't you see them?"

Now that she had a proposal, I thought, she'd suddenly become a saint? I envied her though, and wanted to know exactly what she'd done to get it.

"When is the wedding?" I brought myself to ask.

"Well, his family hasn't come to the house yet."

"Oh?" My world brightened like a star in the midst of nightfall. She might be hallucinating the proposal, or lying about it, or maybe he was tricking her. A Middle Eastern engagement is never valid without the groom-to-be's family explicitly entering the bride-to-be's home and asking her hand in marriage. And if the parties involved are Christians a priest must bless the ceremony to make it legal in God's eye.

"They're supposed to come this Friday," she said and again dismembered my hopes.

I was sweating. I ached to run away, but that would've made my envy obvious.

Maysoon touched her hair and hardened gel flaked off. "I want to grow my hair to my waist before the engagement party. That'll impress his family, don't you think?"

"Uh-huh," I mumbled. She was going to be showered with gold and wrapped in new clothes and for a year or more after she was going to be the center of everyone's attention. For the rest of her life she was going to be escorted by a man. Her luck irked me. Even as she continued to expound her plans I regretted my obedience and longed for her indifference to conventions. I'd wasted my life doing what I was told and now I felt stuck in this personality and in Detroit.

"I hope our engagement is longer than the same old six months," she said. "I want to have fun going out with Tony while we're still kind of single. You know what I mean?"

"Uh-huh."

"We'll be free to hold hands and go into restaurants without checking out who's watching us first. We might be able to kiss." She smiled to herself, lost in an intimate moment. "Aside from orgasm, that's got to be the best feeling ever."

I didn't know what an orgasm was but I nodded in agreement. I was getting dizzy. Her rapture taunted me, and she refused to leave until she rubbed in more details of sex with Tony. Her departure was a relief. One more word out of her mouth and I would have signed myself into hell.

Thanks to Maysoon's wedding news, my loneliness sprawled. I lost all interest in watching my neighborhood, let alone God's life plan. I began recklessly fidgeting. The darkness tying me down had to snap and set me free, I kept thinking, but the darkness was a little devil that wouldn't compromise, leading me to do odd things in the middle of the night: stop my blood flow by tying elastic hair ribbons around my wrists and ankles, poke my stomach and thighs with a nail file and chisel the word "dead" on my arm with a sewing needle.

One day in particular was so disastrous it out-stripped Sinbad's wreck on his third voyage. Sinbad left Baghdad to trade silk, spices and jewelry but his ship was pushed by the wind to the Isle of Apes. There the passengers were held prisoner by an ugly giant who picked out a man every night, roasted him on a spit and devoured him with gusto. Sinbad asked his comrades to band together to kill their enemy. They agreed and stabbed the giant's eyes out with a burning pair of spits, then fled to another island. There, a man-eating snake attacked them but Sinbad was once again able to wriggle out of that mess. Once safe, he undid his turban, tied it to a tree branch, and waved it until a ship came to his rescue.

Unlike Sinbad, I didn't know how to kill the enemies terrorizing me, even though Layla guarded me with twenty-four hour supervision, on the phone or with each other, morning to night. We rarely mentioned Johnny. He wasn't forgotten but he'd stopped being my main concern. Passing judgment on the world was.

I dwelled too long on whether humanity was intrinsically good or evil and was unable to make up my mind which title it deserved. Obsession and shakiness started consuming me.

One day stands out. I was off from work and spent the afternoon folding and refolding clothes, flipping through travel brochures, piling my school books in alphabetical order and Windexing the telephone cord. Such tasks failed to distract me and I ended up turning and twisting in bed.

Later I tried to force myself to get up, but the idea of having nowhere to go and nothing to do harnessed me to the mattress. By three o'clock, I managed to crawl to the floor but could only lie there. At four, I bounced to my feet like a grasshopper and began pacing the room, got dizzy and dropped to the carpet again. Aware mainly of its smells of attar and dust, I lay there, rocking side-to-side.

I considered going to the kitchen and having a spoon of yogurt to calm my nerves but I couldn't get up. Each time I raised my head I felt the weight of a watermelon inside it and had to put it back down. After a few tries I gave up and dozed off. There on the floor, in the late afternoon, starving and deserted, I had a nightmare. I was in a tall metal box and its colorful bright edges were slowly caving in on me. Just before they crushed my bones like a shoe would a cockroach, I blinked my eyes open.

My body was shuddering, my mind frozen, and my heart speeding. Loneliness and fright were tearing me apart. As though there was a fire in the house, I hurried to my car and drove to Layla's. I needed help and trusted she would cure the creepiness that had forced itself on me.

"I'm so glad you're here." She opened the door wide for me. I hoped today she'd have a stronger shield against the storm building inside me than the usual kind words and familiar stories.

Her children greeted me with stained hands and loud voices, but I couldn't return their excitement. Layla began with her usual hospitality. "I just made an eggplant casserole. I still have some of last night's zucchini pilaf, but if you want me to fry potato chops . . ."

Nonsense, nonsense, I communicated to her by taking a deep breath and turning my face away.

"I'll get us a small snack, anyway," she said. "You never know. I just might convince you to eat regular food today."

She returned with a woven basket of walnuts, hazelnuts, acorns, almonds and a plate of uneven coconut wedges. I watched her split the nutshells with a nutcracker, pick out pieces of meat and hand them to her eager children. She offered them to me as well.

I rolled my eyes and sighed heavily.

"Too oily, huh?" she teased. "And since you're this huge bulky girl, you can't afford to taste it, can you?"

I refused to answer.

She turned serious as she examined me closely. "Out of curiosity, Mervat, I'd like to know if you ever plan on befriending food."

"Never. There's too much competition to slack off."

"And who are you trying to impress, may I ask?"

"Everyone! Absolutely everyone!"

"Oh, I see," she began, and the next thing I knew she took out her palette and brushed me with colors of gentleness and proverbs. The phase I was going through was natural and temporary, she said. Better things were sure to come. I need only have patience and gratitude. I listened vaguely even though by now I knew the clichés were useless—rusty and old and without batteries and instructions.

I looked at her with torpid eyes. I was going to give in to tears yet again and explain how badly I wished to die and stop this feeling of nothingness when her sudden raving laughter prevented any further talk of doom.

"Do you remember Sameera's story?" she asked. I shook my head and she reminded me that Sameera was a distant unattractive cousin who'd married a man ten times smaller than her in height and width.

"The morning after the wedding," Layla said, now restraining herself from laughter so she wouldn't choke on the coconut, "Sameera's family rented a bus and drove to the bride and groom's hotel. They wanted to escort the bride to her new home—her in-laws.'"

"They interrupted their sleep? How annoying."

"It's supposed to be courteous and honorable, Mervat."

I rolled my eyes and she described how, when Sameera's family arrived at the hotel, they heard distressing news: the bride said the marriage hadn't been consummated. "*Tila' moo rijal,*" each person whispered to another's ear, meaning he didn't turn out to be a man.

In an outrage, the family declared that they were taking Sameera back to her parents' home. The groom begged for another chance, but they refused. Enough persuasion, however, made them reconsider and they permitted Sameera to spend one more night with him. But first the groom's cousin had a little enlightening talk with him.

"And the second time," Layla said dramatically, "this miniature groom triumphed in performing a man's duty. So both families were content and everyone lived happily ever after." She looked at me and blinked. "The end."

Layla awaited a reaction, and got an abrupt flood of tears.

She automatically began apologizing for having upset me until I sputtered that Maysoon's boyfriend proposed to her and Sameera's husband pleaded with a busload of people to keep her, yet I, who was neither promiscuous nor plain, was as ignored as a moldy loaf of bread.

"If this is how you see things, then doesn't it make you wonder whether you became attached to Johnny simply because he rejected you?"

"I'm heartbroken not attached."

"Why?" she asked. "Did you love him?"

Her question choked me as a clear image of Johnny's fragrance and charm whirled around my heart. My lips quivering, I looked down.

"Did you love him, Mervat?"

"I don't know," I answered, hoarsely. "I liked him very much and could've fallen in love with him had he taken it further."

"But did you love him?"

Rubbing my neck, I raised my bleary eyes to her. "I loved what he could have done for me."

"Some day someone else will come along and . . ."

I laughed, sarcastically. "With all the cussing I aim at God and the praying I never do, I doubt I'll get lucky twice."

"You consider Johnny a lucky thing?"

"That's not the point. If someone can be so beautiful and be so unclean, how can I trust anyone again?"

"Don't trust anyone, trust God."

"God? He's the problem here. I was as good a girl as the Bible asked me to be. I lived up to His standards and He did nothing but deceive me."

"He did nothing, period. It's not His fault. You're the one who doesn't break a single rule, but wants to."

"I don't want to talk about God. All I know is I need a change in my life so I can stop being boring."

"You aren't boring."

"But I am. I'm boring!" I cried, my lips swelling and my face and neck wet with perspiration.

I shrugged off her sympathy, preferring to wrap my arms around my stomach and like a crazy girl bounce my head against my knee. Layla pleaded with me to calm down, caressing my hair and cheeks. She nursed me like that until I nudged her away, ceased all movements and looked fiercely at her. "I'm going to give myself."

"What?" she asked, taken aback.

"I said I'm going to give myself."

"To whom?"

"To a man."

"What man?"

"Any man!"

She was mute for a second, but quickly organized her speech and applauded what I'd said. "Okay, go ahead and do that."

"You think I wouldn't do it, don't you?" I was aware she was trying reverse psychology and it made me angrier. "You think I'm a coward."

"I think nothing. Go and be with a man and see how that'll solve your problems."

"I hate being a girl. It's the biggest responsibility in the world. It's a prison."

She took a deep breath, obviously gathering energy before giving me another tiresome lecture. "Your problem is not that you're a girl rather than a woman," she said tightly. "It's that you put your faith in one man and not God."

I was furious at her mentioning His name again. "What else does God want? What a greedy bastard He is."

I realized my blasphemy was more distasteful than Maysoon's sluttishness. My dignity was shattered.

"All this anger towards God because Johnny walked out of

your life?"

"This isn't about Johnny. If I ever liked God it was because I was afraid not to."

She was quiet. I think I had worn her out.

"But why should I be afraid of Him anymore?" I added to myself. "He's already punished me."

I stood. I was so thirsty for a change that I would have embraced even the worst. My woes were due to my perfectionism anyway; maybe I'd be more at peace if I scarred myself on purpose.

"Then it's settled, I guess," I said mechanically. "I'll lose my honor first thing tomorrow morning and feel better."

"Try surrendering your honor, if you insist," she said, trying to be calm. "Let's see you do it."

"If I don't it's not because I can't, but because I don't have a lover."

She didn't argue my point. If neither she nor I could flip my world right side up, then who could? I continued pacing and fretting. My body itched as I thought of a million ways to bring down unreasonable and everlasting damage on myself. I was ferociously scratching at the scabs of my brain when I at last managed to make a long-contemplated decision. The world was evil and I wasn't going to participate in it any longer.

"I know what to do," I said. The pressure in my head suddenly evaporated. "I know exactly what to do."

I could see that my resoluteness scared her more than anything else I'd said or done since breaking up with Johnny but she didn't ask any questions until I went to get my purse.

"What do you plan on doing?" she asked.

"Nothing. But I have to leave now."

"Where are you going?"

"I have to leave," I repeated and started towards the door. A flurry seemed to seize her as she watched. I'd never seen her look as alarmed as she did that instant. She touched my arm and tried to keep me inside.

"Please, Mervat, stay so we can talk some more."

"No."

"Please, Mervat, stay a little longer."

"No."

"Mervat, please . . ."

"No!"

And like a ghost, I passed through her attempts at keeping me. I was determined to end my suffering and everyone else's.

Chapter 22

Al-adweiya—The medicines

I drove home without my usual headache. Even my depression had lifted. My calm came from my new-formed project. For the first time in my life I was going to break a rule, and as taboo as it might have seemed to anyone else—especially the church and her Boss—my decision brought me more peace even than the stories I'd grown up with.

The house was empty so I had complete freedom. I locked the front door, closed the vertical blinds and prepared for the operation. I cleared my mind of all the junk cluttering it—my parents' rules, my sisters' advice, Maysoon's fortune, Johnny's coldness, my worries about calories and dress size and, of course, God's cruelty. Then I thought about what I needed to do to escape my cage.

I remember the details more clearly than I want to. I began in my bedroom, where I slowly took off my shoes, unbuttoned my blouse and unzipped my skirt, removing each garment with care. I folded them neatly and placed them in their proper places. I treated my nylons, undergarments, and barrette with the same tenderness. I slipped on a white nightgown with ruffles on the straps and around the hem and yellow and purple lilies strewn on its fabric, then prepared myself further by brushing my hair long enough to neutralize its curl. I sat in front of the mirror and looked at myself. For a long while I'd hated my face and size zero body, but now I could prize them again. I put on perfume and when I was satisfied I floated as gracefully as a butterfly to the kitchen.

My movements were too lighthearted for the occasion but I couldn't help it. I was pleased, knowing there was going to be a change in me as big as when God turned Ibrahim's people into stone.

I opened the cabinet where my mother put mismatched china and other junk. She put her medicine bottles there as well. That day she only had two brand name aspirin and a prescription I couldn't identify. The aspirin bottle was full but the other had just six tablets left. I'd have to make the best of it.

I poured a large glass of ice water and began. The first pill was so easy that I went on to tablet number two, number three, four, five . . . It was ironic that it felt so joyful. I fell deeper and deeper and soon discovered I'd swallowed the entire bottle. It wouldn't be enough to hush the entire world. It wouldn't be enough to hush the crowd of ailing voices, so I fed myself the other bottle as well.

With both bottles empty I felt quiet. The malevolence inside me could now be scrubbed out and I would be purified. I went back upstairs and, like a porcelain doll, lay perfectly on my bed. Never before had I experienced such peace. To know that there were no more problems to face or injustices to endure was refreshing. To accept that there was no tomorrow and feel no need to sulk over yesterday was liberation.

I was as close to happiness as I had ever been. I did not believe in a well-intentioned God, but I could have sworn that despite the loud beating of my heart I'd arrived in heaven. Perhaps He'd finally had mercy on me. And even if he hadn't, maybe

Hell wasn't as terrible as the man behind the altar alleged. Its horrible blaze couldn't suffocate me more than loneliness and indifference. Despite everyone's dread I looked forward to the journey.

"Mervat!" I heard a harsh voice thundering over me. "Mervat! Mervat!"

I was in such a deep sleep that it took dozens of Mervats to stir me. Still, I was too distant to react. When I eventually opened my eyes, it was because my father was shaking my shoulders.

"Are you sleeping?" he asked.

My eyes burned from the bedroom light before they opened fully and I saw my father gazing at me in silence.

"Hmmm?" I murmured.

He examined my face for a while. "Nothing."

He walked out, leaving me mystified. My father never behaved this way and I wondered if a guardian angel had tattled. His rescue attempt didn't cease there. I would have returned to unconsciousness had it not been for him having a loud argument with my mother.

I heard several accusations, excuses and denials being hurled in the kitchen before I remembered the pills I'd swallowed. Right then I changed my mind. I didn't want to die or damage my body. Either was a permanent solution to the puzzles I hadn't been able to solve and I wondered if maybe a temporary one would be smarter. If I told my parents now they'd panic, and if I was saved, their opinion of me would be forever altered. Besides, given what I'd done to myself, shouldn't I at least be found unconscious? But what if no one checked on me until tomorrow morning when I would already be in Hell?

Increased indecision would decrease my chance of survival. If I didn't report myself immediately, I'd end up being erased from existence, as King Holaco of Tetter had wiped out the science and literature of Baghdad during the Mongol invasion of 1258, when Iraq stood strong in the Middle East. But the Turkish King Holaco wanted to rule the world. He raided the surrounding countries, killing people, burning cities and destroying all of Baghdad's books by throwing them into the river. It ran black and blue from the ink and Iraq was dead for a hundred years after.

Death seemed awfully long, I thought. Maybe it was shorter when despair wasn't its cause. I suddenly didn't want to be as savage to my body as Holaco had been to Iraq. I gathered my energy, jumped out of bed, dressed and drove to Ikhbal's house. She was my choice of refuge because her husband had been staying at a hotel the past two nights after he lost four thousand dollars gambling.

"Do you plan on staying over?" she asked since it was eleven o'clock.

I was so preoccupied with what I'd done earlier that I silently headed towards the couch. She told me to make myself comfortable and went into the children's room to pull up their covers. I watched television and waited my turn for confession.

"You want a cup of tea?"

I shook my head and she recited the usual hospitality speech. I refused all offers, impatient to disclose my crime. She started to tell me why her husband enjoyed casinos and bookies—they made him feel important and wealthy, she said, and I tried to figure out how to interrupt her respectfully. I came up with curling on the couch and moaning softly.

"Would you rather talk about it, or just cry?"

I wanted to confess, I wanted to shout, but I couldn't be so blunt. To make her understand that I needed her to plead for me to speak, I raised the volume of my moans.

"Tell me, Mervat, what's wrong?"

"I have a headache."

"That's curable. Should I get you an aspirin?"

I grimaced, then laughed out loud.

She smiled. "What's so funny?"

I was laughing so hard I couldn't answer. She again asked what was funny. I pressed my hands against my stomach and went on laughing. She observed me calmly until I sobered abruptly. "I've taken aspirin."

Her smile faded. "What do you mean?"

I folded my arms over my head.

"What have you done, Mervat?!"

I glanced at her for a moment and hid my head again, too embarrassed to acknowledge what I'd done.

"Don't be scared." She said this with cool composure but I knew she was nervous. "Just tell me what you've done."

I still couldn't speak.

"Mervat, I need to know what you did," she insisted. "Please tell me."

"I had a little too much aspirin," I said.

It didn't take more than these words for her to grasp what had happened. She knelt beside me and begged for details. I explained there were none, except for the fact that I'd swallowed some thirty pills.

The number made her wince but she unrolled a what-to-do-in-case-of-a-suicide-crisis map and looked for the fastest route to my salvation. "Wait here a minute."

She disappeared into the bathroom and returned a minute later with a large brick-colored bottle and tried to pour a couple spoonfuls of it down my throat.

"It'll make you vomit," she explained when I complained about its taste. "A nurse told me to keep this on hand in case the children drank poison."

Ikhbal supervised my consumption of the medicine before she called the hospital.

"I live two miles away," she told the emergency room receptionist. She was quiet for a few seconds before adding, "No, an ambulance isn't necessary. I'll drive her."

The person on the other end argued a little before agreeing to let Ikhbal be my chauffeur. I watched blankly as she tiptoed to her daughter's room and whispered that we were leaving. I was feeling fine so far and wondered if my sister and the hospital were making too much of it or if my life really was in jeopardy. I couldn't say this, however, without appearing like more of an imbecile. My credibility wasn't worth much before, but now it was absolutely flattened.

A pink bucket in my lap, I sat in the car and was driven to the hospital. The ride proved I was in greater trouble than I'd thought because I vomited more than any of my nephews or nieces ever had in their entire lives. Walking to the emergency room doors was no different.

Ikhbal informed the receptionist of my overdose and the next thing I knew I was pushed into a wheelchair and asked my name, address, phone number and type of insurance. My sister recited most of the information as I kept my head bent and imagined what awaited me.

As a nurse piloted my wheelchair I heard the receptionist tell Ikhbal confidently, "Don't worry. She won't do it again."

I wished Ikhbal would ask her why she'd said that. I wanted her reasons to convince me. But her replies, regardless of how specific and informative they might have been, wouldn't have been half as effective as what I sampled inside the hospital itself.

I was laid on a bed behind blue curtains. I expected a doctor to come in and reprimand me but it was a big nurse who walked in and did unforgettable things. She roughly shoved clear tubes in my nose, as though I was a chicken being stuffed with rice. I was gasping for air when I felt the tubes travel like a razor into my throat. With all my might I wailed and screamed and pulled and tugged to be set free.

"If you push this up, I'll have to shove it right back in

again," she warned firmly.

That was all she had to say to bully me into helpless compliance. Although my wailing continued, my combativeness drained away to allow its opponent into my un-ripened heart. The tubes assaulted my chest and shredded my lungs. The nurse withdrew from the battle scene without a single scratch on her feelings or body and I was left alone to pity myself and the consequences of war.

Ikhbal came in and saw for herself the mess left behind. She sat on the one chair and said nothing, pretending my defeat wasn't so nearly fatal and humiliating. I knew otherwise. Surely she'd heard my distress echoing through the entire emergency room earlier. The tubes in my nose couldn't have been pretty either. Although Ikhbal may have kept her eyes blind to the sight, I knew her heart wasn't.

She didn't ask any questions, but she did share a funny conversation she'd eavesdropped on outside. A custodian told his co-worker that he ate garlic for breakfast every day, and way? To kill the stink of his stool. "Does that make sense?" she mused aloud.

I gave a weak smile, then glanced at the four women in white uniforms and standing across from us. "I wonder why all these nurses are so big."

"It's surprising, isn't it?" she said, taking a quick peek. "You'd think being on their feet all day, changing sheets and seducing doctors, they'd be slim and trim."

We exchanged a few other meaningless remarks until a young doctor came in. He asked where I felt the most pain. I meditated upon that a minute and realized that physically, I felt none at all.

"Then why are you crying?" he asked.

The question confused me. I hadn't any idea there might be some logic behind my crying. Surely he could see my emptiness. A tear began to slip over my lashes and I looked away.

He stroked my stomach and watched my face with sympathy. It occurred to me that he was probably wishing his medical school diploma could staunch my emotional bleeding.

He left without letting me know the purpose behind his visit. A nurse came and stuck needles in my veins and afterward my sister started dozing off. I watched the clock. Its hands were moving so languidly that my head throbbed. I was desperate for time to pass so I could have a clearer vision of my future. What was I to tell my family? Did they even have to know? And if no one knew, how could I possibly live with myself after having seen such weakness in myself?

My tomorrows looked very bleak, and I wondered if the receptionist was in her right mind when she said I'd never try this again. True, I hated the hospital and the tubes slicing the top half of my body, but I wasn't thankful to have been saved.

A bald doctor, older and most likely more experienced than the previous one, came in. He listened to my heart, took my blood pressure, and performed a few other tests before he excused himself from the cubicle. Ikhbal fell asleep again as we waited for the room the doctor had promised. I tried closing my eyes, but all sorts of fears got in the way, so I watched the nurses walk back and forth instead, and listened to the doctors joke and patients tell stories. The old lady in the next bed explained how she'd fainted after she'd had a piece of toast. The doctor marveled at her being ninety-three and still holding strong while I evaluated her sanity as well as everyone else's. They all seemed as comfortable with this so-called life as Johnny's birds.

In the middle of the night, I was taken into a room where the nurse claimed I would rest better. It was comfortable enough but the tubes weren't. I stared at the ceiling, the walls, the black television set, and my sister sleeping, sweating with guilt as I calculated what I must have caused her. She'd managed to conceal it fairly well.

Hours passed before I got used to the tubes and drifted into a genuine sleep. It was then that a nurse woke me up. "I have to give you this every two hours," she said and made me drink some medicine so tart its taste lingered in my nose and rested on my tongue for years after.

Early the next morning, a doctor came into my room and told my sister what a lucky girl I was. "What she did could have destroyed her liver and put her in a coma."

Only when I heard this did regret strike me. Although I'd sworn otherwise, I hadn't wanted to ruin a fingernail much less my liver. I'd simply wanted a rest from the loneliness and emptiness weighing me down. The doctor acquainted Ikhbal with other principal factors concerning my health and said the tubes would be removed soon. "She should be able to go home tomorrow morning."

"Thank you, Doctor," she said and they shook hands.

Ikhbal telephoned Layla to tell her what had happened and to cover our tracks so Mamma and Babba wouldn't suspect anything. As they spoke, a nurse came in and greeted me kindly. She wrapped one hand over the tubes, leaned over me, and yanked them out.

The pain was so violent I screamed louder than when they had been put in the night before, underscored this time by Layla's sonorous cries over the phone as she heard my protests, making me suffer even more over what I'd put my sisters through. For the first time since I entered the hospital I was grateful to have been saved.

"Are you okay?" Ikhbal asked after the nurse finished the slaughter and I lay as limp as a dead animal on the road. My lips couldn't even part to answer.

I remained sunk in apathy and guilt until breakfast arrived—scrambled eggs, toast, sliced peaches and grapes, a cup of orange juice and a cup of milk. I stared at it greedily and touched their surfaces but dared not lift it to my mouth.

"Aren't you going to eat?" Ikhbal asked.

After all I'd put her through, I knew it would be insensitive to ask for anything else—a raisin bagel and a fat-free yogurt. Besides, I was tired of my rules. So I split half the breakfast with Ikhbal and began chewing food I never would have eaten outside my pre-menstrual days. And soon after, I felt sick. My system was not prepared for things like oil and whole dairy.

My stomachache didn't stop there either because I ate more later. On her way to the rest room, Ikhbal found the cafeteria and bought things she considered treats and I considered dangerous, returning with two croissants. Under normal circumstances I would never accept my share but today I needed something to fill the vacancy in my heart. Of course, when I had finished the croissant I vowed I'd begin the toughest starvation diet yet, first thing in the morning.

Ikhbal and I were joking and gossiping when two psychiatrists entered the room, notepads and pens in their hands. My sister left us and they asked me a series of questions: how long I'd been feeling depressed and what I'd hoped to accomplish by taking the pills.

"I just wanted to rest—" and change my life, I thought, but kept my spoken answers brief.

They scribbled a few words on their yellow pads.

"You didn't think thirty pills could kill you?" the short one asked.

"I didn't think, period."

"What did you want to rest from?" the handsomer one continued.

"Myself. I was tired of myself."

"Why?" the pudgy one asked.

"Because my life is boring."

"Do you think people are boring?"

"No. I think they think I'm boring."

They paused, eyed each other, and scribbled. Then the other man said, "Do you have a boyfriend?"

I looked out the window. "No."

"Have you had a break up recently?" Pudgy said.

"No."

"When did your last relationship end?"

I knew what they were getting at, but in spite of their degrees they were wrong. I wasn't so shallow that a man whom I hadn't fallen in love with could knock me off the earth. Life's passionlessness was what triggered my fall, but in my state I had no room to contradict their beliefs.

"When was your most recent break up?"

"About four months ago," I said, giving in.

They looked at each other again and scribbled. Their interrogation went on for ten more minutes. When it was over, they suggested that, for the sake of my safety, I should be treated in an institution until I was more stable.

"I've told you," I said. "I won't do this again."

"To have done it in the first place creates a doubt about what you might do in the future," Pudgy said.

"I will not do it again," I persisted, refusing to drag my soul's slump beyond this day. "I was simply not thinking."

"That's the problem!" they both answered, and I couldn't help but smile at their synchronism.

I refused to let their recommendation influence me. I might have made a mistake but that didn't mean I was insane. They weren't pleased by my unshakeable stubbornness. They called Ikhbal in and gave her their opinion but her refusal was even more unyielding than mine.

"Mervat has parents, sisters and a brother, nieces and nephews, cousins and aunts around her," she said. "If they aren't enough to help her then we might as well all resign our family titles and be ashamed of ourselves."

They grudgingly consented and made her sign papers saying she took full responsibility for my welfare. Then I was discharged.

At Ikhbal's house I had to wonder whether those tubes had, in fact, punctured my heart. I had another crying jag that spilled tears over my gigantic anthology of relatives' and legendary stories and blurred them so badly that I lost most of the documentation of my past. Then I started all over again.

Chapter 23

Faqad al-nefs—Loss of the self

The croissant I ate in the hospital broke my regime for a year. I gained weight. I had long and lovely periods of buttered popcorn and frosted cupcakes, fried sausage and mayonnaise sandwiches. The food was wonderful but my waistline wasn't. I stopped going to the mall because I couldn't bear skipping over size zeros and twos and trying on sixes and eights. I also retired from the profession of spying because of the thin girls on the street.

My weight fluctuated during those months but at least my nerves settled. I no longer thought about ending my life or the great rest I'd wanted that day. That didn't exactly mean I was happy. I busied myself working at the store, sleeping, reading romance novels and watching television. I'd gotten haggard and fat and hid myself from the Middle Eastern community. The last thing I wanted was for Johnny or any other admirer to see how much weight I'd gained and be smug about not getting involved with me.

The chances of seeing Johnny were slim anyway. I'd made a few stops at the mall and attended a couple of parties before my weight gain and didn't see him once. He hadn't been murdered or jailed or mentioned by anyone I knew. Although I spent much of my time reminiscing about our short romance and wondering what he was doing and thinking now, I wanted him to remain invisible, at least until I recovered.

Meanwhile, a cousin invited us to her wedding. I tried to guard myself against outings that required cheerfulness and dressing up but my mother nearly fell into a swoon when I told her I wanted to stay home. "What will your uncle say? What will his daughter think?"

I finished the last of the Cheetos that were stuck in the corner of the bag and wiped my orange hands together. "I doubt they'll notice I'm not there. Besides, you could tell them I'm babysitting."

"Please stop being difficult. If I was dragging you to the produce market then protest, but a party?"

"You make it sound as though I'm refusing a trip to the Virgin Islands."

"The what?"

I rolled my eyes while opening a box of Crunch-and-Munch. "Never mind."

"Now listen, Mervat. Your cousin is going to be a bride once. Only once."

"I'll make sure then to watch the video tape."

Her eyes and lips tightened. "Your tongue has gotten a meter long, hasn't it? If I let you have your way now, God knows what you're capable of tomorrow."

"Well, if He does know I wish He'd tell me."

Growling and mumbling she headed to the phone. "It's my fault I let your sisters have such influence," she said. "You disregard whatever I tell you."

She dialed Layla, told her what a disobedient daughter I was being and extended the receiver. "Here," she commanded. "Explain yourself."

As dear as Layla was to me, I was too embarrassed to tell her how obese I felt. I didn't even want to acknowledge it to myself. It didn't take much for me to say, "Okay, okay, I'll go." I figured I'd spend the next day planning out a crash diet that would have me looking like I used to.

Customers would sometimes suggest diets where you could lose up to seventeen pounds in three days. One consisted of as much red meat and green vegetables as I wanted with only garlic powder and black pepper for seasonings, an egg, an orange, tea and coffee. Another diet had more variety, but was too busy—accurate measurements and precise foods like hot dogs, exact amounts of tuna fish or chicken, a cup of this or that, halves and ounces. A third diet featured brown rice, but because it required eight days to complete, I scratched it off my list.

I wanted results and I had two weeks so I came up with the ingenious idea of following both three-day diets. I began with the hot dog-tuna fish strategy and lost five pounds. It left me frail and dizzy so I rested for four days before I started the new diet on Monday. With the "eat all the meat you want" plan in hand I was sure I'd be saved from extreme and unnecessary hunger.

I starved myself, dropped only one pound and my face, hair and nails grew dull. The changes troubled me. I was anxious to be thin again so I could burn all the crash diets in one big pyre. Neither diet got me into a size four, and because I couldn't admit that my weight was here for a while, I refused to buy anything bigger. I knew I'd have to adjust whatever was in my closet so I searched until I found a black dress which, although it had a zipper, was stretchy.

It took considerable exertion to slide in and zip it, and the overall look was ludicrous; my breasts were squashed, the fabric creased around the waist, my stomach bulged out and the seven-inch diameter of my calves were apparent. Luckily it flared out at the hem and disguised my kangaroo-shaped buttocks. The experience made me feel foolish but I knew I'd cause a scene if I tried to stay home so I held my breath and attended the wedding.

"Doesn't she look just like a princess, Mervat?" my cousin Nadia whispered as a beautiful young guest arrived at the party.

"Yeah, she's pretty."

I inhaled hard to avoid bursting my tight dress. Either these diets were worthless or I'd gained more weight than I thought. Six months ago this dress was a bit snug, but today it was like forcing Barbie clothes on a Cabbage Patch doll.

The appetizers were served and I became deaf and blind to the world as I raided them, sampling the humus, tabbouleh, dips and tropical drinks. My stomach bulged and I feared the seams would burst, making my cellulite rather than the bride the main attraction of the party.

"Come on, let's dance," Nadia said.

I looked at the dance floor. There were model-thin girls out there, lurching their hips and swaying their bellies. How could I participate in such a dance? I'd be a buffoon, indulging the evil eyes that had once targeted me.

"Come on," my cousin pleaded as I rationalized to myself the reasons I shouldn't dance. "Come on—before the song ends."

"I really don't feel like it," I insisted. I didn't belong in that happy pretty crowd; my duty tonight was to remain in my seat and inhale appetizers, the most fitting conduct in my condition.

"Are you sure?"

"I'm sure."

She shrugged in disappointment and turned to Layla instead. They abandoned the table and after a few minutes, waiters served hot lentil soup. I ate it with bread and butter and finished long before the salad was brought. I ate the salad with bread and butter and the entrée of steak, chicken and potato arrived. It was a magnificent dinner but after I'd cleared my plate it still wasn't enough. Like a plague, my appetite had spread for miles around the epicenter.

"I can't wait until the band starts playing again," Nadia said, setting her fork down after a few bites. "I'm in such a mood to dance."

I couldn't respond because I was burning with curiosity about dessert. My question was answered when the waiters came in carrying ice cream. It was a flat sheet of white, mint and mauve colored rows with pistachio sprinkles. I snatched a spoon and ate like a maniac. No one else in my family touched theirs, engrossed in exchanging love glances and sneaking subtle kisses with their husbands.

Everyone seemed as glamorous and detached as movie stars. My heart had softened and sweetened since the hospital, but the body that I'd worked years to perfect had been hit by a missile. To stop myself from crying and smearing mascara over my dress, I grabbed my purse and escaped alone to the ladies' room. Talk about a horrible sight! Girls primping, wiggling in their dresses, giggling, pretending they weren't satisfied with the way they looked when they were absolutely delirious about it.

"My bra strap keeps showing," one complained while shifting her V-necked top and admiring herself in the mirror. Another whispered something about a boy she liked having said 'hi' to her. I eavesdropped on their conversations, thinking this was where I would have been had I not lost Johnny and stoned God.

Hesitantly, I scrutinized my hair, then the other girls' hair; my lumps, their curves; my two-year-old too-small dress, their fresh imitation Paris designer dresses. I didn't recognize myself anymore. I left, exhausted.

Cake had been served at our table, each piece wrapped in a separate napkin. Although I was full, I badly wanted a piece and I ransacked the dirty dishes for a clean fork. By the time

I finished I was desperate to go home, bury myself under the blankets and binge to my heart's content.

"That girl there," Nadia tapped my shoulder. "That one in red is dating that guy from Macomb—Ibrahim. The guy with beady eyes and a great body."

She was spinning like a ballerina in a music box, throwing glances to the men behind her and flirtatious smiles to those in front as her long hair pranced against her lean arms and tiny waist. I couldn't sit through it anymore. I asked my parents when we were leaving.

My mother was annoyed. "Mervat, why don't you enjoy the party like your sisters?"

I grudgingly entertained myself with figs and dates. My family refused to leave the banquet hall before one, when the music stopped and everyone dispersed.

As though I'd been rescued from sharks, I felt instant relief. Only at home could I comfortably cry, eat and hide. Upstairs I hurried out of my dress, grabbed a bag of marshmallows, a package of cherry pies and Ice Cube chocolates from under my bed, and crawled beneath the sheets. Then I lay my head on the pillow and prayed I'd forget this night forever.

Naturally, my prayer didn't work. The night ended, the sun came up, and I didn't forget a single thing. I normally awoke with a fifteen-pound belly but today my head weighed twice that. The dancing, the ladies' room, the ballerina in the red dress kept running through my mind, and for days I couldn't shake them away. Not with food, not sleep, not tears or stories. Like the queen in a *Thousand and One Nights,* I had kept myself alive through other people's stories. Now I wanted to live through my own story.

I took stock of my alternatives and began experimenting; first I went to St. Mary's. I knelt in front of the altar, crossed myself and took a seat in one of the pews. In the beginning, I felt like a foreigner who didn't know the language or customs of Christianity. I considered returning to my native skepticism but as though I'd misplaced my passport, I felt stuck in this new country. Knowing there was nowhere else to go, I submitted to whatever it had to offer. Soon the strange land of prayer and quiet began to relax me. A part of me lifted in the incensed candlelit air and spoke to the statues and crosses. Questions began to surface, asking various questions such as "Why am I here?" and "How can I belong to this earth?" Eventually the questions were replaced by decisions. I clasped my hands together and begged for a route that would mend my broken heart and show me who God really was.

I began to observe my fragmented lifestyle from a distance. I saw that a cold soul had inhabited me for years. This cold soul had pulled me into a cave until I could no longer stand the cold. My earlier desire to surrender to a man had nothing to do with man, but it had everything to do with wanting to give into an ecstasy that was not man made, one which created a connection within myself and made me spiritually independent. My attempt to die was actually my battle against this cold soul. I didn't want to die. I wanted to kill this cold soul in order to find a pathway to heaven.

I realized months later that this cold soul was not God. This energy was the opposite of God because it wanted to kill. God is about life. He wants to create. The way my father had woken me up that night months ago, that my liver had been left undamaged, suggested He had intervened. He knew I wasn't ready to die. He'd been there for me in the hospital, I reasoned. As I began to sense His positive essence, I now wanted to be aware of Him regularly in order to understand His plans for me. I only wished I had not waited until I was in a crisis because now something was hindering our communion.

Blaming my weight gain for having clouded the dialogue I wanted to have with Him, I stopped eating. I wanted to starve myself back into size five jeans and go to God looking confident and pretty. After a week the scale read 131 and I had to mourn the birth of an extra pound.

My weight didn't discourage me from trying something else. I decided to confront the outside world and went to the mall to busy myself with clothing racks and sales clerks. Instead, I found myself examining what girls were wearing these days. Short floral skirts and skin-tight tops showed off their hips; their laughter and high heels made the windows quiver. I wished I had a wand that would make their bodies as big as mine. Or bigger.

I withdrew into my room to eat chocolate and read more romance novels. It was a good retreat, but not rejuvenating. And then one Monday Maysoon came over.

"My sister's father-in-law died last week—"

"Oh, I'm sorry to hear . . ."

"Yes, thanks but anyway, she has to mourn for forty days so she gave me her tickets to Puerto Vallarta," she pushed on. "Please Mervat, we just have to go."

I was in a daze, partly thinking she was crazy and partly mesmerized by the pronunciation of Puerto Vallarta. She sucked on her chipped bronze nail polish and oscillated through several facial expressions.

"This is a perfect opportunity," she said. "Tony keeps postponing our wedding. He's being the biggest chicken and I want to barbecue his ass."

"Oh, Maysoon," I condoled. I'd never seen her so distraught and I actually felt bad for her.

She pressed her palm to her forehead. "I think his family wants him to marry his cousin from back home. Her cheeks and lips look like a pig's butt."

"He wants to break off the engagement?"

"That's another thing!" she fumed. "We were never officially engaged. The fucker kept postponing that too."

"Oh." Had she told me this a year ago I would have danced

as energetically as a belly dancer at a nightclub, but today it promised trouble. Now that she didn't have a male's genitals to entertain her, she needed my innocence to meddle in.

"Oh, please, please, Mervat," she cried, clinging to my arms like a child. "Come to Puerto Vallarta with me."

She's nuts, I thought. Mexico sounded marvelous but even my midnight dreams were more realistic. My parents would never let me go away with a friend, and Maysoon's reputation deterred me from wanting to. I should call Tony and convince him that she'd make a better housewife than his cousin. If he was suspicious I'd put down my virginity as collateral.

"For a whole week we'll live like mermaids," she said, her eyes shining. "We'll swim, go scuba diving, water skiing, skinny dipping."

How, when neither of us were skinny?

She leaned closer and knelt as though addressing the Pope. "Please, Mervat, say you'll go. Please."

"When?" I asked, knowing I'd never go.

"February eleven."

"Sorry. Not enough time to lose a hundred pounds."

"Jesus!" she lost control. "First of all, it's only twenty pounds, and second, who cares?"

"I care. I haven't been anywhere—ever. Now I get to travel with thighs the ocean won't know how to handle. How exciting!" I was exaggerating, but compared to what I once was . . ."Anyway, Maysoon, my parents will never let me go."

"If they know you're coming with me, they will."

She's amazing, I thought. Half the problem was that she'd be my companion, yet she believed she was the convincing argument itself. "I'm telling you," I insisted. "It's out of the question."

"It's nowhere near that. You're their daughter. You can sweet talk them into practically anything."

"It's not as easy as you make it seem."

"It's easier."

I sighed in frustration and she softened a little. "Okay, then can you do me a favor? Can you just mention the subject to them?"

I kept quiet.

"Please, Mervat, promise me you'll do at least that."

"Yes, yes, I promise," I lied, giving in to her desperation. I knew this trip could never happen. Even if my parents consented, I wouldn't. I had enough troubles without adding Maysoon to my list.

Because I never approached my family about Puerto Vallarta I tried to avoid Maysoon. She was as pushy as the merchants at the Baghdad bazaar, calling me every day. "Did you ask them? Did you?"

"Yes, but they didn't like the idea."

"Why? What's wrong with it?"

"Nothing. They're just like any other Chaldean family—strict and old-fashioned."

"Let me talk to them then. I guarantee I'll have them convinced in an hour."

"Oh no, please. If you do that they'll yell at me for putting them on the spot."

"We have no other choice. This is the chance of a lifetime, and, to be honest with you, if you can't go, then neither can I."

She explained how plane reservations and payments were already made for two, that the hotel was safer with double occupancy, and her parents wouldn't readily let her trek alone into a Spanish-tongued province.

"Uh-huh," I answered. As appealing as Mexico sounded and as loose as my diet rules had become, I still cared for my reputation. I continued to make excuses.

She didn't like my pigheadedness and I could feel her curse me under her breath. She even ignored me for a week. But then she was back, coming to my house in a sleazy outfit and with a stack of dazzling brochures from Quick Pick Travel. We sat in my room and looked over hotels, white sand beaches, blue skies and package deals.

I felt myself weakening. Maybe going on a trip with Maysoon wouldn't be as disastrous as I was making it out to be. No one outside my immediate family would have to know that Mervat Putris had the audacity to make an excursion outside of metropolitan Detroit. As for dilemma number two—well, the natives in Puerto Vallarta weren't really aware of Maysoon's reputation.

Furthermore, February 11 was close to the time Johnny and I started having problems. I didn't want to be here to weep over an unused valentine and a dried rose. More importantly I'd get to go to Mexico without training to be an airline stewardess or cruise director, sign a contract to labor seventy hours a week, and be the talk of the Chaldeans as long as I did it. So the next time I told Maysoon I'd try to convince my parents, I meant it. Who knew what the world had in store? Maybe if I experienced the breezes orbiting the rest of the world, I'd succeed in finally meeting life, the way Abid-Allah had.

Abid-Allah, which translates to "servant of God," was an only child whose parents kept him hidden in the cellar in order to protect him from evil-eyes. He was sixteen when he was introduced to his fellowman for the first time and he tumbled upon the idea of traveling. His parents prepared a caravan and he journeyed to Baghdad. He had many strange experiences on his voyage: a man tried to lure him into bed, Badawi outlaws massacred and plundered his camp, he met a *khalifah* and a king, and he accumulated three wives—a divorcee, a slave and a Christian princess. He also had three sons. By the time he returned home, Abid-Allah had become a proud man.

Maybe Puerto Vallarta, though not as exotic as Abid-Allah's path, would serve me in something the same way. But I wondered if he'd been gifted with luck and experience because he was male and his religious name had flattered God. No Arabic girl I knew took on the role of voyager or experimenter.

I stared at the Pacific Ocean and the six star hotels in the photos and I thought maybe I didn't need the right name or sex to be favored in God's eye. The only way to find out was to test Him.

Chapter 24

Al-nehaya—The end

Confronting my parents would be too required a litigation, so I had no other option than to hire Layla for my defense. Before she took the case on, however, she asked that I disclose certain facts.

"Answer me one question," she said. "Do you really want to go?"

"Yes, I think I do."

"It's either yes or no, Mervat. Avoid in-between answers if you can."

"Ummm . . . it wouldn't be wrong to go, would it?"

She twitched her lips as she considered. "It would be daring, but wrong? No, not wrong."

"Oh?" I asked. The word daring worried me. "I won't take pictures, so there will be no proof. And I could always hide Maysoon's camera so she'll think it's lost." I quickly returned to reality. "That's impractical, isn't it? I mean, regardless of what I say or do, Maysoon's big mouth is going to describe the trip to the whole world."

"If this is how nervous and uncertain you'll be in front of

Mamma and Babba, you'll never see Metro Airport, let alone Puerto Vallarta."

"But I am nervous and I am uncertain."

"Yes, but let's keep it a secret, shall we?" She patted my hand and made a proposal. "I'll come over tomorrow morning for tea and I'll casually open up the subject to Mamma. Then I'll argue for as long as it takes cabbage to grow on trees."

"You will?" I exclaimed. Layla always won whatever dispute she laid her finger on.

Flinging her head back, she laughed heartily. "Honestly Mervat, what kind of question is that?"

"I don't know," I said, thrilled and afraid of what might come of it.

I was excited at the idea of lounging in a place that was tropical and resembling, if even slightly, the heroes I'd put on a pedestal for so long. I'd do something no one in my family had done before and in the future I'd be an example to relatives and grandchildren of how a Chaldean girl defied tradition and traveled with a slut to Puerto Vallarta.

I was committing two unconventional acts with one toss of the stone. It might be riskier than anything Maysoon had ever ventured. Or maybe it would be considered courageous and be applauded, as the princess who was happy until one day she heard of the Talking Bird, the Singing Tree, and the Golden Water.

Suddenly she felt that the gaiety of home was incomplete without them. Her two brothers, who loved her dearly, were determined to hunt for the three priceless articles which slumbered in India. The eldest journeyed there but the path was a doomed one; toward the end of his adventure, he was turned into a black stone. The eldest now missing, the younger prince pursued the same deadly path and the same misfortune befell him as well. With both brothers gone, the princess dressed herself as a man and attempted to accomplish the mission herself.

Unlike the princes, however, she was able to fetch the Talking Bird, the Singing Tree and the Golden Water, and, with their magic, was able to restore her two brothers' lives.

The story's ending was nice but its complications were plenty. Courage could get awfully troublesome.

"Should I even bother?" I asked.

Layla said, so compassionately my heart swelled, "When God offers you a gift, Mervat, it's rude to turn it down."

But what if the giver was Satan? Perhaps this was a trick which would trap my soul in depression again. I would have gone on to darker speculations but I didn't have the energy or even the interest. Deep, deep inside, I wanted to honor this gift, even if it was from Satan himself.

Layla appeared in court the next morning. A trial around the kitchen table immediately followed breakfast but because I couldn't bear hearing the debate of what was good and bad for me, I picked up the dirty dishes and carried them to the sink. I'd barely lathered the sponge before everyone was sworn in and Layla ushered in evidence to support the idea of the trip. All that the court reporter could record then were blasting sound waves coming from my mother.

Not only was her hollering immoderate, but her choice of words in describing me were inaccurate. She defined me in this order: spoiled, unproductive, selfish, stubborn, unrealistic, and most recently, wild.

"You let her become *ghafeefa* today," my mother said, meaning loose, "and she'll scare away all the decent suitors tomorrow."

"That's okay," Layal replied confidently. "She doesn't need to marry a sissy anyway."

"Maysoon is a bad influence, and knowing Mervat she'll fall right into her footsteps."

"Mom, be reasonable. One week isn't going to turn Mervat into Maysoon."

"One week can turn a man against his brother."

"Yes, well, whatever brother is capable of that either has legitimate reasons or was simply born heartless."

"I don't see how your conscience can encourage this without guilt. Mervat is only twenty-one years old. She shouldn't be on her own."

"She won't be on her own. There are guides who will pick them up from the airport and drive them to the hotel. They're staying in a tourist area, where . . ."

"Where all tourists and natives shop for young girls whose brains are no bigger than ants."

"They'll only be gone for seven days. I doubt that's enough time to get into trouble."

"Trouble takes seconds."

"That's true, but Mervat is not a child, Mom. She's more responsible than you're giving her credit for."

"She's not responsible at all. She leaves hair in the tub, spends every dollar on clothes and forgets to shut the window when it rains."

"She went to college by herself, didn't she? She runs the store alone at times, doesn't she?"

My mother mumbled and grumbled.

"I know you're more worried about people's gossip than you are about the danger the girls might get themselves into, but no one has to know."

"That's very reassuring," my mother said with sarcasm. "I'll have shame haunting my house for decades and generations to come."

"What I mean is that it's no one's business to know. Do you think everyone tells us their affairs?"

"A trip with Maysoon is too public to hide."

"I don't want you to hide it, Mom. I just don't want you to treat it like a sin."

"And I don't want my daughter to walk down the street

with Maysoon much less fly across the ocean with her."

"But Maysoon is her only friend and if she doesn't go with her, then she can't go at all."

"She can go when you and your husband go."

"I don't know when that will be, if it'll ever be, and if it did actually happen, which I highly doubt it will, I'd need Mervat to stay here and watch my kids."

My mother started to hyperventilate, or at least pretend to. "What humiliation," she panted. "My daughter, at twenty-one, is already learning bad habits. Today, it's travel, tomorrow it's–" She paused and her breath came in spasms as if to emphasize the hazards of my rebellion.

"Mom, Mervat is beyond learning bad habits. Please lighten up. If she doesn't enjoy her life now, she'll resent cooking dinners and changing diapers in the future. Besides, she's not hurting anyone."

"We don't know that yet." Then she hollered out my name. "Mervat!"

"Yes?" I was still standing over the sink even though I'd finished the dishes twenty minutes ago.

"Come here."

I wiped my hands and went to the table.

"What am I hearing here?" my mother asked before my bottom had touched the chair. "You want to leave your home and have all sorts of freedom elsewhere?"

She meant boys, sex and other naughtiness. Her question embarrassed me so much that I bent my head to conceal my blush. I decided never to set food outside my Chaldean culture. Besides, with my useless crash dieting and the pop quizzes I threw at God, I didn't want to create a third set of unanswered questions in my life.

"Mom, you're making her feel like a criminal," Layla said. "It's not necessary."

"It is when you're siding with her and no one is listening

to me. Don't forget I'm not the real decision maker here. Her father is."

"Oh, that's absurd. When it comes to us, Babba will agree to anything you say."

"And do you think that's fair for me? If I have the last word, I'll also have the burden of whatever consequences follow and I can't handle that."

"You won't have to," Layla said desperately. "Maybe Mervat is the first in the family to travel without a chaperone, but I'm sure she's not the first or last Chaldean girl to do it. And anyway, the consequences might be worse if she isn't given room to breathe."

"Room to breathe?" my mother cried. "It's not like I don't let her go anywhere. She comes and goes—here and there—as she pleases."

"Well, here and there isn't what she pleases–"

And so the argument continued. Despite Layla's polished persuasion, my mother wouldn't totally consent; Layla still had to get my two other sisters and my brother to agree. The vote was "Nae" from Isaam, "Yea" from Nameera, and "Half nae, half yea" from Ikhbal. With the ballots' results so sloppy I was thankful that my father was the licensed magistrate here. His judgment was unbiased and final. So when he slammed his hammer over his bench and shouted the verdict "Not guilty of a shameful ordinance!" (or something to that effect), I borrowed my brother Isaam's honeymoon luggage and started packing.

Meanwhile, I strangely forgot about Mexico, chanting to myself: "I'm going to go looking for God."

Maysoon complained about the turbulence, seatbelts, and babies crying. I, on the other hand, fretted to myself about my failure to lose an ounce of fat, dwelling with special horror on my stomach and thighs, but when I arrived in Puerto Vallarta I didn't have a chance to carp about it. I found myself confronting a jungle, a brilliant sun and the ocean.

I'd never seen an ocean face to face. I stood in front of it like a lost child in front of a lion. My first reaction was to touch it but when I tried I couldn't. It hypnotized me and I feared what coming into physical contact with it could do. I wondered if it could be captivating yet harmless at the same time or if it was as misleading as Johnny.

"I've just met the strangest part of nature in the world," I said, sitting on a towel and inhaling the smells of lotion, salt, wind, and sand.

Maysoon laughed. "You've never watched the Discovery Channel?"

"I have."

"There are oceans in France, Italy. . . ."

"Beirut and India."

My enthusiasm put her off I suppose because she tried to divert my attention. "There are other things to see in Puerto Vallarta."

"I'm sure there are," I said, hoping she would let me be so I could enjoy the freedom of talking idly and randomly to myself. "But for now, this will do fine."

"Ooof!" She was exasperated, rapidly tapping her right heel on the sand. "I'm going to take a walk."

The instant she was out of my sight, I was glad. I returned to watching the sea, resting in its rhythm as I had once cuddled against my mother's breast. I wanted to be a part of it, a wave within its waves.

As I grew more familiar with the ocean, with nature in general, Maysoon found what she'd really been looking for, a Mexican man. We'd quickly and tacitly understood that I'd devote myself to the ocean while she went off with her new man, Ricardo. We made compromises. We bid each other farewell in the morning and didn't meet until night, when we'd eat a delicious dinner and go to the hotel bar. There Maysoon danced the lambda with Ricardo while I made small talk with Ricardo's friend, Jose. He was in his mid-thirties and part Indian.

"Come to my work tomorrow afternoon," he spoke loudly over the meringue. I didn't dance, drink or make out and he was trying to make the best of it. "I'll show you some interesting art."

"You work in an art gallery?"

"Not paintings, no," he laughed. "Come tomorrow and you'll see. I'll tell Ricardo to bring you."

"Okay," I consented, although I had a prior appointment with the ocean.

We left the bar when it closed at three, strolling around the pools and gardens where Maysoon periodically tried to push me and Jose against a palm tree. She was determined to get us to kiss and tumble down to the grass next to the iguanas.

Jose saw I was uncomfortable and ignored her. He walked me to the beach instead and we sat on the big rocks at the edge of the water. In the dark, with only the company of boisterous waves, I was a little wary of being alone with him—he might be a molester or murderer, I thought. But he started to tell me about his father's culture and my doubts relaxed as I got interested in what he had to say.

He told me his people were originally from Central America, where they lived until the Mediterranean people—the Spanish, Portuguese, Italians, Greeks—came, naming it Mexico, which he translated as "mixed people."

"A Native used to call himself one of the people from the south," he said, his eyes distant. "Then the men with the great ships came along and called him Indian."

I took in his dark looks. I didn't think him unattractive but I hadn't been enthusiastic about spending time with him either; he seemed ordinary and temporary. Now I saw he was possessed of a deep stillness and I felt safe.

Jose grabbed a short muddy stick and drew circles in the

sand while I stared at the waves that raised themselves up and then gradually relaxed. "Tell me, Jose, who is your ancestors' God?"

"The Creator, of course," he said, smiling. "I'm sure He is also your God, my God, and our friends' God . . ."

"No, I mean what do they believe in?" I brushed aside his humor.

"That we were sent here to look after nature." He opened his arms wide and looked from side to side. "Because it is all God."

How can it all be God, I thought? Doesn't He only come through the sacraments of the church? Jose' said nothing about the Bible, Moses, the Ten Commandments, Jesus bread. I wondered if his religion was legitimate as he went on. "We allow people to experience growth in their own ways and time. One isn't supposed to be anywhere or anything just because he or she is eight months old, or ten years, or twenty-five."

This sounded too easy. Not enough saints and sacraments and do's and don'ts. I did not share my opinion, though, and spent an hour or so asking questions about life from a Native American's perspective. For once I was getting answers that felt sensible, basic and infinite.

The next day Ricardo and Maysoon dropped me off at Jose's workplace and while he tried to make a sale to an English couple, I looked around. There were table-top sized figures of deer, owls, coyotes and other animals, items made from tiny colored beads. The animal figures had pictures of corn, cactus, grain and all sorts of fruits, plants and vegetables symbolizing prosperity, power, and health. They were priced at hundreds of dollars and Jose told me they were handmade by the Native women of the reservation. I wanted to touch them but a sign on the wall said not to. I wondered whether all pretty things in this world were untouchable or if this was a coincidence. Then

I realized I was mistaken; if I had the patience to save enough money, I could buy such things and keep them at my fingertips forever. In the same way, it hit me; I could create for myself whatever I'd hoped Johnny would do.

"Do you like them?" Jose asked.

"I do." But what I liked more was being closer to the Natives' beliefs. Their respect for nature sounded simpler than spending a lifetime being threatened into avoiding or compensating for sins.

That night I went to bed a foreigner to myself. It was somewhat frightening, even though Maysoon was a mattress away. My mind and heart were getting adopted, like the Indian tribes who didn't fight or kill when there was friction, but absorbed the weaker family into the strong, their beliefs and stories melding.

"For instance," Jose's words repeated themselves in my head. "You were born in Iraq but America will have a greater impact."

"What if one resists, though?" I asked.

He shrugged. "It's okay, but resisting change doesn't help anyone grow. It doesn't."

"How should I let change happen?"

"Be open to ideas. And be patient. When cultures take or borrow something new, they take time to digest it."

I was anxious to be alone the next morning to sort some of this out. I felt myself dissolving and I wasn't sure whether I ought to hang on or let go. It was bad enough that my figure was ruined.

After a breakfast of scrambled eggs and broiled sausages, Maysoon and Ricardo went back to our room and I sat on the beach, keeping well away from the noise of children and from the skinny bikini-wearers. I thought of Johnny and my three days in the hospital: they felt as remote as my first two years in Baghdad.

My history . . . It was short but crowded with thousands of fears. I couldn't remember how I'd accumulated them, especially the ones I had of God. Why should I be scared of my so-called Creator? Did a light bulb quake at the mention of Edison or did the theories of relativity or calculus pale at the memory of Einstein and Newton? No. Since their inceptions, they'd marvelously created and re-created themselves.

I sighed deeply to the sun and sea. No wonder I hated You. With the way they described You—capable of loving this, hating that, getting angry, jealous and punishing—You sounded like a hypocrite, like them. You appeared cruel and tantalizing.

"Show me who You really are," I asked, sweat streaking down my back and dripping from my nose as the day's heat built. The afternoon was hot and sticky. As I closed my eyes, I felt the scorching sun seep into my head and begin to burn beliefs which over the years had stolen my peace. The poor things must have felt like one of the thieves in Ali Baba's backyard whom Kahramana had toasted with her wisdom.

The captain of the forty thieves was determined to get vengeance on Ali Baba for having accidentally discovered their hiding place and taking home a portion of their treasure. So the captain hid each of his men in a jar and, claiming they were full of cooking oil which he planned to sell at the *souk* the next day, asked Ali Baba whether he could sleep in his house. His real scheme, however, was to have his men attack Ali Baba in the middle of the night and kill him. Kahramana, Ali Baba's most faithful and clever servant, heard noises coming from the jars and sensed her master's life might be in danger, so she filled some of her large cooking pots with oil and boiled them over fire, then poured the sizzling oil over each jar. The concealed thieves died instantly.

"Not only did she save her master," Layla had told me, "but she was made the wife of his son and one of the heirs to his wealth."

A statue was put up in honor of Kahramana in one of Baghdad's famous streets. She stands there tall and slim, her figure bending towards a large jar, a jug in her hand and water, representing the oil, pouring out of its nozzle.

Before I return home, I thought, I'd like the sun to play the role of Kahramana, focusing my mind and burning out at least some of my man-made beliefs. Then I could begin, even vaguely, redefining in my heart's terms what was really forbidden and allowed by God and why. I remembered many things I looked away from, like my philosophy professor's lecture about Ralph Waldo Emerson, whose essay, *Self-Reliance,* encouraged a person to "Trust Thyself."

Chapter 25

Al-bedia mara-oughra . . . The beginning again

I was twenty-nine when I saw Johnny again. Between my trip to Puerta Vallarta and that reunion, I'd heard both bad and good tidings about his family. For two and a half years it was rumored that Aunt Evelyn's two unmarried sons were constantly in and out of court for smuggling cigarettes. They had to sell their west-side home and live in an apartment for a while. At one point Nabiel even moved to California with his aunt and uncle.

Listening to this I wondered whether apartment complexes allowed Bolivian macaws and cockatiels. Maybe it wasn't a problem, though; maybe the birds were dead and forgotten. I remembered how much they'd pleased Johnny and hoped they were still alive. Otherwise, Johnny's heart would completely dry out from all the harm, as conscious or subconscious as it might be, he'd caused. The rest of the community, in the meantime, whispered that the young men's lives were in danger because they'd probably been dealing heroine and cocaine.

"They've lost most of their money," my mother said as I served her a cup of tea with orange peel and sugar. "It was a little odd how rich they were."

I picked up my six month old daughter Ieman—Faith— from the kitchen floor and placed her in a baby chair. I peeled a banana and handed half of it to her.

"It breaks my heart to say this," my mother added, shaking her head, "but the truth is both sons might go to prison."

Bringing a plate of clotted cream from the refrigerator, I sighed to myself. I remembered Johnny's dream of becoming a boxer or football player and my heart went out to him. He had everything but the freedom to do as he pleased and to not hurt anyone. Letting me go was a gesture I hoped he'd be rewarded for.

I brought a jar of apricot marmalade and one of honey and placed them next to the clotted cream. "God help them," I said, while silently sending them a sincere prayer. "I hope neither one will have to go anywhere he doesn't like."

Ieman smashed the banana against her bib and smiled at me. I wet a cloth and wiped her hands, face and bib with it. Then I stood back and observed her as closely as I used to the nutritional information on labels. Everyone said she looked like her father and they were right. Not a trace of Mervat in her, although I'd participated in her pre-worldly life for nine and a half monthsut what difference did it make? She was one of the people of the earth, regardless of her gender and background. Besides, she didn't need a certain set of eyes, nose and mouth to know that every one of her syrupy baby breaths was unavoid- ably connected to her mother's heart, as my thoughts, words and actions were to the universe.

About two years later, Aunt Evelyn's family name was cleared with the law, although not with the Chaldeans. Every- one labeled them "involved," or "*bil-hashisha,*" and I thought what a price to pay for a Corvette, a west-side home, and what looked like power. There was no news of them for the next few years. Then, it was bruited about, their family's wealth suddenly doubled. I shut my eyes in regret and said to myself, "He is one of them."

That was Johnny's life from the Chaldean community's perspective. As for me, after I returned from Puerto Vallarta I spent years trying to open my heart and mind through the process of pouring that hot cooking oil into jars of misconceptions and superstitions, learned fears and judgments—not to mention maniacal diets and food binges. I wanted to empty them of what I, my society and environment had filled with mandatory priority, notions of image and book knowledge, then refill them with love, independence, and tolerance.

While the oil scalded quite a number of my darkest thoughts, altering my understanding of the world and bringing me closer to Allah, I searched for a career. I made a lot of small and inactive attempts at being a travel agent, an airline representative, a stewardess. Then one day a customer at the store, a regular who always came in the evenings to buy a pack of Marlboros and occasionally a sandwich, chatted longer than usual and discovered I'd gotten an associate's degree and offered me a job.

"I need an interpreter for an Arabic client," he said. "The appointment is at ten o'clock Tuesday morning. Come to my office half an hour early . . ." He placed his lit cigarette in his mouth and searched his jacket pocket, handing me an ivory card. "This is the address. It's a little far away but call my receptionist and she'll give you directions."

Before I pushed myself to say "No, I can't, but thanks," he moved out of the way and allowed the next customer to approach the counter. He waved goodbye and I rung up the powdered donuts and Philadelphia cream cheese while glancing at the card that had Attorney Richard Matthews engraved in its center.

I felt uncomfortable at the sight of it. Mr. Matthews didn't look like the attorneys I'd seen in the movies or on television.

He was simple in attire and language. The fact that he trusted me to do important work without prior experience cast doubt on his credibility. Law and interpretation was nowhere near my field: I'd have to risk making mistakes in a business that couldn't afford it; I'd have to change my schedule at the store Tuesday morning and perhaps inconvenience my father and brother.

Later, however, I changed my mind. Since Puerto Vallarta, I've been careful not to decline gifts. On Tuesday morning I found myself dressed in a beige suit and sitting with my legs crossed and an empty yellow note pad on my lap, the attorney on my left, a man representing a car insurance agency opposite me, a female Lebanese client to my right and a tape recorder on the table.

Before the deposition began, I'd rehearsed what Mr. Matthews taught me; ask if they prefer you to interpret in the first or third-person. After that question, don't speak unless required, don't add or subtract any words during the translation, and once it's all over, walk away from the building without making any contact with the clients.

"If you're caught mingling with them," he said while I tried to hold onto all his instructions, "it'll look as though you're trying to help them out with their case."

He paused and looked at me questioningly until I nodded my understanding.

"It's best for you to stay as distant as possible," he said. "These clients think you could switch your title just like that." He snapped his fingers. "One second you're an interpreter, the next an advocate."

Once these guidelines were established, I was left alone for ten minutes. Then everyone entered the room and from that moment on and for many years to come, I performed the task of interpreter.

It wasn't as easy as wearing a suit and holding a note pad.

To make a successful career, I took Arabic classes at Wayne State University and learned how to read and write the language so I could interpret documents as well. I also strengthened my Chaldean, which I understood perfectly but spoke little of, by practicing it with my family.

As I continued to empty my jars of unproductive beliefs and refill them with whatever my soul desired—now on a more daily basis—I met my husband. It wasn't love at first sight, and he wasn't as compellingly handsome as Johnny, but he also wasn't affiliated with the mob or any other organization or black market that condemned people to a living death. He owned a produce market.

I saw Johnny a year after I was well settled into my profession, marriage and motherhood, at Nabiel's wedding. He was the best man, looking as attractive in a black tuxedo as when I saw him behind the counter in a white T-shirt and jeans.

My anger had long ago evaporated, and I was curious to talk to him. He had played a big part in my life and I no longer wanted to hide that from him the way I did when we'd been together. However, Johnny was always busy—dancing, chatting with friends and relatives, sitting next to the groom while drinking and eating. Sometimes he was simply missing.

I knew he'd seen me but for whatever reason had pretended not to. It didn't matter, though. I was determined to greet him and make peace. I knew he thought I hated him. Over the years I'd come to understand that his leaving had contributed to my redemption.

I'd unfairly made an idol out of him, relying on him to make me this or that, take me here or there, and I suffered the consequences of my own misinterpretation. I'd wanted to promote Johnny from being a handsome, wealthy man to being God. I was disappointed, of course, because like the Muhammadan prayer, *la illaha ila allah,* there is no god but God. The capacity to manage one's own affairs, make one's own judgments, and provide for oneself are the recipe for life.

I finally found my opportunity to catch Johnny in the lobby. I'd just walked out of the restroom and he was about to enter the banquet hall when I called out his name.

Holding a glass of liquor in his left hand, he turned. He didn't act surprised to see me and I remembered the same coolness ten years ago when he was in an olive green suit, stirring his drink at the bar.

"Congratulations on your brother's wedding," I said.

"Thank you."

I came closer so passersby couldn't hear and so I could get a better look at my ex-idol. We were quiet a moment; since I was the one who'd stopped him, I asked, "How have you been, Johnny?"

"I've been good," he said, but the hint of dullness in his voice suggested otherwise. "And you?"

I didn't answer right away, studying the blue eyes, oddly discomfited, that had once hypnotized me. The pretty and not so pretty details of our affinity knocked on my heart for a moment and I glanced up at the crystal chandeliers, then at the shiny tiled floor until they receded.

"Do you remember us, Johnny?" I asked, unable to waste time with modesty and prudence.

"Yes," he replied reluctantly. I waited further comment but evidently his mind was elsewhere.

"I'm glad," I said. "Not that I'd suspected you'd forgotten."

"No, I haven't," he said and pondered again. "But it was such a long time ago—" Then to himself, "Very long ago."

"Nine or ten years. Not too long."

Johnny frowned, as if disagreeing. "How long were we together?"

I hesitated as I wondered whether or not it was fair to categorize our courting as forgotten history. Either way it shouldn't concern me or hurt my feelings. I couldn't expect him to have experienced the same aftermath as I had, and I was able to answer kindly. "A few months."

He tilted his chin as though calculating how short a time that was. I suddenly felt too foolish for the rest of my speech: that he was my first boyfriend, that until I met my husband no man was able to give me the feeling I'd had with him, and that his departure had both devastated me and led me to a more constructive kinship with God and my individuality.

"It was short but meaningful," I abbreviated my long awaited confession for him. "For me, it was."

"Yes, we had fun."

"Yes, we did."

What a choice of words, I thought, and felt sorry for having cursed God for Johnny's sake. The sleepless nights, crash diets, binges, and evil thoughts—not to mention the pills and the plastic tubes in my chest—hadn't been worth it. Neither his presence nor his absence equaled life. Fruit ripened despite the number of pickers, and sea waves curled regardless of how many swimmers. Souls were no different. They lived no matter what experiences stopped at their door, rented a room and later checked out, leaving either a mess to clean up or a good impression to hold onto.

"We'd better return to the party," I said. "It'd be a shame to miss any of it."

He nodded and backed away to open the door. I was heading inside, thinking how ironic it was that I'd been merely a bit player in Johnny's life when he'd been both hero and villain in mine, when he asked, "Tell me, Mervat, did you get to travel the world yet?"

I paused and smiled. My role in his life was minor but it counted. I remembered the night I'd revealed my wanderlust and how he'd belittled it, forgetting, as I had, that we were living in America where anything, for men and women, was possible.

"Yes," I said, recalling after the break up the various roads my heart had traveled in order to find peace at home. "Some of it."

I bowed, said a final goodbye to my first story and its tall and blue-eyed plot, and walked through the cigarette smoke, prying eyes and dinner tables towards the man in the dark gray suit and thick black mustache, where I'd be able to continue to lovingly tend the story I was participating in right now.

HERMIZ PUBLISHING, INC.

Pick up a copy of Namou's previous novels:

ISBN: 978–0977679003 (paperback)

ISBN: 978–0975295601 (paperback)
ISBN: 978–0975295618 (hardcover)

ISBN 9959–30–079-X (paperback)

Made in the USA
Monee, IL
06 January 2022

88221571R00156